SORROW'S CROWN

TOM PICCIRILLI

BERKLEY PRIME CRIME, NEW YORK

SORROW'S CROWN

A Berkley Prime Crime Book / published by arrangement with
Write Way Publishing

PRINTING HISTORY
Write Way Publishing edition / 1999
Berkley Prime Crime edition / September 1999

The Penguin Putnam Inc. World Wide Web site address is
http://www.penguinputnam.com

ISBN: 0-425-17028-4

Berkley Prime Crime Books are published
by the Berkley Publishing Group,
a division of Penguin Putnam Inc.,
375 Hudson Street, New York, New York 10014.
The name BERKLEY PRIME CRIME and the BERKLEY PRIME CRIME
design are trademarks belonging to Penguin Putnam Inc.

PRINTED IN THE UNITED STATES OF AMERICA

10 9 8 7 6 5 4 3 2 1

Praise for *The Dead Past*

$3.00

"Kendrick is one part Matt Scudder, one part aging Huck Finn, and one part Archie Goodwin . . . The person who summons him home is not a grizzled, but exasperated, chief of police, not a swooning dame in danger—but his own grandmother, who is every bit as snoopy as Miss Marple, and every bit as tart as Joan Rivers . . . [A] blend of hard-boiled and cozy elements gives the book its wit, warmth and appeal . . . one of the best written and most enjoyable mysteries I've read in a long time . . ."

—Ed Gorman, editor of *Mystery Scene*

"Tightly written and plotted, Piccirilli's latest effort gracefully and whimsically navigates through pain, violence, turmoil, and the sundry details of life. At times wisecracking, intense and extreme when necessary, but always driven to find the heart of the matter . . ."

—*Pirate Writings* magazine

"Tom Piccirilli is a genius at characterization . . . His sardonic wit makes *The Dead Past* a great read . . . This novel is simultaneously mesmerizing, frightening, and poignant, turning it into a brilliant who-done-it."

—*Midwest Book Review*

"Piccirilli has got it! *The Dead Past* should give him a vibrant future! Humor, a clear sense of continuity and an unexpected conclusion . . . Put on a warm coat, boots and a mystery mind and join the characters in this well-written, page-turning, thoroughly satisfying murder mystery."

—*Eclectic Book Reviews*

"Tom Piccirilli has taken us places that few mystery writers are willing to visit, and as long as he finds another dark crevice to explore . . . he will have a growing legion of brave readers willing to follow him there."

—*Mystery News*

MORE MYSTERIES FROM THE
BERKLEY PUBLISHING GROUP ...

CAT CALIBAN MYSTERIES: She was married for thirty-eight years. Raised three kids. Compared to that, tracking down killers is easy ...

by D. B. Borton

ONE FOR THE MONEY	TWO POINTS FOR MURDER
THREE IS A CROWD	FOUR ELEMENTS OF MURDER
FIVE ALARM FIRE	SIX FEET UNDER

ELENA JARVIS MYSTERIES: There are some pretty bizarre crimes deep in the heart of Texas—and a pretty gutsy police detective who rounds up the unusual suspects ...

by Nancy Herndon

ACID BATH	WIDOWS' WATCH
LETHAL STATUES	HUNTING GAME
TIME BOMBS	C.O.P. OUT
CASANOVA CRIMES	

FREDDIE O'NEAL, P.I., MYSTERIES: You can bet that this appealing Reno private investigator will get her man ... "A winner."—Linda Grant

by Catherine Dain

LAY IT ON THE LINE	SING A SONG OF DEATH
WALK A CROOKED MILE	LAMENT FOR A DEAD COWBOY
BET AGAINST THE HOUSE	THE LUCK OF THE DRAW
DEAD MAN'S HAND	

BENNI HARPER MYSTERIES: Meet Benni Harper—a quilter and folk-art expert with an eye for murderous designs ...

by Earlene Fowler

FOOL'S PUZZLE	IRISH CHAIN
KANSAS TROUBLES	GOOSE IN THE POND
DOVE IN THE WINDOW	MARINER'S COMPASS

HANNAH BARLOW MYSTERIES: For ex-cop and law student Hannah Barlow, justice isn't just a word in a textbook. Sometimes, it's a matter of life and death ...

by Carroll Lachnit

MURDER IN BRIEF	A BLESSED DEATH

PEACHES DANN MYSTERIES: Peaches has never had a very good memory. But she's learned to cope with it over the years ... Fortunately, though, when it comes to murder, this absentminded amateur sleuth doesn't forgive and forget!

by Elizabeth Daniels Squire

WHO KILLED WHAT'S-HER-NAME?	REMEMBER THE ALIBI
MEMORY CAN BE MURDER	WHOSE DEATH IS IT ANYWAY?
IS THERE A DEAD MAN IN THE HOUSE?	WHERE THERE'S A WILL

For Jenelle and Joseph
—who might not be my children,
but are my kids

Acknowledgments

I'd like to thank the following people for their friendship and encouragement during the writing of this novel: Michelle Scalise, who added poetry to my life; Diana Jackson, for her much-appreciated wise counsel on all things grammatical (though I still think 'snuck' is acceptable); Adam Meyer and Jonathan Harrington, buddies in the trenches who shared their own red-penned fiascoes; Jamie Eubanks, the spy in Palm Springs; Dorrie O'Brien, David Smith and Kim Waltemeyer, who believed in the work and fought the good fight; the memory of David Goodis, Charles Willeford, and Charles Williams, with all my respect and gratitude, for inspiring from dusty shelves and proving once again that the dead past is never truly dead.

"That sorrow's crown of sorrow
is remembering happier things."
—Tennyson, *Locksley Hall*

ONE

PANECRAFT HAD ITS OWN HISTORY, entwined with the secrets and sorrows of those towns surrounding it. Back in the early 'seventies, the mental hospital had housed eleven thousand patients, such a high volume due to the returned vets and end of the hippie movement, when the serious dealers got into the game and brought a trembling house of cards down even faster, leaving runaways without a Haight-Ashbury to head for anymore. Now there were fewer than two thousand faces up there behind the leveled rows of cube windows rimed with ice.

On certain nights, you could head down the back roads surrounding Panecraft and watch how the twining shadows of the complex cut into the skyline and carved down alongside the moon. High school kids performed primitive ceremonies of passage, knocking down barbed-wire fences in pick-up trucks. My ex-wife Michelle and I had made love back there a few times, right before I started noticing hickeys on her throat that I hadn't given her. Echoes rang from the highway, and she liked the noise of the big trucks and the biker packs that roamed up and down the county line in the darkness.

A soft sound faded in, rustling like the hail on the restaurant windows, and after a few moments I heard it again, and once more, much sharper, and knew it as my name. "Jonathan."

I looked at my grandmother, who stared at me with a combination of amusement, deep interest, and general dismay. After we'd returned from Karen Bolan's funeral several weeks ago, one of the papers had dubbed Anna "a lady of silver rarity," and I couldn't quite get the phrase out of my head. I also wasn't completely sure what it meant. Sort of blatant, but accurate enough at the moment, I supposed: her full and lustrous silver hair framed her heart-shaped face, the restaurant's lavish candles reflecting off her knife and fork, light catching in the armrests of her wheelchair. "Yes, Anna?"

"Is there anything wrong?" she asked.

"No," I said.

"Are you sure, dear?"

"Yes."

She smiled one of those resplendent smiles that told me I was doing something wrong and would really hate myself when I found out what. I checked around and spotted sauce everywhere. "Then perhaps you'd like to take your tie out of your lasagna, darling, before you spoil your meal."

Katie giggled and so did Anna's date for the evening, Oscar Kinion, who had the awful habit of slumping against my arm and reaching around in a semi-familial embrace during our appetizers. My father used to do the same thing at ball games when I was nine, and I recalled the warmth it afforded me at the time. Now all I got was a lengthy perusal of Oscar's eyes and a serious whiff of his after shave, a pungent odor that drained my sinuses and smelled like eau de boiled cabbage. The eyes I didn't mind. They sat attentively in his thin, meager face: bright, deeply brown, almost weepy with acute sentiment, and full of seven decades of stolid integrity. When he told me he had four kids, I could see a lot of love for his children in the watery mahogany-colored eyes, and he beamed and came close to tittering whenever he mentioned his grandchildren.

He owned a popular hunting goods store in Felicity Grove, had a well-trimmed goatee, no hair, and a jagged scar under his ear where one of his sons had snagged him with an eagle's claw fishing hook thirty years ago. I got the feeling he'd been trying to impress me when he mentioned he'd been one of the first U.S. soldiers to enter Auschwitz when the allies had liberated the camp. He told a good story, and I enjoyed the fact that he cared enough about Anna that, even at his age, he proved willing to make an effort at impressing her grandson.

The restaurant was about eight miles outside of the Grove, up some rugged, hilly roads that grew treacherous on a fierce night like this. Oscar's treat. The place had a lit fireplace and peering animal heads, with stuffed birds and fish on the wall—compliments of the ammo and rods bought at Kinion's Hunting & Tackle Supplies. It's amazing what watching dead animals scrutinizing you while you ate them could do to your appetite. I had to go for the pasta.

Staring beyond a family of harried, shrill parents and children smothered in ketchup, I could just make out the silhouette of Panecraft on the far ridge as it rose insolently into the glow of the half moon.

Anna turned and looked out the window as well, and I could see how the contemplation snapped so easily in place for her. She refolded the cloth napkin across her lap, making the corners tight and impeccable the way they'd originally been, sipping her wine and settling comfortably into the chair when she realized what was on my mind. My grandmother always remained a mere breath away from discerning all my thoughts, and she must have been passing the aptitude along because Katie was getting pretty good at it, too.

Dimples flashing and giving me only about a thousand watts of her jade gaze, front teeth fit snugly over her bottom lip because she knew it drove me crazy, Katie clearly wanted to talk about the store again. She dipped her own napkin in ice water and found a couple more sauce spatters on my cuff, tsking me while Oscar told Anna, "See the one on the end there, with the chip in his tusk? Kinda looks like he's still pissed off about being dead? A wild boar I caught up in the deep woods off the eastern summit about eight, nine years ago, took him with a Remington 760 pump action in a 30.06 caliber. It's a deer rifle. The first round made him sneeze."

Panecraft had other uses. Not long ago, pregnant teenage girls were sometimes stowed there until after the babies were born and bundled off to adoption agencies. Wealthy men whose spouses troubled them too much over business ventures or children could always pay to have their wives locked away for a year or two, and found to be unfit for alimony or motherhood. More recently, the hospital had taken its turn as a hospice for clergymen dying of AIDS, cloistered on the top floors, hoping to avoid whispers and scandal.

They couldn't. No one could.

Lisa Hobbes, a woman I'd known since grade school when we first learned to finger-paint together, with a baby doll face and a voice like Tinkerbell's, and who'd suffered through four miscarriages I knew of, each loss another presumed failure, now sat in a cell awaiting trial. They had locked her in Panecraft for mental evaluation, and two state psychiatrists had found her competent to stand trial for the murder of Karen Bolan. They would say that Lisa had been of sound mind when she'd placed the barrel of a .22 to Karen's temple and pulled the trigger—carefully cleaning the interior of her El Dorado afterwards, but still not fastidiously enough—all because her husband and her pregnant best friend had been having an affair. But the blood hadn't been spilled for love or sexual jealousy, or any of the many spiteful, bitter reasons everyone else might list. I could remember the timbre of her tiny voice perfectly when she'd said, "But the baby, he needed to have a baby, and I couldn't give him one."

Katie found more sauce on my sleeve. "How does somebody get lasagna on his elbows?"

"You're asking me?" I said. "I thought I was doing pretty good."

"Fork to mouth, you bring the fork up to your mouth. It's fairly simple." She pursed her lips and cocked her head, surveying the damage. "Though for you the end result has somehow become a Jackson Pollock painting."

"Be kind to me, I'm dining-challenged. A bag of chips and a football game are about as high-class as I usually get."

"And aren't I sweet to have never brought that up myself?"

Oscar flung his arm around my shoulder again and pointed out the chipped tusk to me. We had separate conversations going. I turned away from Katie for a minute, and when I glanced back I experienced the same new sense of amazement I always felt seeing her.

We'd been dating for two months, and you'd have thought the twinge of excitement I got from noticing the curls of her hair lying across her forehead, dimples angling at the edges of her smiling mouth, nearly invisible blond down under her ears waving slightly with my breath on her face, would have faded a fraction by now, but it hadn't in the least. More than once she'd had to snap her fingers under my nose to drag me out of reverie. You would think I'd get used to her beauty from moment to moment, while we made love in her small bed or when I watched the side of her face in the glow of coming attractions at the movies, but the draw never lessened. She stared at the ketchup-covered kids without seeming to notice just how stressed and besieged their parents were. She remained a romantic constantly frustrated by my grip on reality, however tenuous it might be at times.

"So?" she said, as sweetly as she could, yet failing to keep the hints of anxiety and anger out of her voice. "You were supposed to give it some thought. You told me we'd discuss it over dinner. This is dinner."

"Or a Pollock retrospective."

"Well, in either case, we should talk."

"You're right."

I attempted picturing it again. The refrigerators humming all day long, filled with tulips, roses, and daffodils, the bell over the door jangling every two minutes. First editions of Wilkie Collins, James Agee, H. P. Lovecraft, and Sartre toppled against paperback originals of David Goodis and Sheldon Lord, everything piled in the corner while plant-growth mix got kicked into the carpeting. Novels smelling like manure.

"A combination flower shop-bookstore?" I said.

She gave this slight sigh of exasperation that ended with a low, sensual growl deep in the back of her throat. I tried to get her to do it as often as possible. "Did I say that?" she asked. "Give me some credit, Jon."

"I do."

"I said there's plenty of empty space at the fringe of the shop, facing Fairlawn. We could set the bookstore up there; it would have its own entrance, plenty of room, and the businesses would be exclusive. Have the two stores side by side. The rent is cheap. There's lots of pedestrian traffic downtown. It would be adorable.''

The cuteness of her suggestion scared me. My store in Manhattan, full of scarce and uncommon books—a great many mysteries since Anna had cultivated my love for the field while nurturing her own tastes—could be considered a number of things: quaint, impressive, atmospheric, well-furnished, all of that, but never adorable. Katie failed to grasp the concept that while there might be room for a bookstore amidst the flora, shelf space was only the minimum of the room I needed. Most of my back stock remained in a storage area twice as large as my store itself. She'd been in Felicity Grove for three months, since her late aunt had bequeathed her the flower shop, and she hadn't quite come to the realization that nobody read much in this town.

Of course, the entire conversation simply provided a front for talking about deeper issues. We were both frustrated that we didn't spend enough time together, but I hadn't worked my ass off to build a reputation as a book dealer and antiquarian in a city rapidly being overtaken by superchains only to toss it all and return to a place I'd spent years getting away from.

"What do you think, Anna?" Katie asked.

"It's an appealing notion," my grandmother said. "And certainly there's an inherent charm. Felicity Grove could certainly use an antiquarian bookstore." Despite being in a wheelchair, she always managed to walk the balance beam between intent and interest. She never came down on some of Katie's more impractical business ideas, but never let me be a pure realist, either. "However, you must be cautious about entering into a business partnership like this, Katie."

"Of course," Katie said stiffly.

"Look, last week I sold a copy of Emerson's *MayDay*, Ticknor and Fields, eighteen sixty-seven, in a clamshell box, signed by Emerson, for twenty-four hundred dollars. You think I'm going to get that from anybody in the Grove? I'll have to start buying books on longhorn sheep and large-mouth bass.''

Oscar nodded. ''Those field books would do well for you, Johnny. I know, I sell racks of them, too. Back stock at least a couple dozen copies of *The Whitetail Deer Guide: A Practical Guide to Hunting America's Number One Big-game Animal*. I sell a couple of them a week, and don't mind the competition if you start pushing them, too.''

''I appreciate that.''

''Jonathan, dear,'' Anna said. ''Your superiority complex is showing.''

''That's just sauce.''

The jade gaze had more heat in it now, Katie's eyebrows arching a little so that her forehead showed a lovely crease of irritation, none of this really about the store at all. ''You can continue expanding your mail order business. That's where you make most of your sales, anyway.''

''I'd have to spend nearly as much time in the city buying and trading stock, Katie.''

Oscar nearly body-checked me out of my seat this time. He might've been seventy, but he had the kind of muscle that was hard-earned and would never disappear or turn to fat. He got me into a friendly headlock. ''You can always come in with me if you like, Johnny. I keep my eye out for men like you who show real initiative.''

Now he was starting to get a tad pushy with his need to impress. He glanced at the animal heads like he wished they'd come back to life again and attack the women so he could sprint into action and kill them with his butter knife. I tried to imagine the quail or moose running rampant and endangering lives, but couldn't quite make it.

''Well, it was just a thought,'' Katie said.

Oscar whispered something in my ear that I didn't hear because Katie was on the verge of either letting it go for tonight or possibly crying. Anna noticed and poured more wine, making small talk. Katie didn't have any. She hadn't had a drop of any kind of liquor for two weeks; she'd started eating more vegetables and staying away from smokers. Shafts of moonlight washed against her back, slender shoulders covered with freckles shruging as if to loosen her neck and dump some of the stress. The shadow of Panecraft fell across my hand as I reached for her wrist. We interlaced fingers. She grinned and let it go for the evening. "I've got the tulips you wanted."

"Thanks, I know how difficult they are to get this time of year."

"Difficult, but not impossible. Not if you try hard enough."

Maybe that was a dig, maybe not. We kissed, and the cool softness of her lips played against mine, her breath in my mouth like ten thousand spoken and unspoken words. Shifting toward each other, we kissed again, more passionately, and it hurt for me not to throw down a credit card and grab our coats and rush back to her place to hold her tightly beneath her aunt's thick blankets.

We heard him at the same time.

Staring into each other's eyes, she frowned, puzzled: a sudden odd, distant humming and gasping stalked nearer, the sound of splashing outside coming closer and closer like a child leaping loudly into every puddle. We knew the noise.

Katie said, "Surely not this far from town."

Clearing her throat, Anna told me, "Jon, I think you should . . ."

"Oh boy," I said.

The door burst open in a flurry of black motion, wind and hail rushing inside with icy streamers twirling.

"I am Crummler! I am here!"

Impossible. He almost never left his shack at the cemetery, and when he did he went no farther than Main Street. To get this far he would've had to walk for hours—who would ever give him a ride? Always in action, even now with the ice crystals so heavy in his wiry beard and hair that his face appeared frozen in place, Crummler erupted into the room with a ballerina's bounce. His coat trailed behind him like a black and ghostly shroud trying to catch up. He smelled of the cemetery, which was only slightly better than Oscar's after shave. His customary mania at once seemed lessened and heightened, internalized so that he twitched even more wildly than usual, blinking in the bright lights, shivering in the freeze.

Bus boys went running. The maitre d' threw menus on the floor, and a young waitress grabbed a fire extinguisher, ready to douse the edgy stranger if she needed to—which I thought was extremely level-headed of her.

"Crummler," Katie told him. "You're freezing. Come sit by the fire."

He jitterbugged and snapped his fingers, following her dolefully. He trembled as much from the night as from his own fiery, burning nerve-endings. "I have been in battle with forces," he moaned. "I have been in battle."

He still wore the same pair of work boots I'd bought him a couple months back. Odd to realize that he'd been there when I'd first met Katie in the flower shop, like the living embodiment of the excitement I felt for her, his eyes blazing with love and madness. He glared at the wild boar's head on the wall, then down at our table and especially at my plate, and I got the unsettling feeling that he was thinking the same things I was.

"I am here, Jon!"

"Want some lasagna?" I asked.

Katie said, "He probably eats neater than you."

"Well, his elbows are clean, anyway."

Melting rime rolled off his neck, and despite the shuddering he actually did manage to eat more neatly than I had, carefully cutting up the pasta and forking it into his mouth with a trained and cautious maneuvering. I could tell a hundred hours of harsh training had probably gone into that conduct, someone at the orphanage forcing him to repeat the action until he got it down perfectly.

"Armadas roared across the roiling waves," Crummler continued. "Met at the shore by the infernal war devices of ancient beasts, pyres burning in the antediluvian skies."

Anna loved listening to his impressive vocabulary that only filtered out when he told tales of ocher nights and ancient empires of other galaxies. It seemed that about a fifth of the patrons in the place recognized him and tried their best not to be bothered. The rest gaped, whispered in a near panic, or hid their faces behind the centerpieces.

I heard the manager in the alcove hissing loudly into the

phone. "Don't give me that jurisdiction crap, he's your loony, you come get him out of here. Yeah, we've heard about this gravekeeper you got. What, if he's three feet over the county line you're going to let him ruin my business?" I could just imagine Sheriff Broghin lumbering to his feet, the gunbelt angled into his belly rolls and leaving ugly welts.

Everything seemed to catch Crummler's interest, so that he spun and wheeled, wet hair whipping like shaggy fur. Brown water dripped off his soaking clothes. He broke from the table and waved to people, some of whom fondly waved back. Forever ignited, Crummler moved and reached. He started dancing with somebody's veal piccata.

"That son of a bitch has my dinner!"

I wrestled the plate away from him and put it back in front of a guy with big teeth, who sputtered and glared at the veal as if it might infect him with lunacy or rabies.

"I'll take him to his shack," I said. "I'll be back in forty-five minutes."

"Jon, be careful," Anna told me. "Something's wrong."

"I know."

"Maybe I should go with you," Oscar offered. "He's sorta the overactive type, ain't he?"

"I have been in battle," Crummler said. "I have been in battle . . . with *myself*."

"Come on," I told him. "I'll take you home."

His mouth fell in on itself and the reckless energy drained from his face. He shivered as though all the cold had finally caught up with him. He stood straight and idle, squinting into the distance, blind to me, his voice thickening with lucidity. "Not to Maggie's."

"Back to the cemetery," I said.

"Huh?"

"Where you take care of our families."

"Yes."

"Where you watch over my parents."

"Yes, Jon!" His eyes re-lit and held their fervor, the wire on fire once more. "They say hello, Jon. They say they love you, Anna." He reached down and embraced my grandmother, rocking gently. She brought the back of her hand to her mouth. We never got used to the way he spoke of the dead as if he'd had recent conversations with them, and I think Anna and I both hoped that, somehow, with his innocence he might actually be telling the truth.

"Thank you, Crummler, that is wonderful to hear," Anna said. "Thank you for telling me."

"Yes!" He shot up and hugged me, too, his hand rubbing my back in gentle and loving circles. "Thank you for the shoes. They fit well. They remain in good shape."

"I'm glad you like them," I said. "Come on, let's go get in the van, okay? We'll put the heat way up for you."

"Like them I do, though they are even more muddy. They suit me well when traveling through the swamps of ten thousand leagues of dwindled empires, fighting the dark orders of ocher nights."

When he talked of ancient obsidian towers in the far reaches of lost dimensions on the borderlands of time, he put so much into it you could almost witness his travels. Crummler snapped his fingers and stomped his heels in a weird but genuine fandango. I didn't know what to do except watch him. Children clapped and got off their seats and danced around with him. A few people left in a big hurry, but most just continued their dinner and conversations without furor, more kids joining in like they were at recess.

"This is why I prefer staying home with a bag of chips," I said.

"Sounds good to me right about now," Katie whispered.

The door crashed open again and Broghin bustled in. His perpetual scowl and flat, bloodless lips were so much a part of him that I couldn't tell anymore if he was truly incensed or if his bran wasn't quite cutting it. Even odds, I decided. The level-headed waitress lifted her extinguisher once more and kept it trained on him, for which I gave her even more credit.

He didn't expect to find my grandmother, whom he'd loved for decades, to be out on a date. It took only a few seconds for all the rest of his usual rage to wash up into his face, veins in his neck and temples suddenly thick and crawling. He stalked forward to our table, kicked some of the dropped menus without noticing, and said, "And what the hell are you doing here?"

Oscar drew his chin back. "That's the way you ask?"

"I'll ask any damn way I please, Kinion."

"Then I'm a damn fool is who I am, because I voted for you."

The sheriff turned to me and said, "Not a word out of you."

I said, "If the forty-percent bran isn't working, you might want to skip directly to a high colonic." I knew he'd miss the joke; he thought a colonic was something you mixed with gin.

Anna reached up and put a hand on Broghin's belly; she didn't have the arm length to get anywhere else besides his stomach. The sweater, recently unboxed and smelling of lost Christmas pine, reminded me of my parents' deaths, as well as Broghin's inept handling of the investigation, the ensuing embarrassment, and my time in jail. "Please, Francis, this is no place for histrionics."

"I might be obliged to agree with you, Anna, except I never know what you're talking about."

"She means you were called in to calm folks and escort a man back to his place, not act like a jackass," Oscar remarked pleasantly.

"Is that so?"

"I believe it is."

Broghin liked poking people in their chests, and I could just imagine his plump fingers thumping the tight, coarse flesh over Oscar's heart. I'd thrown a chair at Broghin's head for doing that to me once and wound up in a cell. I wondered if Oscar had only two racks of rifles out in his truck, or three, or more, and just what caliber he might have tucked away in the glove compartment. He wasn't the kind of man who would take kindly to being poked in the chest. In such situations you needed to count the number of guns within close proximity. Anna and Katie both looked at me imploringly, and I kind of shuffled feet without knowing what the hell I should do. Crummler and the kids came dancing over in an impromptu rumba line. "I am here, Sheriff!"

"You know you shouldn't be, Crummler," Broghin said. "Isn't that right? You should be at home. It's much too cold to be walking around. I think we've talked about that some before, too, haven't we?''

"Yes," Crummler admitted. "We have talked. It is cold."

"Did you walk here?"

"I did. For my boots fit well. I did!"

"Why?"

We'd all asked that question.

"To see my friends!"

Broghin had actually proven to be good with Crummler in the past, and did just as well now. He had a genuine appreciation for him, just as I did, because we were people devoted as much to the past as the present. I called it being moribund; Anna deemed it sentiment. Broghin probably put no name to his feelings, and for a man like him it was just as well. He smiled and touched Crummler gently, and even managed to put a melodic sort of giggle in his voice, bouncing on his toes to match the gravekeeper's dancing. They twirled in a circle for a moment and, leading the waltz, Broghin spun Crummler toward the door, through it, and outside into the police car. He drove off in no hurry, and I saw him put an arm around the gravekeeper, the way my father had done for me, and Oscar had been doing all through dinner. I felt very old in one respect, and too young in another.

A couple of the children stared forlornly through the window, watching the car recede, and started to cry. The guy who'd lost his veal piccata said, "Somebody ought to shoot that psycho son of a bitch before he goes into a second grade classroom and takes over the school."

"Lighten up a little," I said. "He doesn't cause any trouble."

"He ruined my dinner!"

"I'll pay for it."

"You gonna pay for my wine, too?"

"No."

A thousand-yard stare came over him at the thought of his paying for his own liquor bill. "Somebody still ought to shoot the bastard."

Oscar grinned and said, "Kinion's Hunting & Tackle, right on Fredrickson in Felicity Grove, you know where that is? Come on down to my store, I've got a rifle I can show you. A Springfield M-6 Scout, improved and updated from the original U.S. Air Force M-6 Survival Rifle, stainless steel construction, an optional lockable marine flotation.'' The smile dropped off, like it had never existed at any point in the history of his face. ''Of course, it'll be butt stock first up against your peckerwood nose, you horse-faced ass.''

The guy stood and Oscar rose to his feet and Anna went, ''Oh dear,'' the way she usually did when I was about to get into trouble. I found it deeply gratifying that I didn't initiate anything this time, and relished that fact for a moment. The guy with big teeth reached for a bottle of wine on his table, to either throw, drink from, or shatter on the edge of the table so that he could hold the jagged end like a knife. I found myself wishing that the moose and quail actually would go rampaging through the restaurant, anything but something like this. Anna deserved a better night out than this. So did Katie.

I slid out of my seat and quickly slipped in front of Oscar, gliding forward until the horsey-faced guy swung around to confront me, grabbing the bottle like a club. Without really meaning to, and not completely in self-defense either, I just sort of . . . *slapped* him, the way a girl would. It was the kind of silly slap that somebody would give while saying, ''Oh, pooh.''

I looked at my hand and the guy looked at me, and Oscar stopped short, and you could feel the entire situation defuse in a heartbeat. The horsey-face laughed and shoved me away, sat down, poured himself another glass of wine, and started to eat his wife's dinner.

In the parking lot, as we said our goodbyes, I thought Oscar was shaking my hand, but he had actually palmed something to me: a gym membership card. ''They got this guy,'' he said, ''used to be golden gloves, he can teach anybody to box. You should go see him.''

I wondered if, after all the death and blood of the last several years, I'd suddenly become afraid of ever hurting anybody again, and if so, what that would be like from now on.

A soft sound faded in, rustling like the hail on my shoulders.

After a few moments I heard it again, and once more, much sharper. My grandmother, the lady of silver rarity, called to me. "Jonathan."

"Don't mind him this evening," Katie told her, trying hard not to show any dismay. "He's just been a bit put off lately because I'm pregnant."

TWO

ANUBIS THREW ME LONG, TENSE glances as he watched me putting on my sweats, getting ready for an early-morning jog. His dark, thick Rottweiler face seemed to have the same muscles it took to make every human expression. He proved to be especially adept at looking pissed and appearing skeptical and suspicious. Ever since the last time we'd run in the park, when he'd saved my life, he grew agitated whenever he saw me lacing my sneakers. After mauling a murderous punk named Carl who was trying to stick a knife in my throat, Anubis had been through hell; cops and photographers wiped evidence from his face and took dozens of pictures of him from every angle. Some of the townsfolk had demanded to have him put to sleep, and he apparently knew all about it, and held grudges.

"Come on," I said. "We'll stay away from the park, okay?"

It didn't placate Anubis. He slinked off to lie in the corner facing away from me.

Anna wheeled herself in the kitchen, busy with spatulas and cups, rattling pans and bringing platters to the table. She enjoyed cooking enough food for breakfast to choke six lumberjacks: eggs Benedict, French toast as well as pancakes, hash browns, heaps of bacon, and always more coming. She never told me to finish everything on my plate because of those starving kids in China and India. We both enjoyed the morning ritual, despite the disquieting heaviness in the air between us lately.

"Please darling, sit," she said. "Don't wait. Start eating." I did, and had half a forkful of pancakes in my mouth when she leaned in close and asked, "Why didn't you tell me? A child. Your first child."

I'd correctly guessed that small talk remained anathema to her. It also seemed like all the major conversations in my life occurred while I was trying to eat. I stared at the heaping piles of food on the table and knew neither one of us would take another bite.

"We just found out for certain yesterday," I said.

Disappointment threaded her features, and she had a hard time keeping the caustic tone out of her voice. "Even with numerous and various types of birth control available, and the information and statistic on hand, two intelligent people refuse to practice safe sex in the age of AIDS."

"You might want to amend that to 'two people in love.' "

"I'm not unaware of that," she said.

"Okay."

She wouldn't smirk the way some people might have at the idea of two people falling in love after only a few weeks, especially for a man of twenty-eight already once divorced, with an ex-wife who wore enough leather to put cattle on the endangered species list. Bringing up the subject of AIDS proved to be more focused on me than Katie. Anna was aware that my ex-wife Michelle and I had continued to make love on occasion even after our divorce, and nobody liked to think of the quality of health care where her biker boyfriends were concerned, least of all Michelle. Or maybe, least of all me.

Before taking over the flower shop, Katie had been in medical school, leaving the field when she realized that while she had the proficiency, she didn't have the love for it necessary to deal with the stress involved with being a fine doctor. She knew the realities and hazards of our sexual era.

"We were both tested," I told Anna. "And Katie and I *are* in love, and Michelle and I haven't been together in nearly a year." It came out sounding way too whiny and defensive.

"I know that, dear," my grandmother said, as if the knowledge didn't mean much, really. "But you must understand that even love is not an excuse where inescapable realities are concerned." Her smile grew broad and a lot more light-hearted, but her gaze remained firm, maybe even a little cold. She seemed caught between bursting with delight at the prospect of a great-grandchild in her life and wanting to break a wooden spoon over my head. "I know you're in love and happy, and I'm overjoyed for you both, but Jonathan, what were you thinking?"

I didn't really believe she wanted to hear the kinds of things I thought about when I was in bed with Katie. I shut up and drank some milk.

One of the reasons Michelle and I had been driven apart—besides the fact that she'd started growing overly fond of guys named Sycho-Kila and Wrecking Ball—was that she didn't want kids. A strange urgency sporadically possessed me. Some might call that instinct, others ego.

Anna couldn't keep from glancing over at the wall where she'd rearranged some of the photo collages. "Marriage might not hold the same sanctity it did several decades ago, but rearing children is another matter altogether. There is no greater responsibility or commitment."

"Despite the facts at hand not painting me as the most responsible person in the world, do you really think I'd be a second-rate father, Anna?"

"No, you will be a wonderful father." The severity cleared from her face as she imagined Christmas with laughing children again, a season full of presents other than ties, cologne, gift certificates, and cold cash. Lots of colorful paper and breakable parts, with un-followed directions in Japanese wafting to the floor. "But a stable family life is equally important."

"If one can be made, I'll make it."

"Of that I am assured."

"Are you?"

"That you'll do your very best at whatever you put your mind to? Yes, absolutely. Always, dear. However, I fear that these . . . *complications* might work against yours and Katie's relationship.''

"So do I.''

"Lord, that sounded shamefully indifferent. I apologize.''

"Don't. I know what you mean.''

I got up and stood at the collages, witnessing my grandfather reading a copy of Steinbeck's *The Wayward Bus*. I had a first edition at the store that I couldn't look at without thinking of this picture: a man I'd never met nor even heard much about. Anna remained oddly silent about him, and I often thought the worst of him for that. It's difficult to give the dead the benefit of the doubt.

He and Anna had married within weeks of first meeting back in the late 'forties, when they were both still teenagers. He appeared to be a stolid man, lanky, a little thick in the middle but with arms of a mason or blacksmith. Actually, he'd been a milkman, starting his route at four in the morning, finishing by nine, and spending the rest of the day reading. He squinted, refusing glasses, with thick bushy thickets of overgrown eyebrows curling from their edges as if threatening to overtake his forehead. My mother said I'd inherited my love of books from him, my tenacity, and the fact that I was lactose intolerant but liked milk. Fine. Anything, anything at all, so long as I didn't get those eyebrows.

I hadn't spent the night at Katie's, as I'd been doing for the last eight weeks. After dinner she'd suggested a night apart and I'd agreed, though it seemed ironic that we needed time apart to work out our troubles about not spending enough time together. My bedroom felt like an open barn: huge and empty.

Katie hated Manhattan and had so far only spent one four-day weekend with me there. Though she enjoyed fine restaurants and theater, she despised the inherent speed and congestion of New York City, and all that it implied. Currents shifted every second, from street to street, hitting patches of warehouses, underground clubs, and classical brownstones and museums, layered side by side. The Koreans tumbled together on Korean Way, Italians down Canal; condensed passages of shops and youth down on St. Mark's and over by NYU, music and shouting, lots of blaring horns and sirens, and laughter. It annoyed her, turning off one block with a certain atmosphere and suddenly entering another with a completely different charge.

The homeless brought out her generosity, and for the first day she handed a buck out to whoever rattled their Styrofoam cup at us. She couldn't ignore anyone and stared wide-eyed at their approach. She may as well have had her PIN # tattooed on her cheek. At one point, five destitute men were lured from the shadows by her obvious innocence. It was like a scene from a Romero zombie flick, as the circle slowly closed around us and she handed out money.

"I feel sorry for them," she told me.

"I know."

"You don't seem to care."

"You get used to it."

"I never could."

Of course she could, I thought—you had to in order to function in Manhattan, or any major city. You simply didn't have a choice. It wasn't until after we'd made love that night and I saw the quiet panic in her eyes that I realized I'd been wrong. She did have a choice and had already made it . . . to never return to the city. I felt vaguely troubled that the burden of our being together had fallen to me, and that the decision for our future had become mine alone.

Anna took my hand. "You're not interested in moving your shop here, are you?"

"Not in the slightest."

"I didn't think so. Then why allow this façade to continue?"

"Certainly you know the answer to that," I said.

"Because you don't want to lose her. But prolonging the inevitable will only hurt her more in the end."

"I don't know what the inevitable *is*."

Since I hadn't eaten, I didn't need to digest before my run, and I knew of a surefire way to get out of this conversation. "Hey, since we're already speaking about matters of the heart . . ."

She disliked redirection as much as I did, and grimaced. "Oh, please, Jonathan, now really . . ."

"Come on. How serious is it between you and Oscar? And is he going to make you take up skeet shooting?"

"We are friends, as you well know."

"I know he acts like a teenager, and I think I even caught you tittering once or twice."

"I do not," she said emphatically, "titter."

"Yes, you do. I heard it while you were acting giddy."

Her eyes widened. "And I most positively do not, under any conceivable circumstances, act *giddy*."

"Anyway, I'm going to see just how much pedestrian traffic there really is downtown."

"The two of you will work this out."

"Things have to break one way or the other."

I snapped the leash to Anubis' collar and we had a tug-of-war for about five minutes before I finally wore him down. "Not the park," I told him. "Just a little jog downtown. I promise, not the park."

He didn't look like he believed me.

I stood in front of the flower shop. Weather could shift radically in Felicity Grove, and yesterday's storm had collapsed into a warm, sun-packed day. Katie wouldn't get here before eleven; morning sickness had hit her hard, and the daily ritual of anguish left her so drained she usually went back to bed for a while. In those early hours, holding her in the bathroom and watching her suffer, she looked frail and weak and completely incapable of chasing ketchup-covered kids around a restaurant. With her hair sticking to her sweat-stained face, she still tried to smile for my benefit, and I always wanted to make love to her right then.

I tried not to think that Anubis was the reason why people weren't walking by me. He gave frowns of consternation, fully understanding that nobody in this town would buy Emerson's *MayDay* for twenty-four hundred dollars. We walked a little farther down to Fredrickson Street, and I watched the parking lot of Kinion's Hunting & Tackle fill and empty for twenty minutes. At only ten in the morning, a dozen men had already bustled into the store needing to purchase their Springfield M-6 Scouts, improved and updated from the original U.S. Air

Force M-6 Survival Rifles, stainless steel construction with optional lockable marine flotation devices. I wondered if the ducks they shot would know the difference.

I knew that if I ever did move back to Felicity Grove I'd actually have to go to work for Oscar, or someone like him, and get involved with an occupation I didn't want to become involved in, most likely dealing with chickens or weapons.

"Come on," I said, and Anubis trotted beside me.

We headed back to the flower shop. I had a key and let myself in, but I always felt vaguely unsettled being in here without Katie. The floral arrangements had a real style to them, aesthetic with a flair for color and design. The refrigeration units thrummed dully, leaving cold patches and drafts. A slight vibration worked through the floor. The empty space at the side of the store appeared to be too confining for a possible bookstore. I shut my eyes and saw the place the way she always talked about it, then looked around and tried to see the same picture. Nothing came together.

I leaned against a wall and pretended to pull a book from a shelf and read, moving to peruse stacks of Harlequin romances, bird-watcher guidebooks, and football trivia, while coyly giggling at erotica written by "Anonymous" or "M" or "J." The sweetly cloying scent of flowers started to overcome me, that irksome vibration making my feet twitch. I could see myself becoming extremely whiny here.

"What do you think?" I asked.

Anubis remained the perfect partner for such discussions because he always grumbled like an older, more prudent investor. He sniffed around some plant-growth and discovered a patch of irresistibly lickable matter in a spider plant unfurled all over the floor. I had an image of the soil erupting with alien life, tendrils drawing him inside while mutant fauna jaws scarfed him down. I thought my mind would wander a lot like that while customers asked me if I carried back issues of *Playboy* or *Soldier of Fortune* magazines.

Anubis approached, sat, and stared at me as if he also saw my superiority complex showing. His tail thumped twice, expectantly. He grumbled some more.

"Okay."

I went to the refrigerator and took out some tulips, my mother's favorite. He started to growl, understanding their significance.

He didn't like the cemetery. It seemed like I was the only one who did.

At the cemetery, called Felicity Grave, an indistinct odor caught on the stiff breeze.

Leaves whirled. Rocky, root-strewn areas looked equally as well-kept as the flawlessly mowed grass jutting between the rows of markers. Bushes were impeccably pruned, dead branches and stumps cleared and toted away. Lawns remained lush, sweeping trimmed carpets that wound among the knolls and embankments, flowing down into the ravines of potter's field. Even the rubble of ancient angels, martyred saints, and scarred Madonnas wasn't neglected, the stone scrubbed clean.

I left the tulips on my parents' graves, brushing my fingers over their tombstones as I usually did. Certain formalities would stay with me forever. Wildflowers blossomed in erratic strips across the hollows, never hindered by unseasonable temperatures or heavy waves of sleet. The green had returned to some spindly tress growing among the more ornate and statuesque memorials. The old family mausoleums stood like granite condos. Anubis' mouth opened as I let him off the leash. The wind picked up a little.

Shifting breeze brought a wafting pungency.

"I am here, Jon!"

Anubis never growled at children or Crummler, but now he hunkered in the dirt, his head weaving as though trying to shake off dizziness, unable to draw a bead on Crummler. He followed me down the hillock, and the stink hit us at the same time. Crummler waved and pranced, bearing something.

An ugly sound worked free from the back of Anubis' throat, deep and lethal in its animosity. Hard ridges of his outlined muscles rose in the black fur, his hackles stiff; he held his snout low, tongue jutting, showing a lot of fang. The scent worked on him, his nostrils flaring, those black eyes beginning to roll as if he remembered the taste of the guy's throat in the park, and wanted a lot more.

"Jesus, no," I said. "No, Anubis, settle."

Crummler kept cavorting, still doing the dance Broghin and the kids had joined him in. I tried it out too, hoping it would calm him. I bounced around while he capered toward me. The edges of his beard stuck out, highlighted with red where his hair had draped onto his long, stained coat.

When he was ten yards from me I realized he was covered in blood and carrying a broken shovel, his hands filthy, and the coat still very wet.

I jogged down the knoll to him. "Are you hurt?"

"No!"

"Then . . ."

That acrid, burning stench. Nothing else like it in the world. I moved around one of the broad, groomed bushes and nearly stepped into the dead kid's mouth.

Parts of his teeth and features lay nearby. Someone had repeatedly used the shovel on him, making sure they took off every inch of his face. I couldn't tell much about him except that his clothes seemed to be the kind a teenager would wear: faded jeans, sneakers, black T-shirt, and an oversized leather jacket. Anubis stared at the corpse warily but with a strange calmness that unnerved me, as if this were nothing new. Crummler kept pirouetting. His wild, fevered energy and happiness had drained and been replaced by a maddening look of . . . sanity.

He smiled. "I am here, Jon."

"Oh shit," I said.

"I have been in battle . . ." His face fell, and he suddenly began moaning.

His mania meant something different now, with dark streaks of crusted blood on his hands and clothes. The same smile took on new connotations.

". . . with myself."

He brought the shovel up, like offering a gift, hefting it too quickly so that the blade angled sharply toward my face.

A part of me wanted to shout, but for a man too impractical to practice safe sex in the age of AIDS, I wasn't foolish enough to let Crummler get another step closer with his wild grin and bloody shovel.

This time I didn't slap like a nine-year-old girl. I punched him directly on the point of his hairy chin and he went flying backward to roll next to the body of the dead, faceless boy on the ground. He started sobbing, and I didn't know what the hell to do next.

THREE

LOWELL TULLY ARRIVED FIRST, WITH the wig-wag lights on but no siren, so that a strange red sheen from the cherry top spun against my legs and the array of whitewashed angels behind me. He stared at the scene for a minute, squinting as his hair tousled into his eyes, taking in every detail before silently returning to his car.

He made a few murmured calls on his police radio, the wind snapping at his brown deputy's shirt across his broad, muscular back. Crummler had fallen into a deep but fitful sleep not far from the corpse, his arms wrapped around his knees as though he couldn't quite fit into the fetal position. His fingers scratched at the dirt on occasion, like a dog chasing rabbits in his dreams. Anubis gazed about serenely, seated on a grave, comforted by the fact that he hadn't done anything this time. I was sweaty from chasing birds away from the dead kid.

Lowell handled the situation—macabre as it was—the way he handled everything: with the relaxed, easy assurance of a man with four percent body fat and a working knowledge of the body's nerve clusters and major arteries. He still had a football hero's swagger, back from when he'd fractured his pelvis in our last homecoming game. He went to one knee beside the corpse, carefully inspecting the faceless kid without touching him.

He stood and put his fists on his hips, and I decided if there was anything in this world that could rattle him I didn't want to know what it was.

"How are you holding up?" he asked.

"Oh," I said. "Fine."

Lowell took firm hold of my shoulder with one of his massive hands and led me a few yards off. Crummler, Anubis, and I had already done a proper job of fouling the crime scene, and he tried to save whatever investigative integrity remained. There wasn't much. We looked down at the sleeping manchild coated in dried blood, whose fingers kept flashing out.

"Did you touch him?" he asked.

"Only when I hit him."

"Did you handle the shovel?"

"No."

"Or the body?"

"No."

"Are you certain?"

"Hell, yes," I said. "You think I'd forget?"

"Just answer my questions directly and stow the remarks for the time being, all right? Can you work with that?"

"Yes."

"What did you see here?"

I told him, and I made sure I was precise. He listened without a word, without even movement. I was going to repeat myself, and once again felt the odd sense that my fate, and even my love, had become entwined with Crummler's life. "Despite the facts on hand, do you really think he could have done this?"

Lowell had never hesitated on anything in his life, and didn't hesitate now. "He's no different from any of us. Why else would you have knocked him down?"

"I was taken aback."

"You were scared shitless."

"That's what took me aback."

He nodded. "I can see as it might. Tell me everything that happened. Go through it again."

I told him once more, beginning with last night, and the ice-rimed wraith from out of the darkness who had leaped into the restaurant. I expected him to smile when I got to the part of Crummler dancing with the children, but instead he only sucked air through his teeth in a low, unpleasant whistle.

Events had forced a new reality on us. What I'd hoped would paint the caretaker as harmless only led to uglier thoughts: what if he'd snapped last night in a dining room full of children?

"What did you do after you hit him?"

"Called you."

"From where?"

"Duke Edelman's gas station."

Lowell looked over his shoulder at the graveyard path that led up to the road heading back into town. "That's how far? A mile? You left him there like that the whole time?"

It sounded extremely stupid when he put it like that—leaving a murder suspect passed out beside the mangled victim, along with my dog. "He was crying, and fell asleep by the time I got back. I didn't exactly have much choice in the matter. What did you expect, for me to carry him over my shoulder or drop him hog-tied to a tree?"

"You still running them six-minute miles, Johnny? You might consider carrying a cell phone, what with all the shit you get into. You should've borrowed one of Duke's trucks to come back."

"It's less than a mile, and by the time I pulled Duke out from under one of his junkers and found the keys and answered questions I could've run back here anyway. I figured we'd get a lot of unwanted attention soon enough. A cell phone, huh?"

Three more police cars pulled up, followed by Keaton Wallace, the Medical Examiner, in his coroner's wagon. A dull morning for everyone, and the news van crews would be coming soon. Sheriff Broghin sauntered down the hill trying desperately to keep his stomach from getting too far out in front of him, the gun belt riding way too low. He hadn't been able to resist using the siren, and now Crummler slowly roused himself from the mud.

For a moment, Zebediah Crummler looked like any man I'd ever known awakening from a two-night drunk, opening his eyes wide to whatever hell had driven him to it. I could see Lowell there after his fiancée left him at the altar on the eve of his twenty-first birthday. I saw myself when my parents died in their car and Anna remained comatose with her legs crushed; I watched my father on the couch at dawn in his dirty T-shirt back before AA saved what few years he had left. The pain seeped into the air, and it seemed familiar to me. Then the light of coherence faded, and Crummler grinned happily, shuddering and snapping, on fire again, unaware or not caring about the reek of blood on him. He sat up and shouted, "Jon!"

Broghin had a few ways to play it, and once more he surprised me with his gentleness. He reached down and took Crummler by the hand, led him up to the sheriff's car, and gingerly put handcuffs on the caretaker's wrists and eased the yawning man into the back seat.

At some point Lowell glided away from me and conferred with Keaton Wallace and the other deputies as they bagged bits and pieces. I didn't want to look too closely. Anubis remembered the police photographers and appeared ready to engage in lively discourse with them. I pulled him down beside me and we sat beneath the knotty limbs of a stunted white oak. It took a while but eventually Anubis murmured and rolled over, and I watched the slow and steady rise and fall of his chest.

A half hour later, Broghin returned and stepped next to me without a word. We were going to do this gradually. His enormous gut hung over his belt: he had a belly you just wanted to grab with both hands and shake vigorously, then sit back for a few minutes and watch the fun. I wondered if he would question me about Oscar, here over the body of a dead, faceless boy. The sheriff, like most men with high blood pressure who refused medication, couldn't control the flow of his frustration, and would let it out regardless of time or place. His jealousy had to have been prodding him savagely.

"You know him?" he asked.

"The kid on the ground? I don't think so."

"You do or you don't?"

Besides being lactose intolerant I had a touch of high blood pressure, too. "How can I be certain? He has no face. Who is he?"

"You sure you don't know him?"

"What the hell does that mean?"

Broghin was nearly as good at looking suspicious as Anubis. It took me another few seconds before realizing that he actually considered me a suspect. "Oh, well now," I said. "That's wonderful."

"Just answer me, damn it," he hissed, and the slight nub of veins at the edges of his temples suddenly bloated into writhing black centipedes. Anubis caught the ugly inflection and instantly rolled to his feet, giving Broghin his best flat, dead gaze, mouth open a little and showing the barest sheen of fangs. "Goddamn, but I do despise that dog. I never hated a man as much as I do that dog. Now answer me."

"I did answer you. I don't know if I know him, he's got no face."

We both glanced up at the sheriff's car and watched Crummler doing some kind of funky Rockette number in the back seat, his heels tapping out against the window. He saw us and started waving ecstatically even while cuffed. One of the other deputies walked over, trying to pacify him.

"You can't believe he did this," I said.

Broghin's lips skewed into a sorrowful smile that still had a lot of self-righteousness to it. "Jonny Kendrick, I've never heard you sound so unsure of anything in all the years you've been climbing on my back."

"Yeah, well . . . what did he say to you last night when you took him back here?" I asked. "Did he tell you anything?"

"I swear, it nearly sounds like you're questioning me. Yes, I think I hear that in your voice a bit, just a little bit, I do."

Broghin and I could go through the battle of the wills some other time. I wished Anna were here now; she liked it when he pulled out the podunk, and could work him into telling her anything, one way or another.

"You saw all that blood on him, you don't get that covered just hitting a guy with a shovel."

"Somebody took their time with him. The kid wasn't only hit, you saw that."

"Yes, I did, but even so."

He stood smoothing the few hairs on his head as if the wind might have messed them. It hadn't. "Crummler must have held the boy. Cradled him, maybe. During . . . or after."

"Why beat the kid to death, mutilate him, and then hold him in your lap?"

"You want to ask him? Look over there, he's still spouting. I think he's up to the part where the giant alien insects in black robes are robbing Egyptian tombs. You'll like that one, it's one of my favorites."

He grabbed at his hair again and made a show of hiking his belt up, but a moment later everything sagged back in the same place. "Did you hear anything?"

"No."

"Arguing? Sounds of struggle?"

"No."

"You're always at the center of the storm, aren't you, Jonny Kendrick?" That sounded fairly poetic for him, and I could tell he was proud of himself for coming up with it—I didn't argue the point that there was actually calm at the eye of the storm. His mouth curled and twisted. "Did Crummler say anything when you found him?"

"No, he only repeated what he said last night. That he'd been in battle with himself."

"His conscience bothering him? Maybe he's been planning this."

"That's ridiculous."

"Don't go getting involved any more than you already are. Tell your grandmother the same."

I already had. I knew that no matter what happened from here on out, I'd always get back to past misfortunes that followed, and how deeply immersed I became in new troubles because of those in the past.

"What did he tell you last night?" I asked, but Broghin was already stomping off.

They tossed Crummler's shack, wrapped the shovel in plastic and tagged it. Lowell drifted back about an hour later, when the reporters started bustling over, looking to interview me. They kept to a tight but distant ring since Anubis occasionally stalked forward and they were forced to draw back. A couple shouted and asked if the dog had ripped anybody else's throat out. Lowell ordered the other deputies to back them off.

"What about the grave he was lying on?" I asked. "Any connection there?"

"The fella died over a hundred years ago, so I tend to doubt it. Cletus Johnstone, died of tuberculosis in the winter of eighteen seventy-three. His headstone says he fought bravely at Gettysburg. Killed his own cousin, Thomas Johnstone, in the name of God, country, and freedom of these beloved United States. Survived by l' loving wife, Annabelle, and twin teenage daughters, Rachel and Ruth."

"Christ, they managed to fit all that?" I knew Lowell would check the name out further. "Who is the kid?"

"Found a wallet in Crummler's shack. It belongs to Teddy Harnes."

"Teddy? Does that make him the son of Theodore Harnes?"

"I'm guessing so. If it's him at all, and not just a lost wallet."

Theodore Harnes was the richest man in six counties, and though he'd spent most of the last decade out of the country, he still had more news and gossip floating around him than anyone else in a couple hundred-mile radius. The facts though, as I recalled them, included paternity suits and rape charges leveled against him that he'd either been innocent of, or had paid his way out of, and didn't cost him any lasting trouble.

Rumors were another matter. They said he'd used a hammer to murder a turncoat company partner. They said that in the past thirty years he'd helped more people in this part of the state than any of our senators of governors. They said he owed factories overseas where children were sold into sweatshop work. His assembly plants drove all the smaller competition out of business. The, .aid he bought rat poison by the vat and fed it to the Indonesian kids who tried to run. He was a philanthropist who donated millions to hospitals, shelters, museums and libraries. People protested against his factories

constantly, and others reviled the protesters. I could only remember having seen a few photos of him in the paper and
thought him a highly unassuming man. If those rumors were
true, I wondered what being the son of such a man might be
like.

I said, "If Teddy wanted to fake his own death for some
reason, perhaps to get away from his father, this might just be
the way to do it."

"Yes," Lowell said.

"What are you going to do with Crummler?"

"You already know. Bring him to the jail. He'll stay there
for a day or two and then we'll need a psychiatric evaluation."

Broghin got into his car and threw it into drive, languor-
ously easing up the cemetery path. Crummler kept waving out
the back window to me, his hands in cuffs. His gaze, in even
those last few seconds, floated with chunks of madness, innocence, lucidity and rage.

Tomorrow he'd be in Panecraft.

FOUR

ANNA COULD READ A DOZEN mysteries at once and never confuse the complexities of plot lines. She appeared to be in a hard-boiled phase. In the past few weeks I'd sent her Chandler's *Lady in the Lake*, Lawrence Block's *The Devil Knows You're Dead*, Charles Williams' *Go Home, Stranger*, and Andrew Vachss' *Strega*. I'd met Block and Vachss at an autograph party in the city, and liked them personally as much as I enjoyed their work. Anna never cared if she read a signed first edition or not. She wasn't a collector as such, but I tried to get rarities when I could. Block had written, "For Anna, a true lady of mystery. . . ." He'd seen us on the news after Richie Harraday's body had been found in her garbage can.

I tossed the novel back on the pile and got off the couch. Katie and Anna were in the kitchen discussing herbal teas, Lamaze, marriage, and mortgage rates in the Grove. As far as conversation topics went, I was routing for tea to come up from behind and start leading the pack. The world seemed to be sprawling away from me, but not quite violently out of control yet. I felt if I planted my feet and took a firm stance on anything in my life, the sudden shifting of what had been set in motion behind me would rise up across my shoulders and crash over my head.

I looked out the window at the spot on the lawn where Harraday's body had been dumped, and where Lisa Hobbes had left her best friend Karen Bolan's corpse as well, hoping to make the murders seem connected. The tougher reporters, or those less informed, occasionally knocked on the door and tried to peek into the only window with its shade not fully drawn. I left it that way on purpose: when somebody attempted to peer inside, Anubis would draw himself up, lean his front paws on the windowsill, and stick his flat, black muzzle against the glass. The reporters left in a hurry, trundling back down the ramp beside the porch stairs.

Katie and Anna entered the living room, Katie with a huge grin that highlighted her dimples and made my heart tug to the left. Her palms angled evenly across the hand grips pushing Anna's wheelchair—it took a little getting used to, shoving the sometimes unwieldy chair across the wears in the carpet; the smaller guide tires tended to sink and slip. A silver platter of cups and cookies lay across my grandmother's lap. I wondered if we would ever be able to make the break to having liquor in the house again after my father's alcoholism.

Mortgage rates in the Grove, I was informed, were quite reasonable, and the market appeared to be getting even better this fiscal year for homeowners.

I waited it out. Anna would crack soon. We were into something ugly again, and while she didn't feel haunted by it, she did grow more and more enthralled, possibly even delighted. Katie also sensed the change in atmosphere as they talked— my grandmother's attention not only wavering but diverting, leading into another direction. Anna's questions and responses got slower and shorter. She started saying "That's nice, dear," a lot. Katie gave me an amused frown and I shrugged. She sat on the couch, put the television on, and ran the channels, searching for some news.

"Such mutilation of the boy's features has meaning," my grandmother said, sipping her tea, and we were into it.

"Means somebody probably didn't like the guy too much."

Naturally it had significance—you cleave somebody's features off, chances are you're trying to make a pretty big point.

"Did Lowell believe there might be any connection to the grave on which you found the body?"

She knew I'd asked him, both of us traveling along these same paths so often we could second-guess each other's actions. The same way I knew she would go see Keaton Wallace, the ME, tomorrow morning, and ferret more information about the kid's face. "No. An old grave from the Civil War, but not belonging to any of the Harnes clan."

At the sound of the name she stiffened slightly. That bothered me, but before I could say anything Anna continued. "There may be more to it, Jonathan."

"Probably not. That part of the cemetery swings low down the hill into much older sections. You go from the Civil War circles to the present with the rise of the new promontories, spreading back across the fields."

"Perhaps he stood on higher ground, the scuffle took place there, and he rolled down the hill?"

"Maybe he was running for his life," I said. "Whatever it was, it wasn't a scuffle."

This lady of silver rarity, her eyes hardening until she looked a little like Lowell did facing the wind—imperturbable, accustomed to talking and dealing with such matters—stared at me curiously the way my football coach used to when I was off my game. "We need to know more, dear. The wallet disturbs me. Greater suspicion is thrown on Crummler for their having retrieved the wallet in his shack, as much as for anything else."

I thought the blood in his beard was a bit more suspicious, but only told her, "I don't know if that's true, but Crummler wouldn't have stolen the kid's money."

"The wallet appears to be an extra and conclusive touch, without finesse, in order to implicate him."

"Or maybe he found it, before or after he discovered the body, and was simply holding on to it."

Anubis rose, alert to her frame of mind, and paced across the room, moving his broad head beneath her hand, where she petted him absently between his ears. "Were there any wounds on Crummler? Signs of a thrashing or abuse of any sort?"

"No, he wasn't provoked physically, at least not in that manner. He wasn't beaten by the kid."

In a throaty whisper filled with concern, but no real anxiety, she asked, "Do you think he sought us out last night? He said he came to see his friends."

It couldn't be the case, but I kept wondering anyhow, thinking about the way he'd erupted from the night into the restaurant, seething and electrified. Something had driven him there. I didn't believe much in coincidence, but nothing else made any sense, either.

He counted us to be, perhaps, his only friends, and had traveled a long way in the freeze—to find me and Anna?

Or had he simply been trying to escape the Grove, and the ties of circumstance binding him to the cemetery, the town, and even to me and my love, had been stretched to their limit, and snapped him back to where darkness already waited?

"How could he know where we'd be?"

Katie caught a broadcast that showed the murder site, turned to me and said, "I know this will sound ridiculous, but I wish you'd smile more."

"What? You mean in front of the cameras?" I thought about what kind of a day I'd had. "I think that qualifies as ridiculous."

"You always look so angry. Half these people probably think you did it, the way you scowl."

I did look sort of loony, just sitting there on a grave as the camera panned across the cemetery, and I tried to imagine just how many people would be smiling, waving to their mothers, primping their hair. At least she didn't mention that I had dressed sloppily. "Not exactly the best photo opportunity."

"You know what I mean, I care what they think about you, Jon. I don't want them hounding you." She picked up the remote to change the channel but couldn't quite tear her interest from the screen. They were wringing every drop of drama from the story, getting into Harnes' sordid sexual history but not mentioning a word about Teddy's life; we watched the gorgeous newscaster smiling too much and stating that a suspect was in custody and the victim was believed to be Theodore Harnes' son. She dipped her chin to her abundant chest, over-articulated the name, *"Thee-a-door Harnezz,"* as if she were giving you time to gasp, flinch, and wave your hands about your face before she continued.

They went live to the scene, and Broghin, to his benefit, gave only a curt statement. He'd been right to drive Crummler away quickly, before anybody could get a shot of him dancing his Rockette steps against the back window. They cut to a close-up of Anna's house, a tight shot of Anubis' face in the window.

"Oh boy."

Katie's mouth smoothed into a flat, white line. "Why didn't you at least make a statement? You could have explained yourself to them. Anna, you should have handled this. Now they'll be making accusations and innuendoes, angling their reports, like the last time."

My grandmother and I exchanged glances. We'd both spoken to the press in the past only to realize how little of our interviews had actually been used; you could never be sure if your responses and intent would come through as you meant them.

A thin sheen of sweat dappled Katie's forehead. "They kept coming into the shop throughout the day, all these people I'd never seen before who knew we were dating, asking any kind of questions they could think to ask. Some of them reminisced, talking about your years in high school, the way you'd played football. I think most of your teammates and their wives wandered in this afternoon. I didn't think this was the type of town that took high school athletics to such an extreme, but every one of them came in alone but told the same stories."

"Did they at least buy flowers?" I asked.

"No, nobody. Some guy said you botched an easy play against Briscane County? And lost twenty-one to twenty-four, costing the championship. If he's not in therapy he should be. That guy seems to have some unresolved issues."

"Yeah, that would be Arnie Devington. He's still mad. He thinks a scout for Miami University was in the stands, and he missed his shot at the pros because we lost. Did he say anything about his two fumbles in the second half?"

"No."

"That's because he hasn't thought about them since three seconds after I became his scapegoat." Arnie Devington, his mother and father, two brothers and two sisters had badgered me for months after that game, and still the old hurt and anger rose up in me, just as it did in him.

"Was there a scout?" Katie asked.

"Beats the hell out of me, but I seriously doubt it. If there was he would've only been interested in Lowell, anyway. Guys from Miami don't travel north if they can help it."

My grandmother kept patting Anubis in a repetitive, rhythmic motion I could almost put music to. His tail thumped every fifth or sixth beat as Anna turned events over in her mind. Our gazes tangled, and I caught her lips working silently. I cocked my head as if to listen better, waited, and she said it aloud. "Theodore Harnes." She enunciated it with nearly as much affectation as the newscaster. "He is a most . . . intriguing man."

"Oh cripes."

Whenever she said "intriguing" like that I remembered how much I hated her saying "intriguing" like that. I felt a sudden drop in temperature, a rise in pressure.

Anna pursed her lips. "Truly."

"Do you know anything about his son?"

"No, not that I recall."

"If he's anything like his father, from what I've heard, then Crummler might have had provocation."

"So your assertion is that Zebediah is guilty?" She had a slicing arc of astonishment in her voice she could only afford because she hadn't seen him covered in blood. If she'd witnessed that lucidity trying to break through the haze of his burning-wire persona, she wouldn't be half so certain.

"I'm keeping the list of our possibilities open until we learn more one way or another."

Catching the slight edge of guilt in my tone, Katie said, "I'm glad you hit him. I'm relieved you were willing to protect yourself first. Sometimes I worry about that."

"Don't."

"From now on I won't."

I moved to sit beside her and Katie sneaked in close—she

knew how to read me and how to make it better. I'd catch her staring at the side of my face and realize she'd set aside her own worries to concentrate on mine. I slipped my hand onto her belly, which made her sigh, both of us falling into a weird pattern of being preoccupied with something so natural yet terrifying as this. I hoped she'd understand that no matter what happened we'd get through it all. I hoped I could believe it myself.

"Teddy Harnes may have faked his own demise," Anna said.

"Yes, but why?"

"It's something to consider. And you're quite right, Jonathan, I apologize for seeming narrow-minded when it was you who was personally involved with the situation this morning. That was foolish and thoughtless of me. It's correct to keep our possibilities open. Crummler may indeed have been provoked."

"Into defending himself, maybe." I shook my head. "I'm not sure how you can be provoked into shearing somebody's nose and lips off."

Anna's eyes filled with a great distance. A shaft of late afternoon sunlight cut down from the one shadeless window, wreathing my grandmother in rose. "A psychiatric facility like Panecraft will be pure torture for him. . . ." She hesitated in following up, blowing out a thin stream of air that made Anubis' eyelids twitch, and stopping just short of saying, *He'll go mad.*

The bloody blade of the shovel came up toward my face again, with him whimpering about battling himself, perhaps not feeling any differently than I did now, yanked in too many directions at once. He wouldn't make it. Something lurked down inside him—*he's no different from any of us*—and whether it was a weeping boy locked in silence or a burgeoning call to lash out, Crummler wouldn't be able to handle being taken from Felicity Grave and the dead that gave his life meaning.

"I tend to agree," I said.

"Jonathan, are you holding anything back?"

I answered more easily than I would have thought. "I think I saw another side of him."

"Which side is that?" Katie asked.

"A part of him that might be sane."

Anna steepled her fingers and brought them to her chin as though she were trying to figure out which part of *me* might still be sane. "You know as well as I do, dear, that his sanity is not actually in question. Crummler is mentally handicapped."

"Mentally-challenged is the PC term nowadays. And I'm not sure what he is anymore, except that I saw someone else lurking beneath his usual self."

Anna worried her lips and sipped her tea. The chemistry had shifted between us with the introduction of Katie, as it had once before with Michelle. "Theodore Harnes married a friend of mine."

"Who?"

"One of my bridesmaids, Diane Cruthers. They met while I was on my honeymoon, had something of a whirlwind storybook romance, and eloped only days later. Of course, since he did not come from old wealth, this was before he'd amassed his fortune, Theodore Harnes proved to cut something of a deliberate, but shy, figure."

What had it meant when she'd frozen like that before just hearing his name? "So, you've met him."

"No more than three or four times." Her voice both gained and lost an edge, as though she did and didn't want to talk about any of this. My stomach started to knot. She cleared her throat and fell silent for a moment, and I knew she was editing her story for either my benefit, or her own. Whatever she was hiding would undoubtedly be ugly. "A year or so younger than us, actually, he was hardly more than a boy himself. I only saw Diane once again, very briefly. She was expecting their first child."

I scanned the photos on the wall, the large black-and-white of Anna's wedding; my grandfather standing there looking frightened in a bow tie before the rampant forest of his eyebrows completely consumed his forehead; a row of men and women in their wedding party, everyone grinning good-naturedly. I wondered who was Diane Cruthers. The ladies seemed so much alike in the somewhat worn-out, dark pictures, with a sort of glaze to them all. Youth and expectancy, eagerness perhaps. Which of these women would Harnes sweep away to Europe? Maybe he was only a foolish young man with feverish dreams at the time . . . or maybe a monster in the making.

Only rarely did my grandmother allow some prejudice to bubble up and break the surface where it could be viewed by someone who might notice. She gathered Katie's cup and the uneaten cookies back onto the platter and put it across her knees, and worked her wheelchair around and rolled toward the kitchen.

"Where is she now?" I asked.

Anna smiled blandly, one of her few acts of false bravado, and consequently a poor one. "She committed suicide shortly thereafter."

Katie paled and said, "Good God." She shifted against me, folding herself closer under my arm.

There had to be more. I hadn't really heard it in my grand-mother's voice or seen it in the virtually wrinkle-free angles of her face, but the truth had been there, a tiny thing searching for a place to hide.

Anna had been jealous of Diane Cruthers for winning the love of an intriguing man named Theodore Harnes.

FIVE

KATIE STILL LIVED AT THE Orchard Inn, a kind of boarding
house run by the Leones. She'd found no reason to move, and
I didn't blame her. The place was much bigger than my apartment in the city, and cheaper than just about anything else she
might find in the Grove. It had a certain charm, with a trellis
beyond the window, and doilies, floral chintz curtains, and
rosewood everywhere you looked. She'd taken down the crucifixes and some of the statues of saints the Leones had left
around, and politely kept them all in one corner. I'd sometimes
glance over and feel the weight of a thousand years of Catholic
canon upon me.

When we got back to her apartment we spent a long time
in bed whispering and caressing before we finally made love.
Need grew steadily. We worked with the slow madness of
everything we'd been feeling lately, the fuel of frustration and
passion, and wondering how it would all play out. My flight
reservation back to the city had been made for this morning.
I had weeks' worth of backorders to fulfill and auction lots to
scout.

"Boy," she said as we drifted back against the pillows. I
brushed the hair from her face, drawing my fingers in and out
of her dimples. "Somebody had his Wheaties."

Wind howled like baying hounds and rattled the windows, the roof lurching and groaning. The night split open and that freaky hail started pecking at the glass again. Even the weather seemed out of sorts, working to get back on track. Katie shivered, clambered to her dresser, drew on a thick flannel nightgown that had either been out of style for six decades or had just come back in, and climbed back into bed where we huddled beneath the comforter.

She said, "You're looking at Jesus again."

"He's looking at me."

"You want to brood. I can tell. Hey, I know, we'll put on Mozart's 'Requiem,' is it too late for that? What time is it?" She leaned over and checked the clock on the night stand. Beyond her silhouette, the trellis bowed into view, hail driving a little harder now like some kid outside throwing pebbles to get our attention. "We don't want to wake anyone with funeral dirges, somebody might get upset. Why are you still feeling guilty, Jon?"

"Not guilty exactly, just pondering," I said.

"Your choices were limited."

"Yes, they were."

"When in doubt, wallop first."

"Wallop?"

"I kind of like wallop. Better than whatever you did to that loudmouth horsey-faced guy in the restaurant."

"Well, yeah."

"You going to join Oscar's gym?"

"I think I'll take a pass."

She was trying to be serious, but it wouldn't work with that nightgown on. When she turned too quickly the flannel would snap against my knees. I feared burns. She smoothed herself out in front of me and said, "When in doubt, wallop first. A motto to live by, especially when forced with that kind of a situation."

"Which I hope never to find myself in again."

"I think all the major parties involved feel that same way."

"Especially Teddy. If only he'd walloped first." Even in shadow, her beauty carried through, the set of her lips so clear, and her voice giving her so much substance here in the night. "You don't really think it's him, do you?"

"I'm not sure. What was done to his face bothers me. Why would a millionaire's son hide? And if it's not him, then who is it?"

"It's not your problem, and you really don't need to make it your problem."

"I already did that when I didn't listen to whatever Crummler would have told me."

"Maybe he wouldn't have said anything. Maybe there was nothing to say." She took my face in her hands and I took hers in mine, and we looked like some couple in a Fellini film where they talk into each other's noses. "Is it possible we can put this on the back burner for tonight?"

"We'll take it completely off the stove."

"The things you do for me."

"Damn straight," I said. I hoped she didn't mean that we should talk about the flower shop/bookstore idea all over again.

She didn't.

Dawn broke unevenly. A lot of red light, but it was cold again. I wished I had some flannel pajamas. Jesus was still looking at me. I lay staring at the ceiling for about two hours, until Katie lifted her head from my chest and put it back and then pulled it away. Large drops of sweat suddenly rose and began to drip down her ashen forehead.

She whimpered, "Oh hell."

I held on for a second, not wanting to be parted just then. I started to sweat, too. She knew more about this from being a woman, and more still from having been in medical school before deciding she'd rather open a shop and let me steal tulips. Her color drained further, as if somebody with a huge eraser was working down her face inch by inch. I'd been assured this was completely natural, but I still didn't know what to do most of the time, sitting around helplessly while she suffered.

Katie scampered from the bed and nearly didn't make it to the bathroom in time. Her words had a muted echo. "Oh, yuck." I stepped beside her in time to see her legs fall out from under her as she retched and slid against the freezing tile floor. I wrapped her into my arms until she finished.

"It's okay," she said, trying to smile. "Don't look like that. This is normal, really. I don't know why they call it morning sickness, a woman feels ill almost all the time the first three months." I carried her back to the bed and wet her face, breasts, and belly down with a cool wash cloth. At a couple of points she giggled and the hard knot of guilt and stress in my skull loosened a bit.

"You're going to stick around now, aren't you?" she said. "You'll skip going back to the city?"

"I have some things to clear up, but I'll be back in two or three days."

Her jade eyes filled with an irritated charge, and the silence hit like a physical force. She wanted to know why I'd leave Manhattan to return to Felicity Grove in order to get involved with murder, but hesitated when it came to finding housing and happiness with a woman I loved and a child on the way.

That silence followed us while we showered and dressed and got ready for her to drive me to the airport. I was famished, but didn't want to mention food in case she still felt a bit queasy. Her cheeks had the rich pink gleam of stoked anger, even as we made our way down the staircase and past the Leones' living room, where the luscious aroma of breakfast wafted throughout the house. My stomach made one huge gurgling noise that startled me as much as if I'd sat on a cat.

Mr. Leone waved to us as we walked out. "You're not staying for breakfast? Come in, come in here, what, are you *pazzo* making me go in there and eat all that by myself? Hey, did that *schifo* crazy caretaker ever find you?"

I stopped short in the doorway and Katie plowed into my back. She let out a loud *whuff*.

I said, "What?"

They kept their television turned mostly to the Italian cable stations. You could hear *Cella Luna* playing at late hours, all kinds of weird Italian soap operas where the main characters shrieked and wept and tried to bite each others' ears, then threw themselves down on altars at church. Bowling trophies and photos of stern-faced men and women lined the rosewood

shelves. The religious icons weren't kept in a corner down
here, but spread out on every horizontal surface you could see,
with the walls covered by some truly beautiful paintings of
scenes from the bible, giving the room a vaguely funeral-home
feel to it.

"He came here a couple nights ago looking for you. I told
him you two went to that restaurant, what is it called, Frank's
Bistro? How can you eat at a place called Frank's Bistro I
have no idea. I went once, tried their *frutti di mare* and it
tasted like they boxed and mailed the fish over from Genoa,
fourth class, on a slow boat, took maybe two months to get
here. Tell me you didn't have that, please, couldn't be anything worse. Hey, I already told you, come in here, want some
pasta fagioli? Just made it yesterday. It's good even for breakfast, hot or cold. Jonny, tell this girl she's got to eat. She's
too skinny and looks pale to me all the time." His wife
shouted something in Italian from the kitchen, and his eyes
got very wide. He said, "You forget the basil and she goes
for the cleaver, *scusi*," and wandered off.

"Crummler was looking for me," I whispered.

"Call Lowell."

"Anna was right. He needed my help."

"Listen to me. It still doesn't have to be your problem. Call
Lowell, notify the police. If Crummler really needed help he
would have told the sheriff."

"Maybe he couldn't for some reason."

We were still stuck in the doorway, the screen open with
leaves swirling in a circular drift around our feet. A white
Mercedes limousine idled at the curb, with a shine so thick
you could have thrown buckets of gravel on the hood and
never dented the coat of wax. Both front doors opened, and
two men climbed out and stood rigid, waiting and staring.

"Now what?" Katie asked.

"I think I can guess."

An Asian woman stepped up the walk and took a long bead
on me. Her straight, shining black hair fell longer than any I'd
ever seen before, down beyond her waist in a perfect crest.
The rising wind hadn't dislodged a strand. She wore only a
tightly fitted, sleeveless red dress, and I saw the slight rise of

goosebumps on the back of her arms as she approached.

"Mr. Harnes would like to speak with you." I expected an Asian sing-song cadence but there was only an Ivy League thickness of voice and manner. She added with a note of demand and finality. "Now, please."

Katie kept the quiet fume going and said, "Go do what you have to do."

"I'll be back in a few minutes."

Except for the curiously dead gaze of the woman, she was the most exotic lady who'd ever stepped foot into Felicity Grove, and looked like she could teach a man the secret sensual pleasures of the Orient even if he were on the rack. If she had been one of the kids in Thailand forced into sweatshop factory work at the age of six, then somehow it had paid off for her.

"That won't be necessary. Please allow us to drive you to the airport."

Katie asked her, "You want to tell me how you happen to know where he's going?"

"Please." There was no query or room for discussion in the woman's tone. She simply stared, her lips not notched so much as a millimeter toward a smile or frown. Her face seemed fabricated from cloth or plastic, smoother than flesh should be. I didn't spot a single line in her skin, not around her eyes, not at the edges of her mouth, not even between her eyebrows where we all get a furrow.

To know I was leaving they had to know my schedule. I tried to placate my paranoia by accepting the possibility that Harnes had simply made a few inquiries about me in the past twenty-four hours after all the news broadcasts. A man of his wealth and position wouldn't find it too difficult to garner information. It made more sense than the idea that he'd been hovering over me—or perhaps Crummler—for weeks.

"What's your name?"

"Jocelyn."

"I'll be with you in a moment," I said, and turned my back to her. I didn't like being accosted, checked up on, and followed right to the door of my girl's place. Jocelyn hardly made a sound walking down the walk to the Mercedes limousine again, but Katie watched her leave.

"Call Lowell," she said. "Whatever is happening, you're going to need his help. I'll call him now."

"No, it's all right."

"You have to do everything alone, in your own way, don't you?"

"It'll be fine."

"You're going to get hurt." She stood quickly on her toes, threw a kiss at my lips that sort of missed, spun back inside and shut the door.

The driver was hardly more than spectral: a thin, ashen-faced man in a bad-fitting black suit who smelled like he'd gotten into Oscar Kinion's bathroom and used up the rest of his cologne.

Another guy with a white crew cut stood half out of the passenger seat, as if ready to come in and get me if I hadn't been persuaded to follow the woman. The etched lines of his face bent around his mouth like a poorly folded map—his sneer had been affixed to him for decades. He looked a very healthy, fit, and forceful sixty. His upper lip dipped at an improper angle, almost like a harelip. Once he'd been punched in the mouth so hard that he'd bitten out a large piece of his lip, and the sew-up job had mauled him further. The lower half of his front teeth showed through, yellow and dry. He said, "Stop looking at me."

The woman opened the rear door of the limo, and I got my first glimpse of Theodore Harnes.

Nondescript was the best description I could come up with. Nothing about him stuck with me, no simile or metaphor came to mind. I sat beside him with my body slightly twisted in case he wanted to shake hands. He stared straight ahead. Jocelyn got in beside me, pressing me over until I sat in the middle between her and Harnes. If this was a Chandler, Block, Williams or Vachss novel I'd have been "scrunched between the heaving shoulders of two guys named Vincenzo and Popgun Rolly." The woman felt like smoke beside me, a presence but not a pressure. Harnes, though we didn't touch, was the opposite. A live pressure but no sense of a living presence.

I was starting to think that getting into the car was a bad idea.

Theodore Harnes, who had married one of my grandmother's bridesmaids, said, "I want to thank you."

"You do?"

"Yes."

"For what?"

"Catching the man who murdered my son."

An autopsy report wouldn't be completed for at least another day. The kid's teeth had been broken and scattered and it would take a while for him to be identified by his dental records or whatever other means they had. I wondered why, under these circumstances, a father wouldn't reach out with both hands for even the slightest hope that his child wasn't dead.

"It might not be your son. There's no real evidence yet that . . ."

In a tranquil, toneless voice, he said, "He did not come home."

"But there's a chance that . . ."

"My son always came home."

I could see he was a man who brooked no opposition of any kind, not even by natural events. All things had to follow in the same course, at his insistence. What he expected must come to pass. His demands would be unrealistic and unobtainable. Only death proved to be an acceptable excuse for Teddy. What would having this man for a father do to a boy? To what lengths would someone forced to live in that shadow go to get away?

"I don't think Crummler did it," I said.

He showed no bewilderment, as if prepared for my response. "A raving lunatic covered in blood holding the murder weapon? He is guilty."

"Crummler wouldn't hurt anyone."

He ignored my comment and said, "I've heard of your past, helpful interests in certain investigations. The kidnapped Degrasse child. The sheriff's recent troubles. You found the murderer of your parents. You and your grandmother, I believe.

You are a formidable pair. She sounds like a most intriguing woman.''

"Oh cripes."

So, he would take the tack that he didn't know Anna, or perhaps he'd forgotten her, or only remembered her in a haze from before he had such power to wield.

"Why was Teddy at the cemetery?" I asked.

Jocelyn gazed at me, the driver glared into the rearview mirror, and the other guy kept his grin up, as if nobody ever asked Harnes a question, or maybe nobody ever mentioned Teddy.

"His mother is buried there," Harnes said.

"Was he visiting her grave?"

"I believe so."

"Tell me about him."

"Why?"

"Why not? Who were his friends?"

"You should have murdered that madman," Harnes told me, and a static charge built around him. I thought if I reached out and touched him, sparks would skitter off my fingernails. He gave me a sidelong glance, showing nothing. "Believe me, Mr. Kendrick, it would have been worth your while, if you had killed him."

He said it the way anyone else would talk about turning in their recycled cans for cash. I stared at the side of his face, trying to get a bead on him, but he moved in and out of focus from second to second.

"Is there anyone I can talk to?"

"Talk? About my son?" Harnes snapped back into himself, so unassuming that he seemed to fade in and out of existence. "No, there is no one with whom you can talk."

The guy in the front seat turned to grin at me some more with that scarred mouth. He had the air of a man who knew a secret and wanted everyone else to know that he knew it. Whatever he wanted to tell me, he'd eventually get around to it. I smiled pleasantly at him, showing off my nice upper lip. I wasn't getting anywhere with Harnes anyway. "What's your name, Sparky?"

He opened his mouth slowly and I saw that part of his

tongue was missing as well, leaving it slightly forked. He said, "It sure as hell ain't Sparky," just as we pulled up to the airport. Jocelyn got out and I followed.

Harnes said nothing, and didn't even glance toward us. Jocelyn slipped back into the Mercedes, slammed the door, and they left me there.

I realized that Harnes hadn't given me a lift in his nice limousine to thank me for finding his son's killer, not at all.

He hadn't even seen me, really.

He'd been looking right through me and staring at Anna.

I called my grandmother from the airport but got my own voice on her answering machine. I said, "If Harnes comes around call Lowell immediately." Then I called Lowell and told him that I thought Theodore Harnes was going to be great misfortune in one form or another.

He laughed and said, "You giving me a bulletin, Jonny? Guy's got kids in Indonesia, Hong Kong, Thailand, Nicaragua, all the places you can't even point to on a map—"

"I think I could get Nicaragua."

"—they do nothing but work on the line making shoes for sixteen hours a day that are sold on Rodeo Drive for six hundred bucks a pair. He has a house full of Burmese servants who probably get paid off in table scraps and half the minimum wage. He makes the old men in the sawmills and out on the road camps thank their stars they've at least got shooters and beer to slump into in their dirty trailers at night. Thanks for the advice, I can't express in words how much I appreciate it. Why don't you go shelve some more books out there in the big bad city, Jonny Kendrick? What's that noise, you dropping change into a pay phone? What, you didn't get your cell phone yet?"

SIX

FOR THE NEXT TWO DAYS I sat in the store fulfilling orders I'd received from the Internet. More and more of my business was actually done through the mail and over the Internet, now that I'd hooked up with several online bookseller databases. I'd list most rarities and first editions, and within a couple of weeks I'd generate orders and I'd send the books off. It was much easier to reach collectors who knew what they were after and were willing to pay, rather than relying on the chance that someone would come in off the street who was probably only interested in finding a cheap paperback copy of a recent best-seller. I had three locked glass cases filled with books over a century old, and it felt nearly that long since anyone had browsed and asked me to unlock the cabinets.

My assistant Debi Kiko Mashima finally realized that the way to fame and success was not to work in a Greenwich Village bookstore, but to quit NYU and marry one of the leading software writers on the face of the earth. His name was Bobby Li and he liked to rollerblade and always wore hockey jerseys. They'd met at a computer expo at the Jacob Javits Center. Despite the fact that he, too, was of Japanese descent, he'd lived in the San Francisco area all his life and now owned a large portion of it. He was Debi's age, twenty-one, and worth roughly half a billion dollars. They'd had five dates before he proposed and she accepted. I did not consider her leaving my employ to be a great betrayal.

If I moved the store to Felicity Grove and went in partners with the flower shop, I could still make a living, but I'd have to get a door with bells on it that chimed or jangled or rang or tinkled whenever anybody came in. Maybe I just had a low distraction threshold, but the idea of having a clanging noise interrupt my thoughts and work every few minutes didn't appeal to me. A door opening and somebody entering made more than enough clamor to alert you to the presence of a potential customer. And every once in a while somebody came in hoping to sell me a few rain-soaked paperbacks they'd nabbed out of the trash.

Or so I thought, until I turned in my seat and saw a guy standing there only two feet away, staring intently at me.

He'd entered without a sound.

No way to judge how tall he might be, crimped as he was, low to the ground like an animal tensed and coiled. He wore remnants of a dark three-piece suit, ripped and patched with different pieces of fabric, a frayed black overcoat hanging open so that he looked like an Old West gunslinger waiting to draw. He had the hard, confident, but wary edge the street imbued those whose brains hadn't been turned to tapioca by drugs, self-pity, sexual abuse, or the unending loneliness of the outcast. His eyes had a black, shrewd, and discerning energy to them, but I might have just been mistaking malicious aptitude. He had a poorly trimmed beard, thick in spots and showing cuts in other places, as if he'd used a pair of broken scissors to slice off hanks.

He took his time sizing me up, shifting now until he stood in front of the counter, glancing down at my fists filled with invoices and mailing labels.

Despite his silent entrance, I should have noticed the reek. The stink of rotting fruit and vegetables followed him in. His torn, gaping pockets were stuffed with lettuce leaves and a few bruised apples and old legumes. I smelled no alcohol. He looked fifty, but might have been a decade younger or older. A sharp look of feral intelligence lit his face, and I thought he must be one of the rare breed who had chosen the street instead of the street choosing them. He could have been a cop taken down low.

"You're Kendrick," he said.

"Yes."

A bell over the door might not be such a bad thing after all, I thought. One that jangled and rang up such a storm that nobody who looked like they wanted to yank a Colt strapped to his thigh could walk in while I worried about how distracting bells over the door would be.

Even if I'd wanted to wallop first and ask questions later, he stood just out of arm's reach. Keeping a fair distance, yet staying close enough so that if I had a weapon handy he could whirl over the counter and leap into my chest before I could do anything about it.

"I'm Nicodemus Crummler," he said. "Nick. I know you're my brother Zeb's friend. I need your help."

"Who's Maggie?" I asked.

His eyes lost their protective black shale aspect, the dead sheen lifting for a second. That seemed to be about as close to a flinch as he was capable of after living so long in the refuse. He chose to ignore the question for the moment.

I'd rolled with it pretty well myself, I thought, but he'd still shocked the hell out of me. I'd known Zebediah Crummler most of my life and always believed that in his childish mind and burning-wire mania resided truths not even the rumor mill of a small town could ever churn free. But a brother? He'd been in orphanages, hospitals, and foster homes before coming to rest in Felicity Grove, that much was common knowledge.

Now that I looked harder I could make out similar physical characteristics: the same wiry hair, facial muscles spread wide as if battling tics forever, an equal amount of intensity there, although Nick bit his down hard.

"How did you hear about him being in trouble?" I asked.

"You make the news, you and your grandmother, and now him, too. The son of Theodore Harnes murdered, that's what they're saying. Did you think they'd only hear about it in Buffalo?" That wasn't what I'd meant at all, and of course he knew it. "Oh, because I don't have a pot to piss in or a win-

dow to throw it out of, you think I can't buy and read a paper?
I can only wrap my feet in them?''

I cleared about twenty pounds of books from the chair beside me, but he didn't sit. The idea that he might have once
been a cop hit again, the way he stood with such a sense of
authority. He reminded me of Lowell. There was no anger
behind his words, everything fell out with a perfectly composed and even tone, as if whatever might have been heated
had cooled before he said it.

''He never mentioned a brother,'' I told him. ''I thought he
was an orphan, a ward of the state.''

''He was. You're talking about when we were six and seven
years old. A brother who's a year younger doesn't count as
family in the eyes of the law. We were separated. That's what
they did back then. Still do, I think. Besides, he's special, they
call it. They couldn't wait to get him into the system.'' He
leaned back against the cabinets of rare books and my heart
hitched a little to the left, imagining him with shards of glass
raining on him, my stock destroyed. He had a dancer's spry-
ness though, and the fragile doors didn't even rattle in their
frame. I couldn't quite picture him jitterbugging with children.
''It's not hard to track somebody, not as hard as they make
you think it is, anyway. I've kept in touch with him, best as
I could, best for him.''

''Why haven't you ever shown up before?''

''I do, but that's between me and him. Not you, and not the
rest of that place. He's better off with the dead, and a whole
lot safer. At least he was until now.''

We stared at each other for a minute. I thought of the guy
I'd sissy-slapped in the restaurant, and the way he'd wanted
to shoot Crummler. I could imagine him raising his fist and
shouting in delight the next day after reading the paper, vin-
dicated for his beliefs that the ''psycho son of a bitch'' had
proven to be a killer.

''Did he ever say anything about Teddy Harnes?''

''No.''

''He said he'd been in battle with himself. Does that mean
anything to you?''

''No.''

"Are you sure?"

"Yes. How do you know that name?" he asked, again without any inflection in his voice, so that it hardly sounded like a question at all. "Maggie."

I focused on his hands. Although small, they were thickly veined, and appeared powerful, like Lowell's. For some reason I didn't like thinking of Lowell and this man together, but couldn't help myself. "He mentioned her."

He nodded, resettling himself against the glass cabinets, and again not even making a whisper of noise. "She was our aunt, a wonderful woman. Wanted to adopt us after our parents were killed, but she died not too long after. He talks about that?"

"No, the sheriff offered to take him home and your brother answered, 'Not to Maggie's.' "

"Not there? He didn't want to go to Maggie's?" He squinted, pondering it, and looked like Lowell.

"Were you ever a cop?"

The black shale broke off again, his eyes filling with real humor. "Me?" He smiled, showing off a few spaces between amazingly white teeth. "Are you insane?"

"Was he abused?"

"No."

"Are you certain?"

"Yes. Don't ask me again if I'm sure or certain about something, I wouldn't say it if I weren't."

"All right. Were you abused?"

"No. I understand why you're asking, but you can quit this track. It was the happiest we've ever been in our lives."

I wondered what Aunt Maggie had done to them.

Nick Crummler said, "That town scares me. I need your help. We've got to get him out of Panecraft."

"I'm going back tomorrow. You're welcome to come with me, sleep on my couch tonight if you like."

"Thanks for the offer, but I'll pass. You'll see me around, though."

Of that I was certain, as he eased back toward me and shook my hand. He appeared to be a man who could take all the city had to offer, so I wondered what in the hell there could be about Felicity Grove that could scare him.

"How do you know about Panecraft?" I asked.

"How else?" His voice, like the stench, wafted off him even as he slid out the door. "I've been in there."

Teddy brought them in. Hundreds of people showed for his funeral, their whispers crowding us like a constant brush of the breeze, though I didn't hear a single person crying. They milled and wore their best suits and dresses, everyone overly-aware of the newscasters beaming around us.

Another rainy day, but the drizzle had petered to a fine mist an hour ago, so that Felicity Grave appeared well watered, as if by a troupe of loving gardeners. Katie must have been extremely busy the past couple days if even a small percentage of the flowers on view had been purchased at the shop.

My grandmother hated the cemetery. I saw the soft flesh beneath her ears bunch because she kept her teeth clenched. She obviously hadn't been sleeping well, and I didn't know whether she'd come out with whatever was on her mind about Harnes or if I should prod her the way she usually did me. We were both good at it, and both susceptible.

She wore a black kerchief which accentuated her silver hair. Because she was in a wheelchair the crowd parted to allow us nearly to the front of the casket. When we got close enough she reached up and tightened her hand on my wrist, not willing to get so near that Harnes might see her. We could also talk more easily at a little distance, backed away by ourselves off to one side.

I stood over her with a closed umbrella in my fist, just in case it started raining again. Anna had a healthy pink in her cheeks, and she made me point out the area where I'd tripped over Teddy's body. I heard a mild huff from her when she realized it would be extremely difficult for me to wheel her to the spot. Small running threads of water streamed down the hill, forking against gnarled, erupted roots.

"Ironic," Anna said. "That he should be put to rest here, of all places, where he met such an appalling end."

"And that his grave is the most sloppily dug."

"Yes, they have two men here, with another overseeing, and still it hardly compares to a plot worked on by Crummler, who has a real sense of accomplishment, and a respect for the dead.''

Teddy was apparently being buried beside his mother. The grave angled down from an embankment about twenty yards from where I'd found his body. Her headstone read Marie Harnes, but the name didn't mean much to me. After Nick Crummler had left my store I'd gone over to the main branch of the New York Library and spent a few hours checking through the reels of microfiche for whatever I could find on Theodore Harnes and his family.

Outside of business articles and brief accounts of mergers and other financial ventures, there were only vague reports of mistresses and sexual lawsuits handled out of court. He must have paid plenty of hush money to put down the gossip so competently. Most sources were unconfirmed, identities never revealed. Marie Harnes, his wife following Diane Cruthers, died giving birth to Theodore Jr. The date made Teddy twenty-one, a little older than I'd originally suspected. Theodore Harnes had married and divorced twice more in quick succession, and there had been hardly any information on either woman. His fifth wife, whom he'd divorced years ago, had been notably in and out of drug and alcohol rehab centers all over Europe. It didn't seem like Harnes was a man who knew how to please women much.

He stood staring straight ahead, at an angle from the casket, without a glimmer of expression. He might as well have been watching a sunset in the Bahamas, or an ant farm, or kids in Nicaragua making shoes for fifty cents a day. Some people might think he was in shock, paralyzed with heartache, as though he might crack at any moment and fling himself down into the grave, tearing at the mud and howling. The most human response I saw was when he blinked.

''You are right, Jonathan,'' Anna said. ''He has changed radically.''

''What's different?''

''He once exhibited a powerful presence. The kind of man who commanded a fundamental admiration. He exuded a natural ease and charm in his youth. Now, he hardly moves at all. I'd suspect tranquilizers.''

"Or tranquillity."

"No, a man like him never finds peace."

"I know. He acted the same way a few days ago, but was in full control of his faculties from what I could tell."

The newscasters were on the move, getting better coverage than at a raging fire. They were being particularly brazen, even for Action Team Channel 3, sidling up behind the priest and getting a view of the tombstone, panning around at the throng, tight close-up of the father. The thought that Harnes was a mannequin posed in a window struck home again.

"Anna, I've only seen him once or twice in the paper . . ."

"Yes, he relishes his privacy, to the extreme. Curious, then, that such a recluse would allow a personal tragedy as this made into an exhibition."

"Maybe he doesn't really consider it to be very tragic."

She folded her hands in her lap and slowly rubbed her knuckles, which either meant she had a touch of arthritis acting up in the rain or all those hard-boiled novels were really getting to her and she wanted to jab someone in the jaw.

She wet her lips. There are times when you want to say something like, *Impossible, no father would ever kill his own child, no friend would betray a friend,* and the words die in your throat because you know the bitter truth. She would never take another step again and my parents were dead because of a friend.

My grandmother merely said, "Dreadful."

The priest grew annoyed with all the camera equipment and started motioning for them to be set aside, or at least backed out of his face. He waited another moment before beginning the final service. His voice didn't carry far into the wind. Harnes' lack of emotion bothered him as well, giving him no one to comfort. He murmured in Harnes' ear and gripped his arm in a gesture of sympathy. Leafless branches bowed in the breeze. Harnes didn't move or reply.

"His utter indifference is almost a cruelty to those around him," Anna said. "What kind of effect might that have had on a child?"

"I was thinking the same thing when he picked me up in his limo," I said. "I'm getting a hint as to why five wives left him, taking the hard route.'' I wondered where Diane Cruthers had been buried. "You told me Diane Cruthers was pregnant. Did she have the child before she committed suicide?''

"No.''

Jesus, I thought. "Harnes has had several lawsuits brought against him, sexual harassment, palimony. Do you think that we . . .''

"That we might find Teddy's bastard siblings in this assemblage?''

It bothered the hell out of me when she finished all my sentences. "It'll be a good chance to find out something about him. What did you learn from Wallace?''

She didn't bother to ask how I'd known she'd spoken to Keaton Wallace. He stood a dozen yards away, fiddling with his dentures the way he usually did. Even from here I could see the spotting of burst blood vessels in his nose, his drinking almost as bad as my father's had been. They'd both gotten on the wagon together, though Wallace continued to leap off.

"Virtually nothing. The wounds are consistent with being attacked with a shovel. Teddy was indeed killed by blunt trauma to the head, the cleaving of his visage induced either as he died or just post mortem.''

"Do you think Wallace might have missed something?''

"No.''

"If he released the body to Harnes, then Wallace is satisfied the corpse is Teddy. He must've matched the fingerprints to Teddy's passport.''

"My thoughts exactly, but passports can be faked. Wallace may have been deceived.''

"Or bribed.''

"No, I don't believe that.''

We were silent for a moment, each of us lost in thought, disturbed by the fact that the killer had taken the time to eradicate his victim's face. It didn't sit well.

I looked over at Wallace again: in his mid-fifties, the barbershop quartet haircut and bristly mustache made him look like a man reaching backward to the day of Teddy Roosevelt. He grinned too widely because his dentures didn't fit well, and his generally jolly nature could make you forget that he'd once had a mean streak that landed his ex-wife in the emergency room a few times. I liked him a lot, and as a kid I especially liked him when he was drunk.

I wondered where he stood on the road of his life, and if he was proud of what he'd accomplished or if he felt like a failure, still full of hate, the anger hiding within him the way it had hidden inside my father. He and my Dad hadn't been especially close friends, but they had been devoted drinking buddies, and gotten into brawls that landed them in Broghin's jail more than once. The broken blood vessels lining his face depicted all the regrets and remorse of his life; and a lot of the fun, too, I supposed.

Could he have made a mistake? Could a faked passport have gotten by him? He rubbed at his mustache, smoothing it as he licked his lips. He might still go to the occasional AA meeting, but he was so far off the wagon at the moment I could tell he was already starting to get thirsty. Could Teddy, trying to escape his father, have paid off Wallace into faking the autopsy? And if so, who was the dead man I now watched being buried?

"We may just be dealing with a jealous psychopath who hated Teddy so much he cut the kid's face off for no real reason," I said.

"Doubtful."

Lowell moved off to one side, wearing a black suit and sunglasses, weaving among the crowd.

"Deputy Tully also suspects something is amiss," Anna said. "He's studying the crowd."

"He knows the killer might be here."

"As does anyone who has ever seen a television police drama or read a mystery novel."

"Yes, but only a real genius would do it covertly," I said, putting on my sunglasses.

Finally we heard a heartfelt wail, and a girl at the front slowly drew nearer to the casket. She sobbed loudly and was comforted by a young man who looked on the verge of tears himself. *Okay*, I thought, *now I have something to do.* Harnes didn't even turn to look at her. Jocelyn didn't either, or the chauffeur. I didn't see Sparky and wondered what else he might have to do that was more important than attending the funeral for the son of his employer.

"A girlfriend?" Anna asked.

"Or his sister."

"Did you hear any of the names of his personnel?"

"More like an entourage. Just the Asian woman. Her name is Jocelyn. The others never addressed each other, and the lipless guy didn't take the bait."

"This Jocelyn looks quite"—she searched for the right word—"formidable." There were a lot of other adjectives I'd use in describing her, but formidable worked just fine for the moment. "Regardless of the men in his company, I believe she might actually be Theodore Harnes' bodyguard."

I wondered how many copies of Emerson's *MayDay* I'd have to sell in order to have enough cash to pay a body like hers to guard a body like mine. "She could certainly wallop me."

"Oh, dear."

I knew a lot of the people and when we caught each others' eye I understood that we all shared the same thought: *why are you here?* Harnes hadn't even been in the country for most of the last decade, so what kind of hold did he have on the town? Vinny Matalo and John Trusnick and Pete Wilkes, Jessica Sperling, Daphne Kupfer, some other friends I hadn't seen in months, neighbors, all of us here for whatever reason, to pay our respects to a dead kid and a wealthy man whom nobody even really knew.

"Not like Daphne Kupfer is a business associate of Harnes, being a waitress in Pembleton's Diner, and how would she know Teddy?"

I watched the girl crying. It was the only noise heard outside of the priest who mumbled through his service.

I waited a while longer before I finally asked, "Do you think Harnes killed Diane Cruthers?"

Anna remained silent. Her lips parted, but she soon closed her mouth again and cleared her throat. She looked beyond Harnes into their shared history, and I knew it hadn't only been bad, it had been awful. It took a few seconds but she eventually shook the question off.

She didn't want to deal with the dead past, and said, "The truth of Teddy's murder lies with Crummler."

"Yes."

I had to go to Panecraft.

SEVEN

PEMBLETON'S DINER HAD BEEN DOWNTOWN on the corner of Broome and Maiden since nineteen-twenty-eight and looked every minute of it. Arthur Pembleton himself had stepped in front of a southbound freight a couple months following Black Monday, but none of the successive proprietors had ever decided to change the name, including the current owner, Harvey McCoy. Pembleton might not have had any luck business-wise, but he sported a properly high-class name, and lending it to the diner must've been thought to raise the general level of class in the place.

A few coats of paint would have gone a lot further to that end, I thought, and might've even made a dent in the seventy years' worth of grime clinging to the walls. Maybe not. I'd been in worse-looking places in Manhattan, but none that served meals as bad as Pembleton's. No one liked to eat here, and the regulars appeared to have mutated two levels further down the food chain, but the next nearest diner was several miles uptown and the lunch crowd hated to travel.

If anybody ever went into direct competition with Harvey McCoy they'd make a fortune. I thought about a flower shop-bookstore-diner and wondered if we could get the Leones to come and cook for us, with Katie putting fresh flowers out in

the booths and me going table to table selling first editions of
A. E. Houseman, Francois Mauriac, Thomas Wolfe, and books
on longhorn sheep.

Already the fumes in this place were starting to get to me.
The hostess seated me with nod of her head and slapped a
menu down in front of my face so hard that it bounced off
the table and hit the floor. I reached down and had a perfect
view of Daphne's legs as she shouldered the kitchen door open
and stepped out carrying two plates of what might be passing
for scrambled eggs. I didn't know what the purple stuff was,
and I would make it my mission in life never to know.

Daphne Kupfer had never stopped being twenty-one. She'd
held thirty at bay with skin-tight clothing and a physique she
worked hard to keep with at least four nights a week spent in
the gym. Those angles and stone-hard contours of her body
stuck out whenever she moved in the slightest; just turning
her head or shifting her stance brought curves and veins up
from all over. She still had a little girl space between her two
front teeth and wore dangling earrings of unicorns leaping
through hoops that jingled like wind chimes.

Twice while Katie and I were in line at the movies we'd
run into her and her dates. She went in for the boyish types
who weren't so much boyish as they were boys. I thought that
if anybody I'd seen at the funeral might have actually known
Teddy, it would be Daphne.

She swung by my table carrying a pot of coffee, and though
she caught my eye she drifted away quickly, unsure of how
to react. My skills at covert operations needed to be improved
upon. I'd left my sunglasses at home.

I beat the lunch rush by a half hour and the place was nearly
empty. She spotted me again as I sat staring in her direction
and a ripple of tension moved through her face. I smiled and
turned up the wattage of my natural charm. She ducked her
head and hurried back into the kitchen. I tried hard to recover
from the blow to my ego.

It took a few minutes before she came back out. She didn't
have any choice but to eventually come over. "Jonny, hi."

"Hi, Daphne."

She didn't need a pen and a pad to take my order, and just

kept smiling widely as annoyance continued to slip in and out of her eyes. The muscles in her sleek neck bunched. In a fair fight she'd probably kill me. "What can I get you?"

I glanced down at the menu. It all looked about the same so I just pointed toward the middle, hoping she wouldn't bring me the purple stuff. Her smile down-shifted into a grin and she sort of bopped her head to the side so that her hair did a wheeling twist in the air. It was a gesture that might have been cute when she was fifteen. She nabbed the menu from my hand. "Coming right up."

When she returned I was thankful to see nothing purple on the plate. There was also nothing edible. "Can I talk to you for a minute, Daphne?"

She tilted her head again and her hair swept back in the other direction. "Can't, Jonny, the boss might see me."

"You've been working here for twelve years, Daphne. You think Harvey is going to fire you anytime soon?"

"I don't like the way you said that," she told me, and two thin bands of red spread in straight lines across her cheeks.

"I'm sorry."

"What do you want?"

"To talk about Teddy Harnes."

"Teddy?" She drew her chin back and frowned.

"Yes."

"I didn't even know him."

"Why were you at his funeral then?"

Now the real heat came up, and I heard something crack in her, maybe her knees as she grew rigid. Even the unicorns looked pissed off. "And what the hell business is it of yours?"

"Listen, I . . ."

"Why, do you think I killed him?"

"No, of course not."

"I'm a suspect? Funny, I don't remember you ever wearing a badge, Jonny. Exactly when was it again that you became a cop?"

I was beginning to have serious concerns about my abilities to glean useful information by merely smiling. So far, I'd done nothing but rile her into throwing up a defensive wall. Her hair wagged back to the other side again. Time for a new tack. "You didn't know Teddy?"

"I just said that. I never met him."

"But Theodore Harnes?"

"None of your business." Her arms crossed and appeared strong enough to break two-by-fours. "You like to think you're smooth, don't you?"

"Uhmm, no, actually."

"Slipping back into town, nosing around until you find something ugly you can yank out and hold up for all the cameras and newspapers, right? That's your action? Funny thing is, didn't you ever think that some people might think you're a suspect? The way you're always in trouble? Watch where you point that finger, Jonny, because there are plenty of folks around who are pointing one right back at you."

The lunch crowd began to pile up, doorway filling, the hostess seating more customers and bouncing more menus. I'd lose Daphne in another minute.

"The young woman at the funeral who was crying. Do you know her?"

"Her name is Alice Conway, lives out on High Ridge. Her father was a competitor of Harnes' in some local merchandising business, I don't know what. Her old man got driven out pretty quick, lost everything. Her parents are dead. Now leave me alone, and when you see her, give the little bitch my regards."

She caught herself at the last moment and realized she'd said more than she'd cared to say, but really didn't care that much. A nasty smile nicked the edge of her mouth as she stared at me.

I thought I'd better turn off the goddamn charm, and I got the hell out of there.

High Ridge seemed draped against the foothills overlooking the country, falling back one level upon the next farther and higher into the hillside: huge homes sparsely dappled the entire area, some huddled together and others keeping their distance like squatting, cagey brutes.

The houses all appeared to be at least a century old, and I

saw several Historical Society preservation plaques inlaid along the sides of boulders. Wrought-iron signs standing beside stone lions kept proclaiming which great people had done what great things in bygone eras. A statue of a revolutionary war hero stood on an empty bluff looking lonely and very confused. I knew just how he felt.

I still didn't have a car in Felicity Grove, and all three of Duke Edelman's station trucks were up on skids, so I kept borrowing Anna's van. The hand controls were as familiar to me as using foot pedals, almost more so considering I drove her van more than I drove a standard. I hadn't owned a car in the six years since I'd moved to Manhattan. I had a CD of Pachelbel's "Canon and Other Baroque Favorites" playing, and the winsome classical music didn't match the approaching vista as I made a sharp turn onto a private road.

Alice Conway's house brooded behind a thick line of oak and hickory, dark except for one foreboding yellow light that shone gloomily through the shadows of abundant trees. The driveway had chipped and rutted in several spots, and last autumn's rotted leaves lay strewn against the porch. Rain gutters on the east side of the house had torn loose and hung askew, bouncing against the split wooden shingles in the breeze.

I stepped up the porch and the stairs wobbled and creaked under me. I waited for a black cat to leap at my face or an unkindness of ravens to burst from the attic window. A '68 Mustang that looked like it had scraped every highway divider from here to the Holland Tunnel sat at an angle facing the house. Behind it, nearly kissing the bumper, was a GTO that somebody had spent a couple hundred hours restoring to mint condition.

I rang the doorbell and then knocked loudly. It seemed like the kind of house where people might quite often say, "I didn't hear a thing." I waited a minute and repeated the process. And then again. No cats crept along the porch rafters.

The young lady who'd wailed at the funeral finally answered the door. Only one side of her face was visible as she peered through the crack at me. We both looked at each other for a little while. Slowly she opened the door wider, exposing more of her face. She was eighteen or nineteen, with large, pink lips made for pouting that nearly drew complete attention from the deep brown circles under her eyes. A rowdy group of curls hung into the corners of her mouth. Her nerves were clearly shot, and when she said ''Yes?'' her voice squeaked curiously, hauling the word out and snapping it in half.

I saw the outline of a man next to her behind the door and I dipped forward to get a better look. She jerked back and the young man who'd been comforting her during Teddy Harnes' service came into view. She said ''Yes?'' again and kept it to one syllable this time, the curls edging in and out of her mouth. We watched one another some more, and I understood that the depth of her sorrow was real and I suddenly felt very sorry for her.

''My name is Jonathan Kendrick, Alice. I was hoping I could talk to you for a few minutes.''

Her eyes grew wider and I got to see just how bloodshot and raw-looking they were from all the hours of crying. She gasped and pointed at my nose and said, ''It's you!''

''Me?''

''The one on television. You're the man who found Teddy.''

''Yes, I did.''

She appeared to be lost for a moment, and glanced indecisively from side to side. The kid hiding in there with her muttered something in a harsh tone. She shut the door in my face with a heavy blast of air. I heard more quiet but urgent talking as they argued. The door popped open again and she told me, ''Please, come inside.''

I felt certain the guy would be out of sight but near enough to eavesdrop on everything Alice and I might say. I was wrong. He stood in the foyer with his features tautly drawn like a bow pulled too tightly. He had the grimace of a man holding back a well-stoked rage just waiting for an excuse to set it loose.

Alice Conway introduced him. ''This is my friend, Brian Frost.''

''Hello,'' I said.

We shook hands and he glared at me and tried to crush my

knuckles. He kept scowling, and I could almost here his brain
cackling and shrieking *"Die, die, die!"* I had no idea why, or
whether it was focused at me or if he hated the world at large.
He had hair so yellow and short that it looked like a huge
lemon peel sitting on top of his head. He wore a black sleeveless T-shirt and had the excessive musculature of a serious
steroid user. He didn't work his shoulders or stomach enough
though, so he also suffered from a somewhat swollen appear-
ance. The enormity of his biceps forced him to sway when he
walked.

Alice led us into a spacious and barren living room that had
deep grooves in the carpet where a lot of furniture had once
rested for many years. Brian leaned against an achingly bare
wall where you could see the outlines of paintings that had
recently been taken down.

"Did he . . . did he try to . . . say anything?" she asked.

"No, I'm sorry, he was gone by then."

"Oh, my God."

She wanted to cry more but didn't have anything left to
give. I could tell by the way her shoulders shrugged inward
and hands drooped to her sides that she must have felt as if a
fist were barreling into the center of her chest. I've felt that
way a few times myself.

"How did you know Teddy?" I asked.

"I was his girlfriend."

Teddy's presence, unlike his father's, seemed to be solidi-
fying. He grew around me, a ghost taking on a more substantial form with each person I met who knew him. Here was
someone who sobbed and trembled at his loss, those beautiful
lips had touched his. It felt as if Teddy stood at my shoulder,
urging me on.

I took a deep breath. I couldn't shake my odd doubts that
he might still be alive; that Wallace may have been mistaken,
duped, or influenced.

The boy's face—why had they taken his face?

"Do you know of anyone who might have had a reason to
hurt Teddy?"

"No!" she said. "There was no one."

"Are you sure?"

"Teddy didn't even know that many people. He was . . . shy. Reserved. For most of his life he traveled around the world with his father. He never had a stable home life, and there were a fleet of stepmothers. Spending so many years in the Orient and South America, without being able to speak much of the languages, he learned to live comfortably with his own company. They really didn't settle back into New York until two summers ago."

"Did he like it here after being gone for so long?"

"We didn't really go out much at all, and when we did it was up to the mountains or to the preserves. Or bookstores. He loved to read, and read everything he could get his hands on. He returned all the books for credit or else just gave them away. With his money he could have bought anything he liked, but he didn't believe in materialism. A few weeks ago he started getting involved in volunteer work, some community service. He was interested in nature, and started to take up painting. He loved Chinese brushwork. He learned a lot about being . . . spiritual, I guess you would call it, in China, by watching the monks and the people at their shrines."

"He was religious then?"

"He loved Eastern culture. He cared about aesthetics."

Brian Frost snorted loudly.

"You disagree?" I asked him.

He said nothing, but his face tightened even more until I thought his chin and forehead would meet.

I turned back to Alice. "What did he think of his father?"

"He loved his father, of course. Very much."

"Did Teddy ever mention Crummler?"

Alice hesitated and grimaced at Frost, who continued to smolder in silence. "Yes, he liked the man," she admitted. Her voice continued to strain and splinter, wavering from a whisper to a whimper. "Teddy thought Crummler was blessed, in a way. Crummler had the proper sense of respect for the dead, and made the cemetery into a beautiful place of worship, the way they do in the East. Teddy's mother is buried in Felicity Grave, and he said that Crummler not only understood the beauty of the land, but the reverence for the departed."

Respect for the dead. Anna had said the same thing.

"That's all such shit," Brian Frost hissed. They were the first words I'd actually heard him speak, and about what I expected. "That Crummler guy is a bum. Just a crazy bum who tried to rob Teddy."

"Do you have a photo of him?" I asked Alice.

Frost tipped himself off the wall and took a step toward me. "You don't have to show or tell this guy anything."

"It's okay, Brian," she said and quickly reached behind her to a breakfront where some knickknacks and pictures still rested.

"He isn't a cop, you don't have to let him stand here and question you." Frost started flexing. Actually, I was surprised he'd managed to contain himself this long. "You sound like the police, but you aren't, are you?"

"No."

"You sound like that deputy. Tully. We had to talk to him, but we don't have to listen to your questions."

I figured Lowell would have beaten me here, and knew that after having been questioned already Alice would be a lot more reticent with me. "It's just that I never got a chance to meet Teddy," I said.

"So, why the hell do you care?"

Alice touched him softly on the back and handed me a framed photograph. "This was taken last summer."

Frost looked like a nice kid when the lines of his face weren't folded into a blazing hatred, trying to use psychic powers to make people shrivel up. He hadn't indulged in steroids then and was almost skinny. No wonder he was so angry. A side-effect of overindulgence in steroids can lead to aggressive, combative behavior, what they used to call "roid rage" back when I was in high school. We had some players on the football team who would smuggle the stuff in. They'd also get the chills and have a hell of a time getting even minor bleeding to stop if they happened to get cut during a game.

In the photo Alice appeared extremely happy, with a bright smile that reached her eyes and ignited her whole being with exuberance.

Teddy Harnes stood between them.

Unlike his father, Teddy appeared to have a glowing personality to him, leaning into the camera as if wanting to launch himself forward, one arm around Alice and the other around Brian's shoulders, pulling his friends to him. He had black hair with large looping curls that spilled down his collar and hooked against his forehead. I had no way of telling if this was the kid I'd found dead on the ground, but I kept staring, hoping that something would trigger.

"Do you know his father well?"

"Why would you ask that?" Frost said. He flexed a little more, his pectorals heaving. "Now why would you want to know something like that?"

"I'm just trying to find out what might have happened."

"He's dead and they arrested the killer who did it, and I hope they fry his ass even if he is a retard."

"Look, I think—"

"That's enough," Brian Frost told me. He was the kind of guy who raged up to the point when he was about to cut loose, then grew calm. All the fury left his face and I knew our sociable, amicable time had about run out. "You can leave now, you son of a bitch."

He put his hand on my chest and shoved me backward, then did it again as I backtracked step by step down the hall. I stumbled and Alice's eyes grew wide with terror.

"Don't push me, kid."

"Screw off, creep."

Frost got ready to prod me once more but I dodged out of reach and opened the door. I couldn't see any point in arguing, fighting, or bothering them further. When I got out onto the porch, Frost lunged and elbowed me in the kidney, slamming the door and locking it.

I floundered down the steps and landed on my ass, then sat with the wind blowing and piling leaves against my back. I looked up at the highest dark window far above. I saw nothing, but could imagine a hand slowly releasing a lace curtain, and a ghostly figure quickly easing away.

I couldn't shake the stupid feeling. I wondered if Teddy Harnes was alive and hiding somewhere in the bowels of the black house or someplace else, and if so, what he was running from, and who was buried in his grave.

EIGHT

KATIE TURNED TO THE DOOR as the bells jangled, smiled at me, and said into the phone, "Carl, you're not listening, you hate to listen. Do not send me irises. No, I am not imploring, I am simply telling you. Stop buying irises. You always get stuck with inventory and then try to unload your rotting over-stock on me. Yes, Carl, always."

She swung back and forth behind the counter, checking through papers, opening drawers, and began packing together a bouquet. She had a fluidity of motion that I could watch for hours, a combination of ballet, aerobics, and erotic dancing.

Her eyes, as usual, flashed with unrestrained feeling, show-ing everything that was going on inside her, perfectly expres-sive and easy to read. She smiled again and my chest loosened; brick by brick the rest of life fell away, and I got a little heady again with my love for her. She scratched the tip of her nose and cocked her ear away from the phone because Carl the jughead was fouling her orders again and whining loudly about it. I heard his high-pitched pleas and yammering from across the room. She needed to connect with another supplier but hadn't managed to find a competent one yet. I never re-alized gardening could lead to such a cutthroat industry.

Katie's dimples came and went as she worried her lips for

a moment. "I send the check when I receive the orders. That's how it works in this world, Carl. Goodbye." She hung up with a slam. "Jerk."

"Carl has not exactly established himself as reliable," I said.

"As a matter of fact, Carl has established himself as a grade-A moron, is what he's done."

I sat and pulled her onto my lap and kissed her for a long time. I stroked and smoothed the line between her brows, caressing her face, and gently touched the length of her soft, cool neck. As I pressed my lips on her throat she sighed. She grinned her crooked grin at me and my breath hitched in the same way it had when I'd first seen her, and every time since.

"I missed you, too," she said. "Been a long day?"

"You could say that."

"Want to tell me about it?"

I shrugged and shifted her farther back into my arms. "I got yelled at by a lot of people."

"Well, if that's all they did . . . for you that's not too bad, actually."

"I think I have to agree."

I checked the refrigeration unit to my left and saw through the glass doors that most of her stock had been emptied in the past couple of days. Except for the irises. "How've things been here?"

"About what you'd expect with a funeral that size. And hey, did Anubis eat my spider plant?"

"Only a little bit."

Lots of people walked by the shop. A few hovered in front by the door talking excitedly, either because of all the media coverage in town lately or because the purple stuff had escaped Pembleton's and was currently rampaging down Main Street.

"I had a raid on white roses and lilies," Katie said. "They didn't even want wreathes. Folks trying to outdo each other with larger and more elaborate arrangements, hoping to impress Theodore Harnes."

"Or just each other."

"Strange what people take pride in."

"City image, maybe," I said, thinking about the neighbors I knew at the funeral, without understanding why they were there. "Nobody wants the reporters to think we don't throw nice funerals for all the murdered kids who get their faces sliced off."

I shouldn't have said it, and especially not with such an offhand tone. Katie paled, her jade eyes appearing even more intense and luminescent as she lost her color.

"I'm sorry, it was wrong of me to joke that way."

"No, it's not that, Jonathan, I'm only sorry you were the one who had to find him."

"Me too."

She looked at me for a minute as if she didn't want to tell me something. I waited. I wouldn't push it. She grew more rigid on my lap. "He didn't order anything, you know. Harnes. All those flowers at the funeral and that wealthy man didn't have anything to do with it. I thought it was odd, but maybe not. Since Carl screwed up my orders so badly this week I called around to most of the other shops in the county, working out exchanges. Harnes didn't order anything from them, either." She tried to give me the grin again but couldn't quite pull it off. "Is that a clue? Did I just give you a clue?"

It made sense if Teddy wasn't really dead. Why would Harnes waste his efforts on whoever had taken Teddy's place? But that would mean he and his son were in it together, spoiling my idea that maybe Teddy had planned his own death to escape his father. Harnes had the news teams there; he'd opened the ceremony up to a public that knew nothing about him. He'd gone through all the appropriate motions, even if he found himself incapable of properly playing the bereaved father. Or was it possible that Harnes so loved his son that his grief had fashioned him into the colorless man I'd met?

Katie stared at me, and I saw the fear nudging everything else aside. "Let Lowell and the department handle it. As much as you dislike Broghin, he is the sheriff, and I can't believe he'd ever allow Crummler to come to any harm if Crummler is innocent."

"And if he's not?"

"If he's not then it isn't your fault." She kissed me lightly;

it was the kind of peck you give a crying kid when you want him to shut up and go watch cartoons. "If you keep getting yourself involved where you shouldn't be it's going to cost you a lot one of these days."

A veiled threat of an ultimatum might be lurking in that statement, but I chose to let it pass. I looked over at the other room, thinking of workmen putting in bookcases, a neon sign in the window, and wire spin racks that squeaked and never rotated correctly. I could just see the Leones serving *pasta faglioli* to anyone who came in.

"Listen, Katie, I . . ."

"I'm not talking about me. I'm talking about you. You're going to get hurt, and I don't ever want to see that again." She'd actually stitched me up only a few days after we'd first met, using her background as a med student one last time before she'd fully left it behind to take over the shop. "Sometimes you just need to let it go."

"Crummler needs all the help he can get right now."

"And have you found anything to help him?"

"No," I admitted. "Not yet."

"So what happens next?"

"I didn't listen to him when I should have. Now I'm going to try to make him tell me whatever it was he needed to say."

"You're going to visit him in the hospital?"

"Yes."

"What if he says that he murdered Teddy?"

"Then I want to know why."

She traced the lines of my face for a while, and I did the same to her, stroking her hair. So many huge decisions loomed nearby, and it seemed like I was the only one who felt any pressure from them, a coward at heart. I let my fingers continue to glide across her throat in the playful way we sometimes did when not thinking of so much that might come between us. I ran my palm lightly over her belly and could almost sense our child growing there, heading toward the world.

"He came back in," she said.

"Who?"

"That football player who still hates you. Arnie."

"Devington," I said. "He came here again?"

"Yeah."

I thought of him unchanging through the years, emotionally and mentally stagnant while his body grew to fat, balding prematurely, his knees probably not in the best of shape, so that they sounded full of sand when he got up in the morning. Perfecting his pettiness. "What did he say?"

"Nothing. He just watched me."

"Watched you?"

"Stared a little while he wandered around the store. Don't get upset. It was nothing, really. I sort of feel a little sorry for him. He seems like he's trying to find something he already knows is gone, but can't help checking for it anyway."

"Okay," I said.

Watched her.

I spent a half hour downtown shopping until I found what I needed, then called Lowell.

"What's that noise?" he asked.

"A Suburban with a bad transmission in the left lane."

"So you finally bought a cell phone. Keep a set of fresh batteries on you. I've got a feeling you're going to be on that thing a lot."

"It's a rechargeable."

"You buy two. Keep one always charged so when the other starts going you just switch them."

"Oh."

"Give me the number."

I gave it to him. I also gave him the doubts that had been stacking up like firewood in my mind. "Listen, this might sound stupid—"

"Hell, when you admit it yourself, I know it's going to be bad."

"—but are you sure it was Teddy?"

He sighed heavily and there was a long pause that kept lengthening until I thought he might have gotten into his car and was about to drive up behind me. "You're dogging my steps, Jonny Kendrick."

I couldn't argue, and waited until he decided whether he'd

threaten me, give me a lecture, or let it roll. We'd played it every way in the past. The cell phone had clear sound, and I could hear his slow, regular breathing while he ran it through his mind and wondered if I'd trip him up on this. He'd stand for a lot, but never that.

I thought I might have stepped over the line this time, as the silence thickened, but eventually Lowell said, "Cause of death, about what you'd expect. Multiple blunt trauma to the head. We matched fingerprints from the victim to Teddy's passport."

"Dental records?"

"No dental records on Theodore Harnes, Jr. that we could find. They spent most of their time in Asia, Africa, South America, and the Netherlands. The kid didn't put in a single grade in our school system. Harnes had private tutors, he's a certified tutor himself, and taught Teddy at home when they were in the country, which wasn't often over the past twenty years. Teddy was born in Roggeveldberge, Cape Province, South Africa. He'd never been in jail or the service, never been printed outside of his passport."

"You matched him to latent prints found in the house? In Teddy's room?"

"Hey, 'latent prints,' you been reading Ed McBain novels again, Jonny? You even know what 'latent' means? The mansion has six maids from Burma who can't speak English and have nothing to do all morning and night except cook, scrub, dust, vacuum, and do little things like pluck hairs out of brushes. Entire place gleamed like a sheet of ice, and smelled of four daily coats of furniture polish. They're teenage girls, and not one of them can so much as raise her chin high enough to look a person in the eye. More than likely, they're also Harnes' personal harem and he uses them to keep business associates happy."

"Jesus."

"Harnes probably bought them from their starving families for twenty bucks total. The man makes his fortune off slave labor." Lowell's tone didn't waver. "Not everybody is lucky enough to grow up in Felicity Grove."

It sounded like sarcasm, but he meant it sincerely.

"Okay," I said.

"Teddy wasn't murdered in his bedroom, there was no legal impetus to perform a full forensic investigation there once we established his identity. Sheriff Broghin was satisfied with the passport match. Why wouldn't he be?"

"And you?" I asked.

"I got Harnes' permission to inspect Teddy's room, but there were no grounds to bring in the lab boys and start dusting and pulling hair samples. I searched around, but didn't find much. Kid lived like monk in a cloister. Just a few books and some clothes. No posters, videos, or CDs. No love letters from Alice Conway, none of the usual stuff you'd expect from your average twenty-year-old."

"Art supplies?"

"No, though Alice and Harnes both mentioned that Teddy enjoyed painting. He didn't have any brushes or easels in his room or anywhere else I looked in the house."

"What about his driver's license?"

"Didn't have one."

"A kid rich enough to own a fleet of Lambourghinis, and he couldn't even drive? So Alice Conway wasn't exaggerating about him being a recluse."

"He sure didn't go to any father-son picnics."

I knew my time was running out; I could tell I'd just about reached my limit with Lowell, and was surprised he'd allowed me as much leeway as he had. He would be about *this close* to hanging up on me, anyway, so I went for broke. "Teddy could have faked his passport if he needed to get away from his father badly enough."

Lowell had considered it, of course, and any other angle I could possibly come up with. "Badly enough to kill somebody and cut the guy's face off? No, it doesn't play out. Not like he just found a hitchhiker and laid him to waste. He would've needed the accomplice in order to use his prints on the passport."

"But—"

"Like most people, you think it's easy to get a solid print. You have no idea how easily they smudge and smear, and how difficult they are to get off an unwilling party, or a corpse.

Like some talcum powder and scotch tape are all you need."
A passing eighteen-wheeler drowned him out for a couple of
seconds. ". . . assume he did want to get out from under the
old man. If even half the rumors about Harnes are true, you
know you're dealing with someone capable of cracking your
head open or poisoning you in your sleep. He's not on any
corporate boards, he runs his shop the old-fashioned way.
Alone, and in complete control. If I had a millionaire father
like that, a man who makes most of his money from slave
labor around the world, and my father was pissed at me about
something, I'd probably run—"

"No, you wouldn't, but Teddy might."

"—but nobody would do it by leaving a faceless corpse in
the cemetery. If he had the money and resources to fake a
passport, he's got the brains to go for the long haul. A fire, a
car explosion, a rock-slide, those are more effective ways to
erase yourself, if you wanted to play dead. Why leave room
for questions and doubt afterwards? No, it doesn't play out.
Teddy Harnes is dead."

How did any of it fall back to Crummler? What had he seen
the night before the murder that brought him miles out of town
in the middle of a freeze searching for me? What had scared
him that much?

"Can you get me in to see Crummler?"

He thought about that for a while too, turning it over. He
was right, I should've bought an extra battery. "Beats the hell
out of me. I'm not sure I can. Why?"

"I don't know. But if I'd talked to him before I'd started
pounding him, maybe we'd have some answers and understand what happened."

"Understanding isn't a word I'd associate with Crummler.
Talking, either, really. Prattling is more like it. He babbled
and jabbered gibberish non-stop before we transferred him.
Gave the guy in the cell next to him the crawling heebie jee-
bies, this drunk British silverware rep from Briscane County
we nabbed on the turnpike doing triple digits. You should have
heard Crummler carrying on about ten thousand leagues of
evil swamps in dark orders of ocher nights, fighting the dwin-

dling obsidian empires. Dragons and knights kissing and fighting.''

"I have heard him. I like listening to it. He mixes in fragments of the truth, sometimes. Bits and pieces.''

"Maybe. Sometimes. But can you tell the differences?''

"On occasion something sings out.''

"If that's singing, it must be a Wagnerian opera. Along the lines of 'Twilight of the Gods.' ''

It impressed me that he knew Wagner, and I could hear a soft, angry rattle in his throat because he knew I was impressed. Listening to that rattle coming from him made my scalp prickle. It became startlingly clear to me that one of these days Lowell would probably beat the shit out of me over something like this.

"Do you think he did it?'' I asked.

"I'm not convinced he didn't,'' Lowell said. "You're not either. Either way, something else is going on. Crummler may have had cause, but that will never come out.''

The guilt had been hanging on my back since I'd first raised my hand to Crummler. I had to make a choice.

There are times when the hedging is over and you must make a decision despite confusion. You've seen blood and sharpness coming up at your face, and you react without thought, and the rest follows the way it must, with the shadows already cast.

If I'd handled it differently, if I hadn't struck first but instead danced with Crummler for a little while, calming and reassuring him, I might know who was dead and who had committed murder. My fear had forced my hand.

I had to put my faith back in him. I couldn't effectively work to free him if I didn't wholeheartedly believe he was innocent.

"Crummler didn't do it,'' I said.

"You just keep telling yourself that, Jonny Kendrick.''

And that was it; there wasn't a sound on the other end but I could hear Lowell shut down completely and pull away. He hadn't gone this far out for no reason. He knew how it looked to the outside eye, and how it would play out in front of a judge and jury. Crummler would be buried in court, incapable of even giving his own testimony. Nick Crummler had been right, the system just couldn't wait to get a hold of a man like his brother.

"By the way," Lowell said. "We got a complaint on you."

"On me? From who?"

"Alice Conway."

I guessed that Brian Frost put her up to it, and wondered what that meant.

I pulled up in front of Devington's house.

Watched her.

"Yeah, well, you're about to get another one."

Some folks, when they retire, take up a perch in their front windows and wait with the stony patience of the Sphinx for something to happen. Mrs. Devington was such a person, set like a guardian over a king's crypt, with only her diligent, scornful face visible through the parted velour drapes. She spotted me and her eyes filled with expectation and excitement. She drew back and her bottom lip began to quiver.

She was already freaking me out, this lady.

The drapes folded shut and she ran through the house shouting for Arnie. I waited on the front lawn and glanced around at the overgrown bushes and untrimmed trees, the dilapidated garage that looked like it would fall over any second. A rusted tool shed with a corrugated metal door appeared eager to slice a finger off anyone stupid enough to try to get inside. There were a lot of shingles scattered across the grass, and a sizable amount of mold and ivy crept up the brick and crumbling gingerbread trim.

Last I'd heard, Arnie had gotten married and relocated to the Midwest for a couple of years, then returned after a bad divorce and moved back into his parents' house just before his father died. The old man had apparently taken with him whatever love for the place there'd ever been. Arnie's disdain for his home was evident. Perhaps its poor condition proved a testament to his laziness, or merely confirmed his self-disdain.

Mrs. Devington burst from the door in such a flurry of motion that I nearly dove for cover.

Arnie came charging out on her heels and pleaded with her for a minute, trying to get a hold of a skirt the way a five-year-old would. He'd gone even further to fat than I'd thought, with male pattern baldness leaving him with only a horseshoe of fluff that he let grow too long so he could feel something dangling down the back of his neck. "Ma, go on inside, I'll handle this. C'mon, go on back inside."

Rounding in at about two-eighty, I thought Arnie's mother could thrash me and Arnie both without breaking a sweat. If she were a thin woman, one might've noticed the rabbit teeth first, but with so much ballast to her and a nose like a dollop of wet clay, she was more like an enraged wild boar. I wished Oscar Kinion were here with one of his high caliber rifles.

"You!" she shrieked, pointing at me. "You always been trouble from the first, now get off our land!"

She said "land" like we were out on the Ponderosa and I was trying to rustle a hundred head of cattle, instead of standing on a quarter-acre of crabgrass covered with wind-blown trash and uncleared brush.

"Sure," I said. "Right after your son and I discuss the finer points of civil conduct."

"What's that? What'd you say?" She made a face I don't think I've ever seen on a human being before, and doubted I'd ever see again. A few beads of cold sweat rolled down my back. "You, always thinking you're so superior to everyone else."

Arnie kept trying to get a grip on the situation, alternately scowling at me and working hard to calm his mother. He put his hands on her broad shoulders and tried to shove her back up on the porch. She wobbled a bit, and the meat under her beefy arms swung back and forth. Eventually she decided to just stand and glare, and my old football teammate Arnie Devington stomped on over.

Devington's younger sister, Kristin, pushed through the screen door and pressed past their mother. I'd dated her a couple of times in high school, and had even taken her to her junior prom. Margaret Gallagher, Katie's aunt who'd owned the flower shop before her, had let me go a few bucks on the corsage and boutonnière.

Though Kristin and I had never really connected I'd always enjoyed her company. There was something about her I found solemn and intriguing, even after that final game when her whole clan had come after me like crazy hill folk. She'd bad-mouthed me a little for a couple of years but eventually let it drop. I knew she did it more out of some loyalty to her family than any real deep-seated hostility on her part.

She watched us both closely now and I could see the way she worried her bottom lip. She worked the makeup counter at McGreary's discount store and used an attractive vermilion on her mouth. She'd missed out on nearly all her mother's physical characteristics, but I could see some of the same fleshiness in her face, the softening of her chin. On her it almost looked good, though, the gentle humanity rising in her eyes as she watched me and Arnie on the lawn, each of us harboring resentments that went back to a decade-old football game, knowing something was about to end completely and something else might get kick-started back into motion. She'd root for him, I thought, but I had no real trouble with it.

He said, "Get the hell off my property, you shit heel."

"I accept your offer of the olive branch."

"The hell you talking about, you bastard?"

"Arnie," I said. "You can growl and glower at me all you like, I really don't mind. But if you bother my girl again we will no longer be able to remain amicable."

My peripheral vision filled with the wide shadow of his mother stalking closer again.

"Ain't you done enough?" Arnie asked.

"Enough? Good Christ. I dropped a pass, I didn't back over your legs with a cement mixer!"

"You might as well have. I could have been with the Dolphins."

"Arnie, scouts from Miami don't come to iceberg towns like ours without a reason, and even Lowell wasn't good enough. It was just a rumor. You've been stewing in your juices for ten years over nothing."

"I could've been with the Dolphins."

"You couldn't have been water boy for the Dolphins, Arnie. You were a scrub, we all know it. I wasn't much better, but it's time to—''

Not like I didn't know it was coming. You call an unstable, hypersensitive, borderline psychopathic wretch a ''scrub'' when his days are built into a shrine for his glory years— which consisted of three seasons spent mostly on the bench and a couple of flounders and fumbles in the mud—and you can pretty much count on.him lunging.

His footwork was about the same. He came at me with his shoulders low, throwing a bad block, looking for a tackle by keeping his eyes on my face instead of my hips. I wondered if he'd raise his fist, knee me, or do anything you might do in a real fight, but he wasn't interested in punching me out anymore. In his head he wanted to knock the ball out of my hand, recover it, run it down to score in the last ten seconds, invite the scout from Miami home for some of his mother's beef stew, talk about the color of the car he wanted, five-speed, fuel-injected, cherry red.

I set myself, wondering if he really thought he'd find salvation in knocking me down in the dirt and crabgrass of his yard. For a second I felt a great sympathy for him, watching his lumbering charge, his mother's eyes wide with anticipation and pride, hoping he'd find himself again over something as small as dropping me on my ass, letting all the venom pour out of him in some cathartic moment when he might finally jump-start his thoroughly wasted life.

Then I thought, fuck that.

We hit the way we had in a hundred practices on the high school field, grunting shoulder-to-shoulder. He'd gone to pot but he had a lot of weight behind him, and the ground was still wet and slippery in spots. He slammed into me like a charging . . . sea lion, maybe . . . and his forearms came together hard on my collarbone. It hurt and a red blaze filled my head as we clung together and grappled. I drove hard into his barrel-chest, digging my feet in and working him back one step at a time.

A sharp stab of pain pierced my back and a loud crack like snapping bone twisted me around. I wondered if the old lady had actually stabbed or shot me. I turned and saw Kristin holding half a broom handle, the other splintered piece lying at my feet. She screamed, "Leave my brother alone!"

"Kristin. . . ."

There was a lot more in her face than anger and worry. She spoke under her breath out the side of her mouth. "Sorry, Jonny, she was gonna bash you with a wrench."

"Oh," I said. "Okay, thanks."

"You should go now."

"Your brother hasn't quite seen the error of his ways."

"Have you seen yours?"

Arnie lumbered to his feet, set himself and started to grunt and growl. His hands were bleeding and tiny shards of brown glass stuck to his palms. The yard was in worse shape than I'd thought, a couple years' worth of broken beer bottles scattered in with the rest of the refuse.

I told him, "If you ever cared this much when we were in high school and didn't always quit after half-time, Arnie, we would've won more games too."

It drove him berserk and he howled in rage, lunging for me again as if the quarterback had just shouted "Hike!" He kept his head too low, the way he'd always done, so that he couldn't properly judge speed and position. He caught me low but not low enough to actually shove me back, and his ham-hock fists worked ineffectually against my thighs as he tried to find my kidneys. Mrs. Devington shrieked some more, urging him on. This was not exactly the *tête-à-tête* I was hoping for.

I rolled out from between his meaty arms and wove aside a few paces. "Don't look at the ground, Arnie, I'm up here. You always used to do that, go for a guy's knees, that's why they could always dodge you."

He worked his lips as if he wanted to chew them off and spit them out at me. His cheeks inflated and deflated like a blowfish until he managed to yell, "You screwed me!"

"I did not screw you."

"You did!" his mother chimed in.

"I dropped the ball. In one game. Ten years ago. You people need a serious reality check, you're both a couple of quarts low."

Kristin groaned loudly and rolled her eyes at me. I shrugged.

Arnie was catching his breath, and starting to feel good again, his mouth working into a pretty ugly parody of a smile. "I should've taken care of you a long time ago."

"How many articles did you ever clip out of the *Gazette's* sports section, Arnie, huh? How many times were you singled out for ever winning a game? For Christ's sake, get over it. Have you really been like this for ten years? Or did you need me to be the scapegoat again when your marriage fell through?"

"You son of a bitch! I'll kill you!"

He swung wildly and caught me on the temple. The red haze returned and I flopped over onto my knees and scrambled. His laughter could hardly fit through that weird smile of his now, coming up hollow and like a gurgle. He sprang, grabbed the back of my head and hauled me to my feet. He pulled his arm back and drove a fist into my stomach twice in quick succession, and I yelped and nearly vomited. He tried it again and I seized two handfuls of his sweatshirt, yanking him around and around, then let him go. Arnie slipped in the mud but tried to stay on his feet, did a couple of fairly graceful spins before he fell on his face. Mrs. Devington held a wrench and Kristin wrestled with her shouting, "No, Ma, no!"

No matter what our respective intentions had been, we were all beginning to border the farcical. Arnie took a crawling lunge at me and I put my palm down on his bald head and held him at bay.

I said, "Couple of things here, Arnie. First, I shouldn't have made that crack about your wife, that was low. I'm sorry." It brought up another snarling cough. "Next, get over that damn game and get on with your life." He'd bitten the inside of his cheek and blood dappled his lips. "Last, and listen good, this is the important part, you can forget the rest but not this . . . if you have any intention of bothering my girl again, don't do it. You hear me? Don't do it."

He said nothing, as his mother continued to screech. Kristin looked at me as if she knew this wasn't over, and might never be.

I had the same feeling, got in the van, and went to buy more batteries.

The old photo albums had a primitive type of plastic covering the pages, now yellowed and split in places. They made a distinctive crackling snap when you touched them, like freshly cut pine popping in the fireplace. Anna sat with two of the albums on her lap and another few piled atop the precarious tower of hard-boiled Gold Medal paperbacks on the coffee table. I tried to keep things in perspective and not let my usual anal nature take too firm a hold of me, but it wasn't easy. My stomach clenched at the thought of those rare novels from the 'forties and and 'fifties being crushed beneath the weight of Christmas and birthday pictures from those same decades.

Semi-conscious and lying flat on the floor, Anubis caught the scent of blood and nervous sweat and reared to his feet in one sinuous wheeling motion. He opened his mouth, mumbled like the priest at Teddy's service, and stalked closer to me. He sniffed my bruised knuckles and stared into my face impassively, but somehow managed to convey the impression that he was rolling his eyes.

"You've been walloped," my grandmother said.

"Repeatedly."

"That much is apparent. Was it the Asian woman? Jocelyn?"

"I wouldn't be looking so dejected if it had been."

She nodded with enthusiasm. "I suspect that's true. I also fear you wouldn't be quite so jaunty afterwards. Let me get an ice pack. Sit down on the couch, darling, you've got quite a lump." She rolled into the kitchen and made up an ice pack. Again I failed to control myself and wound up shifting items all over the coffee table, moving the albums aside.

My cell phone rang and both Anubis and I jumped. It was the guy who'd sold the phone to me, checking to see if it worked to satisfaction. I told him yes even though I thought the shrill, twittering ring was as bad as jangling bells over the door of a flower shop-bookstore.

Anna returned and gently set the ice pack against my temple. She took the phone out of my hand and fiddled with it, flipping open the receiver and pressing buttons that made pretty green lights blink. She appeared agitated and so did Anubis, who continued to mutter. I got a pad and pen out of the drawer and gave her the number. We both realized that the world had suddenly gotten a little smaller.

"A cell phone. This reminds me of when you were eight and cried unabashedly for weeks on end because of your insistence on walkie-talkies."

"I never did get them."

"You did, but we refused to address you as Agent X-49, and you proved to be far too petulant to speak with afterwards." She handed the phone back to me and rubbed her hands together as though touching it had made them cold. "Who did this to you? Tell me what happened."

I told her about Devington haunting Katie, and my seeing Kristin again, and the amount of animosity and displaced malice that could still rage inside even the mothers of failed football heroes.

"And was this fight analogous to your letting off a little steam?" Anna asked.

"No, it was analogous to me punching an asshole in the head."

"And being punched."

"Yeah, well, that too."

She left for a minute and returned with cotton balls and a bottle of hydrogen peroxide. "You might consider taking up stamp collecting as a more beneficial way to pass the time."

"It's something to think about."

My grandmother swabbed my bruises and made a huffy noise in her throat exactly like the irritated grumble that everybody else had been giving me lately, including the dog. Two of the photo albums remained in her lap and after she finished cleaning me up, she rested her forearms over them, staring out the one window with the shade up. The ice pack felt good against the rising knot on my head. Anubis kept looking at me with anticipation, like he was expecting a detailed catalogue of the afternoon. I told him to go lie down a couple of times, but he sat stolid and sedate, waiting for something to happen.

I sort of felt the same way, and knew that Anna did, too.

"It is your assertion that Keaton Wallace was duped with a false passport into incorrectly identifying the corpse as Teddy Harnes?" she said.

"I'm not certain. Lowell sure doesn't think so."

I couldn't get over what I'd seen in the cemetery. The boy's face—why had they taken his face?

"But you considered the possibility that Teddy might be hiding in the Conway house on High Ridge?" she asked.

"If he is then Alice Conway is brokenhearted about whoever was buried in his stead. Her grief was real."

"As was Daphne Kupfer's anger? Or do you feel it was resentment? Jealousy, perhaps?"

"I don't know."

"Possibly Daphne planned to woo young Teddy, and her plans were derailed by his relationship with Alice?"

"Makes sense. From what I've seen she mostly woos young men, and none of them are as well off financially as Teddy . . . was . . . would have been . . . might have been."

"Has Nicodemus Crummler made contact with you yet?"

That took me back a step. "Made contact with me? Anna, you make it sound like we're in a James Bond flick."

"Be that as it may, have you seen him since your arrival back in Felicity Grove?"

"No." I had the feeling he was sitting back waiting until some major play was at hand. I looked down at the albums and said, "Show me Diane Cruthers. I want to see her."

Anna reacted instantly, like she'd been waiting all night for me to ask that. She knew where to look and turned to it without having any trouble locating it among the array of snapping pages and hundreds of photographs. Years crackled and swept by. I spotted my grandfather in his pre-sagebrush eyebrow period. Other smiling faces spun past, along with children, weekends at the lake, houses, pets, windswept hair, lots of dimpled knees.

She stopped abruptly and her index finger tapped out a tattoo on the plastic. "There is Diane."

The two large black-and-white photos on the page had that extra-sharp contrast and crispness that the old-time cameras gave—that wonderful light, shadow and shine effect that made everyone look so damn good, straight out of film noir.

Diane Cruthers, for all time, remained on this page a statuesque woman with shiny luscious lips that formed a knowing, honest smile. In the first shot she had her palm up to the camera as if to wave it off, her head slightly turned like she was about to burst into laughter. She wore her hair in a nearly full-blown bouffant. Beside her stood my grandmother. Anna had on a plaited flower dress, with her teenage gawkiness on the cusp of shifting into womanly grace. I noticed a slight roll of her shoulders, as though she hunkered before a more weighty personality. Her smile was nothing more than her teeth clicking together. Her face was partially obscured by Diane's arching hair as they both sort of dipped their chins in opposite directions.

In the second photo Anna had begun to lurch to one side, leaving the scene without realizing another photo was being shot, the smile softening and becoming much more natural. Her eyes focused as she spotted someone across the room, her attention directed away from the photographer. Even at the age of eighteen she'd hated to pose. Diane Cruthers looked more solemn in this one, the smile less structured. She and Anna both had long sleek legs, and kept their hem lines lifted an extra few inches as the post-war years edged into the hipster abandon of the 'fifties.

"Do you have any photos of Harnes?"

"No."

"He's not in any of these?"

"No."

"Are you telling me the truth, Anna?"

If I'd smacked her I couldn't have gotten a more hostile reaction from her. My grandmother's chin snapped up as if a gunshot had gone off. The air filled with such an atmosphere of disappointment that I suddenly felt more afraid than when Mrs. Devington had come after me with a wrench.

Anna said, "I've never lied to you. Never. Nor would I begin in this instance. You ought to be ashamed for asking."

"I am. I'm sorry."

The cell phone rang and both Anubis and I jumped again. I knew I'd never get used to the damn thing.

I answered and Lowell kept it brief. He said, "Go see Crummler tomorrow. In the evening, after most of the staff have already left for the day. We're sending protocol to hell on the bullet train so just fake it when you have to." He didn't say "if" I had to. "Try to get something useful out of him."

I hung up and told Anna, "I'm going to visit Crummler tomorrow."

"Good, Jonathan. He needs to understand that he hasn't been forgotten inside that awful place. Discover whatever you can from him, and I shall attempt to do the same directly at the source."

"The source? What source?"

She drew an envelope from her pocket and handed it to me. "What is it?"

"An invitation. I've been invited to Theodore Harnes' home for dinner tomorrow night."

"Dinner?"

"Yes."

"Is this a dinner for the two of you or a party?"

"A small gathering, I believe."

"I don't suppose one arrived for me?"

"No."

"You're allowed a guest?"

"Yes. Oscar will be accompanying me."

I sat back, sighed, and snapped the envelope against my knee. "You're trying to shut me out on this one. Why?" She cocked her head, but I had my answer already. "You're trying to protect me from him, aren't you? For a guy with his resources, capable of making people disappear, I don't see why he'd get so sloppy in murdering his own son." She seemed a little too pleased that I couldn't be in attendance, so I grasped at straws. "Maybe my invitation went to Katie's."

"No, I'm afraid it didn't. I took the liberty of phoning her earlier, and she mentioned that nothing had come in the mail for you there."

"Oh. Well, then."

Guess I'd just have to crash the party.

NINE

PANECRAFT CONTINUED TO RISE INTO the darkening sky, silhouetted in the lustrous moon as black and silver clouds roiled
onwards. Not even five o'clock yet and already the day had
drifted into a deepening night with the approach of another
storm.

Looking up at the hospital, it didn't take a great leap of
imagination to believe every rumor about this place was true,
and that even greater secrets prowled within that had never
even been whispered about.

Yesterday Lowell had made calls. To whom I didn't know,
and had no clue how effectual they might actually be. The
institute had a black-and-white striped semaphore arm at the
front gate checkpoint. When I told the guard my name he
made a big show of flipping page after page of lists on his
Lucite clipboard and not finding me anywhere. He said, "Wait
right here. Turn off the engine," and picked up a red phone
in his little booth. He muttered unhappily for a while before
finally palming a button that opened the gate.

He dismissed me without a word or gesture, pulled out a
men's magazine called *Gozangas* and turned back to the cen-
terfold he'd been staring at before I'd disturbed him. I drove
through thinking of every low-budget horror movie I'd ever

seen where madmen in asylums leaped onto the hoods of visiting cars and giggled maniacally, their insane faces splashed
against the windshield.

I found the parking lot and got out. There were a great many
people walking the grounds, some accompanied by nurses or
guards, others alone or with visiting friends and family. Regardless of the dusk, several patients still read beneath trees,
and a couple of guys threw a football. At the main doors there
was another checkpoint where two guards looked over my
identification. I was frisked and told to turn out my pockets;
they nabbed my cell phone and went through more pages on
other clipboards.

I looked up and down the long, well-lit corridors: they were
completely empty. I wondered where all the other people listed
on the clipboards might be. The guards pointed at a bench and
told me to sit. I waited and they made a couple more phone
calls, first on a red phone and then on a yellow phone.

Eventually one of them said, ''Dr. Brent will allow you
access to non-restricted areas B and C. Your visit will be limited to Sector Seven.''

I nodded because it seemed the thing to do.

I was escorted to the elevators and up to the sixth floor to
a sterile-looking white office so bright that I had to shield my
eyes until I got used to it. The ceiling buzzed loudly with
fluorescent lighting. There was nothing on the burnished white
walls, not even a calendar with the days neatly X-ed out or a
poster of Freud. Three clean white chairs formed a half-circle
around a clean white desk. The clean white floor didn't have
so much as a shoe scuff. Maybe the room was supposed to
make the patients feel comfortable, passive, secure and con-
tented as if they were back in the womb, or ascending toward
heaven. I thought that sitting in here for any length of time
would drive me to scrawling all over the place with Dayglo
paint, just before I broke out and hung onto the hood of a
visiting car, giggling maniacally with my insane face splashed
on the windshield.

Dr. Brent sat at his desk smoking a pipe despite there being
two No Smoking paperweights in front of him. He said to the
guard, ''Thank you, Philip. Proceed with your rounds.'' Philip

spun on his heel with the well-practiced maneuver of a country music line-dancer and slipped down the hall.

Dr. Brent's first name turned out to be Brennan. He had a large badge on his white button-up sweater with his name printed evenly in big block letters. Maybe I'd just missed orientation at the asylum, or somebody was having a party on another floor. Maybe that's where all the other folks listed on the sheets were, everybody off having a bash on the ninth floor. *Hi! Welcome to Panecraft! My name is Brent! What's yours?*

He stood five foot five or thereabouts and wasn't sure whether he felt more empowered standing behind his desk or sitting there. He sucked his pipe loudly, leaned forward, fell back in his chair, stood in a half-crouch, and went through the motions again. When I sat he abruptly followed suit and dropped heavily into his seat. He was sweating and couldn't quite meet my eyes. A mustache like an unhappy insect skittered beneath his nose, his top lip wriggling as if he had an itch in the middle of his head. He didn't have Tourette's Syndrome and wasn't exhibiting any other signs of psychosis.

He was just very nervous.

"I'll have you know this is highly improper, Mr. Kendrick."

"I understand."

"You are not a peace officer?"

"No, I'm not."

"Then I'm afraid I must object."

"You must?"

"Yes."

"Why must you?"

That threw him, and he frowned uncertainly. "Why? Because I don't see the value in your visiting at this time. It is severely disruptive to the nature of the situation at hand, grim as it is."

Doug Hobbes, Lisa's husband, had visited her every day for the week-long period it took the doctors to conclude that she could be tried for the murder of her best friend Karen Bolan. Willie Bolan, Karen's husband, had come to see Lisa as well, before he'd moved out of town.

"Your duty is to determine if Crummler is legally competent to stand trial for murder, isn't it?"

"Well, yes, of course."

"But he is considered innocent until proven guilty in a court of law. Isn't he allowed visitors?"

"Technically, yes, but these circustances are exceedingly unusual. Though Zebediah Crummler has held a position of some . . . uhm, trust and respect in the community, his inability to clearly articulate the day in question and circumstances thereof have left many unanswered questions. Questions not only pertaining to the crime itself and such events occurring before, during, and directly following the homicide, but also to his state of mind at this same time."

I got the sinking feeling that Dr. Brennan Brent was seriously trying to snow me.

"I'd like to see him," I said.

"For what purpose?"

"Because I'm his friend."

The mustache kept crawling until I thought it would scurry right out of the clean white room. "I'm afraid I don't understand." The pipe had gone out but he continued to gnash it, teeth clicking repeatedly.

"What's to understand? I'm his friend. I'd like to see him."

"But he . . . that is, Mr. Crummler . . ." The words trailed off, but I could see he wanted to say *Crummler has no friends*.

"You appear nervous, Doctor."

"Don't be ridiculous."

"Is Crummler all right?"

"Certainly. What kind of a foolish question is that to ask? What are you implying? How dare you make such an insinuation."

I stood and said, "Take me to him, please."

"And in what capacity are you working on this investigation with the police?"

"In no capacity."

He smiled, and showed that the teeth on one side of his mouth were little more than stubs from all the pipe chewing he'd done in his life. He had a presumptuous sneer hiding beneath the skittering bug. "You speak with a fraudulent authority, Mr. Kendrick. You have none here."

"I never said I did."

"Well, then . . ."

"If you deny my request to see Mr. Crummler I can assure you I'll notify the National Board of Psychiatry, the American Medical Association, the American Academy of Psychiatry, and the respective staffs of the *Journal of Research in Personality, Psychology Today,* and *Mental Health* magazines."

"See here, now, if you're attempting to discredit . . ."

"I'm not finished." I didn't know what the hell I was talking about but it sounded plausible enough. Lowell had told me to fake it, so if we were sending protocol to hell on the bullet train, I might as well be the engineer and ride that sucker all the way down the line. "I'm personal friends with Dr. Asa Hutchings of Channel Three News, and he's been considering a four-part series on the history of Panecraft Hospital and its current standing. There are quite a number of questions surrounding procedure at this facility."

"This is simply outrageous."

"Will you let me see Crummler?"

I thought of Lisa Hobbes in here, being asked questions about her miscarriages and her desperate want for a child. They'd go round and round about when and how her husband's affair had been discovered, and exactly what had brought up the rage that carried her to murder her friend and dump the body on my grandmother's lawn. I also wondered how she'd fared in the clean chair beneath these boiling white lights, and what she'd felt when faced with this kind of overwhelming arrogance, finding her name at the top of the list of the first page of every clipboard in the place.

Dr. Brennan Brent kept staring at me and sweating. He champed the pipe a few more times and finally assented. "All right."

I followed him back into the normally lit world, down the hall to the elevators. We passed a huge room where someone had just finished reading bad poetry aloud and others were commenting on how powerful the imagery of smashed frogs had been. Beautiful murals of cliffs and cloudscapes covered the walls, designed to take the patients' focus off the bars on the windows. I was surprised to see so many young people seated in a semi-circle among other, older, more harried and plagued faces.

Brent said, "Volunteers working with our non-violent patients. Mostly church-affiliated, though sometimes we get high school students or college freshman hoping to earn credit before formally applying to the psychology department."

We went up to what I suspected were non-restricted areas B and C of Sector Seven. It was also the twelfth floor. Two more guards met us there, and I was frisked again. We were led down a series of corridors to a cell that looked like little more than the drunk tank in the jail where I'd visited my dad. There was a small plastic window and a slot in the door. I didn't know what I expected, but I didn't expect such overbearing silence. The lights were tapered so that one corner proved to be a bit darker than the rest of the room. I didn't see Crummler anywhere. A guard unlocked the door and ushered us in.

Brent gave a cheerful greeting that sounded excessively loud as it rang around the cell. "Good evening, Zebediah, you have a visitor!" He started to chortle but gulped it down at the last second. "Zebediah? Would you like to see your visitor? Are you awake? Did you enjoy your dinner?"

A thick brown blanket rustled on the bed and a figure slowly began to unfurl like an animal awakening from its lair.

The blanket slid back to reveal, inch-by-inch, the pale shape of a baby's face, eyes wide with confusion and tears. Two streams dripped down the cherubic cheeks to land on the quivering bottom lip, hanging there before dropping off. A tiny gurgle escaped, and another, and another, until they became sounds that were almost words, but I didn't know what those words might be. The blanket clung like a robe as he got to his feet and took a few halting steps forward.

They'd shorn him.

"Oh, good Christ," I whispered. I swallowed repeatedly but my mouth had gone desert dry.

Crummler shuffled almost into my arms but didn't seem to

recognize me. The happiness and the fire, his ecstatic energy and fervor, all of it gone, and nothing remained but unbridled terror.

His, and now mine.

I spun on Brent and could feel every muscle locking up one by one, even my elbows popping as I began to shake. "What have you done to him?"

The guard moved in as well, one hand resting on a billy club and the other on something I'm sure I didn't want to get sprayed with in the face. Brent's self-assurance grew here, surrounded by his men. "Do not take that tone with me, sir. Shaving is a requirement of this facility. He proved to be quite wild when placed in confinement and physical restraints originally proved to be necessary. Remember, he is charged with murder."

"You keep leaving out the important part," I said. "Innocent until proven guilty in a court of law, Doctor. A court, Brent, and this *facility* isn't one."

Crummler kept staggering forward, sobbing and muttering harshly now, and rested his face against my chest.

I'd have given anything in the world at that instant to have been Lowell Tully. Lowell would have known what to do, how to play this round, how to lash out or bide his time waiting, and he wouldn't have tipped his hand. I took the blanket and wrapped it around Crummler's shoulders like a shawl and walked him back to the bed. A barred window showed rain pulsing against the glass.

I said, "I want to talk with him alone."

Brent saw the value in not pushing this scene for more than it was worth. He champed his pipe once more and followed the guard out of the cell. The lock latched with an unbelievably loud clack that sounded like a bear trap snapping shut.

I checked Crummler thoroughly for bruises and welts, under the arms and on his thighs and lower back where someone might think they could get away with pounding him. In a little while he stopped weeping and just sat there staring out the window. All I found was a slight discoloration on the point of his chin, where I'd punched him.

A slab of ice collapsed within me as I looked at the manchild, his mouth open and stunned face so much like a toddler's.

"I've seen your brother," I told him.

Crummler's voice flattened and hardened, and became serious and full of understanding. It scared the hell out of me. "Nick? You've seen my brother Nick?"

"Yes."

"He shouldn't be in town. Tell him to stay away. If they catch him they'll put him in here. They'll put him back in here."

"He'll stay away," I said. "It's all right. We're both going to help you."

"I am cold."

"I'll tell them to give you more blankets."

"They won't listen. They don't listen. They never listen to anyone, and never have, and never will. I don't want more blankets, I want to go home. I want to go home, Jon."

"Crummler . . ."

"Please, Jon, make them let me out." Tears welled in his eyes again and I felt a furious animal scratching inside my chest trying to scrabble its way out.

"I'm going to try. Tell me what happened that day in the cemetery."

"I like it there, Jon. I want to go back to the cemetery."

"You will, I promise. Crummler, tell me what happened. Do you remember that day?"

"An errant night fallen before the dragon."

"How did you get covered in blood?"

"He was coughing."

"Teddy?" I asked. "Do you mean Teddy was coughing up blood?"

"The knight."

"Teddy was coughing?"

"The dragon kissed and bit him to death."

"The dragon coughed? How did you get covered in blood? Did you hold him? Did you cradle him?"

"He was coughing."

Part of me wanted to shake him into answering me, and the rest of me realized that if I hadn't been so quick on the draw in the first place all of this might have been avoided. "Did you know Teddy Harnes? Was it him? Had you met him before?" He continued to look out the window and *tsked* with a groan, as if hoping the rain and wind wouldn't mess the cemetery much in his absence. I thought he might recognize a headstone more easily than a living person. "He was visiting his mother, Marie Harnes. You take care of her grave."

"I take care of all the graves. I do a good job. I want to go back to the cemetery, Jon, please."

I could feel what span of attention he'd had to give quickly dwindling away, so I started throwing everything at him, hoping something would connect and make an impact. "Was another man there? A big man named Frost? A girl? Do you know Alice Conway? She says she was Teddy's girlfriend."

"He kept coughing."

"Who killed him?"

"The dragon's bite."

I sighed and sat back on the bed and saw motion outside the cell door. They'd be coming in to tell me that my time was up any second now. "Tell me about Maggie."

"Maggie?" Crummler said. He snapped up straight as if I'd passed a torch over his back. "Aunt Maggie?"

"Yes. What happened there?"

"Oh no. No, oh no."

"Tell me, Crummler, I need to know."

"I was. . . ." The muscles of his face tugged in every direction at once and his eyes filled with the fragments of his lifetime. His breathing sped and faltered. A mass of emotions slithered and scaled. Twin veins in his forehead bulged in a V pattern. I'd never seen his ears before: they were large and almost pointed. They turned crimson until I thought they might bleed. The corners of his mouth lifted and drooped as if fishhooks tugged repeatedly at his lips. He sat frozen, trapped by his own dead smile. *"I was happy there. I was so happy there!"*

Crummler bent forward and dropped to his knees, and crawled into a ball in the corner of the room sobbing wildly.

. . . .

I knocked on the door and no one came. I knocked again, and
played another scene in my mind, imagining them outside
planning their strategy and filling out forms and giving me a
new identity, never letting me go. I saw myself bald and in
rags, ancient and mad, clambering in the shiny white rooms
and subsisting on spiders and flies. I pounded harder. They
could do what they want, claim I never arrived, drive the van
into a lake.

In a near-panic, I hammered some more and the door
opened slowly. Brent whirled past and a guard stepped into
view.

It was Sparky.

"You," I said. "You did this to him."

"You know what the beauty of this moment is?" Sparky
asked. He smiled, and the etched lines around his mouth and
eyes continued to bend and twist—his upper lip dipped toward
me at that strange and ugly angle. "Seeing that look on your
face. Christ, I wish I had my camera. Hey, I'm just doing my
job, now ain't that right, Doc?"

"Please, Mr. Shanks," Dr. Brennan Brent said.

I thought about that for a minute, how the head of the hospital would call a guard "mister." Shanks. The name fit.

With an intense clarity I realized Theodore Harnes had
bought them both, and that Panecraft was his to use as he
needed. But was it to torture Crummler or to kill him and hide
the truth of what happened that day in Felicity Grave?

"Hey, Doc, call me Freddy. Everybody does, except this
asshole here, he likes to call me Sparky. Doc, you got a Po-
laroid around here anyplace? Look at his nostrils, I think
they're quivering like a bunny's."

"So," I said. "Harnes has the hospital in his pocket."

"Sure," Shanks told me, more gleeful than anybody over
the age of five ought to be. "He put three wings on this place.
Mr. Theodore Harnes is a gen-you-ine philanthropist." He
stopped and tried to appear thoughtful. "You know how much
money this institution earns for this town? This county? How
many employment opportunities that comes out to be? Nurses,
doctors, pharmacists, custodians, security officers?"

"Patients," I said.

He smiled with that ripped mouth and said, "Oh yeah, lots of patients. Well hell, wouldn't be a hospital without them."

"No, I suppose not."

I kept looking back and forth from him to Brent, thinking about how much time there was before something awful happened to Crummler. Shanks let a little of the ferocity ease though, jabbing like his namesake.

We drew a bead on each other and he said, "Hey, asshole, I told you once already, quit staring at me."

"With pleasure. Where do you keep the violently insane?"

Brent knew his place and kept silent. He'd been given his tasks and orders over the last few days. Maybe debts had been owed, and were now being paid. I didn't even guess at how many of them had been collected over the years. Who else had Harnes hidden away here? Pregnant girls, irritating partners, mistresses, his ex-wives . . . Teddy?

"The fifth floor, actually," Shanks said. "Always been partial to it myself. They got this water therapy tub down there, a big basin with one of them massagers, you know?" He put his hands on his lower back and stretched. His spine popped like pulling up a bath mat. "I get twinges on occasion, ain't young anymore." His white crew cut and corrupt persona didn't make me think of him as old and infirmed. "Me and this little nurse I know, we sometimes get together and we get to washing each other's backs and such. Better than a hot tub, I'm telling you. Next door, there's this cell, rubber all over, you get my drift?"

"Tell me later," I said.

"Anyway, it's the fifth. Why'd you ask that?"

I could picture him cutting off somebody's face, starting at the upper lip and carving outward from there, peeling back flesh as he unwound a boy's good looks. "I just wanted to make sure I knew where to visit when they lock you up in here." I turned and we stared at each other, and I thought about how much more of his lip I could ruin with my fists when the proper time came. "See you at the party tonight, Sparky? Or are you working late?"

•   •   •

Rain spattered down as heavily as syrup, smearing angry shadows across the streets. Despite a relatively cold night, lightning still occasionally speared the riled, cresting sky.

The bloated moon, fiery and flickering, bobbed in the clouds like a luminous buoy set adrift in the rolling ocean.

I expected an even more abundant security force at the Harnes estate than there'd been at Panecraft, but only two life-size stone lions rising to roar in the wind greeted me as I drove down the private road. The imposing electric gate had been left open just wide enough for the van to squeak through, as if daring me to enter. The name HARNES arced above, each letter an intricate piece of ironwork art. I continued on the road for a couple hundred yards more, the moon sliding down the wet trees and appearing in the sheen of windows haphazardly glinting through the woods. Backlit by lightning, the mansion loomed: four floors, perhaps thirty or thirty-five rooms, and yet hardly any lights on at all.

Oscar's truck sat parked out front in the impressive brick drive, along with several luxury vehicles, limousines, and Sheriff Broghin's police car. I noticed Alice Conway's mauled '68 Mustang directly across from a new Ferrari with so much wax on it that the rain beaded into thick pools gliding like mercury over the hood.

Quite a dinner party.

Dormers and colonnades filled the roof like a dark play ground where glaring gargoyles could cavort and hide. The streaming panes of glass gawked like hundreds of bleary eyes gauging my approach.

I pressed the doorbell and the first several notes of Bach's "Air on the G String" played distantly within. There was no overhang at the front door. I waited and continued to get rained on. The six Burmese servants didn't scurry to let me in. I pressed the doorbell again and another classical piece seemed to play; it sounded like Mendelssohn. I'd never heard of a doorbell that switched tunes, but if such a thing existed I thought Theodore Harnes would be the man to have it. Then again, I was completely soaked, my ears were filling with water, and everything was beginning to sound like rain and my own breathing.

I tried the door, opened it, and walked inside.

Jocelyn stood directly in front of me.

She took a station at the foot of a magnificent staircase that wound to a landing filled with a line of sculptures. The statues receded into the murkiness like escaped convicts making a break. A chandelier burned dimly overhead, and most of the light seemed to drop down onto her like columns pitching forward. Her incredibly long, straight, shining hair continued to fall in a perfect crest. The dead gaze also hadn't altered.

Wearing a tight black dress and with her intensely black hair framing her pale face, she appeared cut from the fabric of darkness. She said nothing as I dripped on the marble floor. I realized immediately that she was actually a Ninja warrior, and in half a second my chest would be stuck with nineteen throwing stars that had earlier been dipped in poison.

"Your invitation?" she asked.

"Surely lost in the mail," I said. "Wouldn't Mr. Harnes have invited the man who captured his son's killer? Or should I consider the ride to the airport to be thanks enough?"

"You have extremely poor manners, Mr. Kendrick."

I simply nodded. "Not always, but tonight that happens to be the case. I apologize."

"Leave."

"No."

"I can have you arrested."

"Just try to interrupt Broghin during the main course. He'd arrest you for bothering him."

She remained completely expressionless, showing no anger, no warmth, no clemency. I speculated again about what kind of childhood she might have had. Had Harnes bought her for table scraps from her starving family? I wondered where she fit into this game, and whether she was another of Harnes' lovers or just a captive like all the kids in Thailand and Nicaragua working themselves to death for him.

She took a step toward me and I could feel the welling of her presence, as though a crowd of people moved with her. I was amazed by the sudden shift in atmosphere and waited for her to take another step, but she didn't.

We stared at each other for a while longer and thunder

growled as the wind tore at the door behind me. Finally Jocelyn took another step, and whatever ghosts had flocked
around us receded into the gloom of the foyer. I reached and
found some switches on the wall and hit them. The chandelier
blazed. She lifted her chin as if to give me a clearer view of
her face, displaying those exotic features and mysterious
chemistry that comprised her being.

"I'd like to see my grandmother."

"Mr. Harnes and his invited quests are currently enjoying
their dinner, and you shall not disturb them." A Chinese em-
press couldn't have said anything that sounded more detached
and indifferent, yet abiding no opposition. "However, they
will be taking drinks in the library shortly, and I shall announce you then."

"Thank you."

We stared at each other some more. The discord running
between us grew even heavier. In a romantic comedy we
would be adversaries who would now begin slapping each
other and then break down into frantic groping; the camera
would cut to the two of us entwined in bed with the covers
drawn up to our armpits, fondling happily, and the audience
would get a laugh. I did not foresee such a scene occurring
for us anytime in the near future. Though nothing registered
in her face, I thought I noticed a slight uncertainty in her eyes,
as if she did not know what I was, or what to do, or which
can of spray to use on me.

Where were the Burmese servants who cleaned the mansion
daily? Who knew what happened at night? Jocelyn's duties,
whatever they might be, would not include the taking of
guests' coats.

I said, "I guess we have some time on our hands."

"What do you want here, Mr. Kendrick?"

"To find out more about Teddy."

"For what purpose?"

"To find out who killed him."

"You captured the man yourself."

"No," I said. "I made a mistake."

"I see."

I noticed that she hardly ever blinked, her black eyes filling with jagged incisiveness and emptying again. Her face was completely unmarred by lines of any kind, as if she were incapable of smiling, frowning, or showing a hint of what went on inside. In that moment I would have paid ten grand for a joke that would have made her giggle.

"I see," she repeated. "You feel guilty about the fate of your friend, the gravekeeper, and now you seek to incriminate someone else."

"I like the sound of 'to cast aspersions' a little better."

"Do you?"

"But you're wrong. I want to find out who killed Teddy, and why."

We continued our standoff and the wind continued its mad caterwauling. Thunder provided a nice contrapuntal cadence, as rhythmic as a backbeat. Jocelyn had much more patience than me and would undoubtedly win our staring match unless she forfeited by falling over dead from boredom.

"What nationality are you?" I asked.

"I was born in Hong Kong."

"I'd like to see Teddy's room."

Without hesitation she said, "All right."

That was too easy, and I wondered why.

She dimmed the lights once more and led me to the staircase. Again she faded into the shadows, reappearing only when she turned her head enough so that I could catch a glimpse of the pale angle of her cheek. She glided so smoothly up the steps that she appeared to be floating.

Maybe it was the darkness, the company, or the leftover edginess from Panecraft, but threads of cold sweat trickled down my chest.

I strained my ears hoping to hear Anna's voice or the clatter of silverware, but there was only silence.

"How long have you been with Harnes?" I asked.

"Quite some time."

"Did you know Teddy well?"

"No, not especially. No one did. Teddy was quite reclusive. He preferred to remain remote. Solitary. He found solace in philosophy. Theology. Other more cerebral pursuits. He recently took up painting."

"Did he care about his father's business affairs? The factories? After all, eventually he would have inherited it all."

"Teddy did not care much for possessions and finances."

"How did his father feel about that?"

"It made no difference whatsoever."

"A multi-millionaire didn't mind that his son followed more aesthetic pursuits and had no interest in taking over a vast family fortune?"

"Not at all. He cherished Teddy and put the highest value on his son's happiness."

She stopped in the darkness and I brushed against her back. A switch clicked and a portion of the second floor ignited as though lightning had struck nearby. On the walls were several Oriental tapestries and paintings, representations of myths and seascapes mixed side by side with family portraits. A number of beautiful women gaped down at us, some poised, and others who looked highly uncomfortable and even angry.

"Which is Marie Harnes?"

"I don't know."

To the side, separated from the others and at eye level, a much smaller painting showed the face of Diane Cruthers; her shiny luscious lips were turned into an honest but not so pretty smile, gazing out across a mansion she hadn't lived long enough to step foot inside. Her face was slightly turned, like she might be on the verge of laughter, exactly the same way as in the photo in Anna's album. A character trait, then. Her hair was much shorter.

What pregnant woman commits suicide?

We continued down the corridor to Teddy's room.

It hardly looked any different from Crummler's shack. Entirely bare except for a bed, dresser, desk, and a small bookshelf with a dozen or so books lying on their sides in stacks. Lowell had been right, if felt like a monk's cell. The stink of polish was overpowering; every surface sparkled. I drew my finger along the shelf and found it totally dust free.

Since we'd already established that I was completely rude, I decided to open a dresser drawer. It slid back too easily on its rollers and slapped me in the knees. There were only two shirts within.

Jocelyn's hand wrapped around my wrist and she squeezed until the tiny bones in my fist started to grind together. It took all my effort not to yelp. I let go of the drawer handle and she let go of me.

"Why do you insist on this type of behavior, Mr. Kendrick? I allowed you access to this room because I don't want you pestering Mr. Harnes with these ridiculous antics."

On Teddy's shelf were three books lying on their sides with severely cracked spines, as if he'd taken them down and reread them many times. On top, with a few dust jacket chips, lay *Lao-Tzu Te-Tao Ching: A new translation based on the recently discovered Ma-Wang-Tui texts* by Robert G. Hendricks. Below rested Kwo Da-Wei's *Chinese Brushwork: Its History, Aesthetics, and Techniques*, and an older copy of Ta T'ung Shu's *The One-World Philosophy of K'ang Yu-Wei*, published in London by George Allen & Unwin in 1958.

I flipped through them and spotted extensive handwritten notes in tiny, clear print on the subject of painting. Beneath the back flap of the *Brushwork* dust jacket I found several neatly folded papers. I opened a few and saw they were ink drawings of women. He'd even drawn on the end pages and on the inside back cover with pencil: fruit, junk boats, seascapes, and more women.

I recognized the books as fairly uncommon titles. My former assistant Debi Kiko Mashima used to handle a great deal of my foreign first editions and their translations, and took to stocking volumes on Japanese culture and society, as well as other books on Asian thought, craft, and history. Just inside each front cover a cardboard strip poked out: bookmarks. I checked and saw the store stamp.

It was my store.

I would have remembered an online order if I'd mailed it to my home county. There hadn't been any. That meant Teddy had come into my shop sometime in the last few months.

I'd met him and hadn't even known it.

"You look disturbed," Jocelyn said.

"No."

"What is it?"

"Nothing."

"Put those down." She didn't wear a watch and there were no clocks in the room, but as though some silent alarm had gone off Jocelyn stiffened and lifted her chin. "They will be taking desert and drinks in the library soon. Follow if you must."

I looked out the window and saw a figure lurking in the darkness. I took a step closer, peered down, and watched Nick Crummler standing on the front lawn in the rain, staring back up at me.

TEN

DESPITE THE HISTORICAL FIREPLACE, DARK pine paneling, a huge finely detailed wooden globe of the ancient world, and marble chess pieces set upon a mahogany table-board, the library held all the appeal of a diorama. It lacked any real ambiance, and came off more like a setting in a wax museum.

The room spread out large as a ballroom, and guests milled as though ready for the countdown to New Year's. Built in shelving ran sixteen-feet high, with two rolling ladders on either side of the library. Instead of rare originals, most of the books were cheap facsimiles, faux-leather-bound sets of the *Masterpieces of Literature, World's One Hundred Greatest Novels*, encyclopedias, and a ton of outdated law books, as well as several duplicate series of novels and journals. Harnes simply wanted to fill the shelves, and didn't care with what.

Chatter enveloped the room. No one seemed puzzled or surprised as to why they'd been invited here in a time of supposed grief. There was a lot of laughter. Nobody took any notice of me. Jocelyn drew attention, chins snapping up around the room. People turned and watched as she glided past. The smarm factor rose a thousand percent as wealthy single men swarmed and surrounded her. They didn't seem to mind each other. I hoped she might smile, out of courtesy, as she was offered lit cigarettes and snifters of cognac, but the band of grinning attendants couldn't garner so much as a grimace from her.

I walked among them listening to the small talk, gossip and tattling. Anna spoke with Harnes off in the farthest corner where nobody bothered them. Clearly they were in deep discussion and had been for some time, perhaps the entire evening. Harnes wore an artificial smile, his hands out in front of him hanging emptily in a gesture of unconcern. They had the ease of old friends, or very good new friends, which perhaps they were. My stomach tied into timber-hitch knots.

Sheriff Broghin glared and glowered at Oscar Kinion among a group of laughing land barons from the southern edge of the county. Oscar appeared to be enjoying the fact that he upset Broghin so much, and sat drinking and smirking a little. Still, he kept checking over his shoulder at Anna, and I could tell he was growing more and more disconcerted. Alice Conway stood alone near the globe, forlorn and on the verge of tears, also watching the corner where Harnes and my grandmother kept talking. I wondered where Brian Frost could be. Harnes hadn't made the mistake of inviting Lowell here tonight.

Others told bad jokes and discussed economics and got drunk and ate desert, and I couldn't see any way to get anything from anyone.

A woman wearing a little French maid outfit wandered among the guests serving drinks. Talk about a thankless job; she wore a *bustiere* and her hair up in a French twist, the little skirt and apron giving an extra-fine inch here and there. She wasn't from Burma. When she got a bit closer I saw it was Daphne Kupfer, her lips set so tightly they were colorless.

"Hi, Daphne," I said.

"Jonny," she said, and her eyes narrowed into two short angry wedges. I'd never seen anybody do it quite that way before, her entire face thinning and becoming redefined by the squint. "What are you doing here?"

"Just dropped by."

"You're not on the guest list."

"How long have you worked for Theodore Harnes?"

"Every once in a while to make some extra money." She

tried to answer naturally enough but the words caught on barbs. Harnes made her wear the maid outfit in order to use her as thoroughly and openly as he could, complete with the frilly little headpiece. A punishment of some kind? For talking to me? For causing some kind of stir when he'd passed her over for the embraces of Alice Conway?

Daphne shifted nervously, hoping to recess her cleavage. "What the hell are you after?" she asked, backing away and drifting off. "Whatever it is you're just going to get yourself in trouble."

"I'm sorry," I said softly, and I was.

I could smell Oscar's aftershave from here.

Broghin and Oscar were both drunk and slurring and miffed, but appeared to have reached a deadlock. Broghin could only stick to his juvenile jealousy, and Oscar could do nothing about it but take exception and note a resentful man's grudge. "You've got no call to take that tone with me, Sheriff."

"I'll take whatever tone I want."

"Not with me you won't. I've had enough of your hateful manner."

"You have, eh?"

"You heard me, I think. You have something to say, then let's get out with it."

"I've got nothing to say."

"Hell, that much I already picked up."

"Is that a fact now?"

"It is."

Broghin mopped his brow with a wadded dirty napkin, the high-priced smooth liquor bringing out two large round red circles on his flushed cheeks. He kept blinking and looked wobbly on his feet, not nearly as angry as I was used to seeing him. He started teetering just enough to get his belly moving, picking up momentum. His heartache was evident, and I knew it wasn't all because of Anna and Oscar. It had cost him something to lock Crummler away, the joyous man he'd danced with.

"She's a fine woman," the sheriff said.

"I know it."

"And a good friend of mine."

"So she's told me, though I hardly know why."

Oscar kept glancing around at the walls as though expecting wild animals heads to suddenly appear instead of all these books. He blinked a lot too, and although he didn't teeter, he had a tremble working through his legs, as if an awful chill had grabbed hold of him and he couldn't get free.

"You don't need to know much besides that," Broghin said.

"Is that so?"

"It is."

"You always this damn sociable?"

I walked off. Alice Conway looked even more lost and scared as the night went on. She obviously wanted to talk to Harnes and continued to float around him, wafting in and out among the other guests, but she didn't want to impede on his conversation with Anna. I could only guess at what he'd make her wear if she ever made him dissatisfied. Every time Daphne spun by Alice sparks passed between them. I wondered if they had both been Harnes' lover at one time or another, and if Daphne had been completely ousted by Alice, intentionally or not, or if they'd both only been after Teddy. For some ugly reason, I also wondered if their mothers had been his lovers as well, and if, in fact, Alice and Daphne were actually his daughters.

People brushed shoulders with mine and continued talking without skipping a beat. Pompadours had sneaked back into style, and several white-haired gentlemen wore their hair up high and thick with sculpting mousse like Baptist televangelists. Conversations circulated around me, discussions ranging from stocks and politics to the latest sitcoms and sports statistics. The strata of the county could be noticed as clearly as striations in an emptied quarry. Nobody mentioned Teddy.

Time ran at a new pace as I waited for Shanks to join the party. Over an hour passed and I still felt wet from the rain. I circled back and Oscar and Broghin were talking guns and duck hunting and had reached that point of being drunk when the world is a happy place and you love absolutely everybody in it. Before long they would settle into a friendship of sorts, maybe even before they passed out, but they needed to do so if they both intended to remain close to Anna. She could deal with the male rivalry, but not with petulance.

My grandmother finally caught my eye.

Years dropped to the floor around us like dead leaves, or bodies. I couldn't read anything in her features, and that frightened me. It seemed as if our lives unfurled for an instant until we were both the same age, eighteen or so, neither of us more secure or smarter than the other. I saw her in the photo again, side by side with Diane Cruthers. Harnes had drawn her back into the dead past. When Anna spoke to him did she see a murderer, or a man she might have loved? Or a fate she had barely avoided? I tried to read her eyes but something kept shifting there.

Jocelyn appeared at my side and I backed out of the room with her gaze sutured to me. With Alice here I had a chance to check out the house in High Ridge, and see if Teddy actually was alive and hidden or snared inside, the way Crummler had become trapped in the heart of Panecraft. I backed out another step and Harnes turned now as well, and we made a pact of sorts. Again came the live pressure but no sense of a living presence, less intimidating than Oscar's aftershave. Harnes quickly snapped back into himself this time, no longer unassuming and fading out of existence. He grew more substantial as the seconds flew by. Shanks would have called him, and seeing me must have proven to Harnes that I wouldn't be letting go of this. A part of me reeled thinking that perhaps Anna had actually had an affair with him—and more than that, so much more than that, the idea that I might be his grandson. I looked into his eyes and took my time to dig deep, hunting through whatever it was he wanted to show me, and I saw that down in there, with all the rest of his coiled malice, rested the dormant, but still deadly, dragon.

A dark and thrashing animal, the night continued to squirm with wind and rain. I sat in the van praying that Anna knew what she was doing, and that I had at least a little more time to get Crummler out of Panecraft. I still had the vague sense that somehow I was too slow and standing outside the rest of the world, watching everyone else cruising along. I needed to pick up my pace.

I drove down the slick private road and reached for the cell phone. I should have called Lowell after I left the hospital, but I'd been too worried. I hoped Brent could keep Shanks in line for a few more days. Crummler would fail his psychological examination, and instead of going to jail he would be kept in Panecraft for the rest of his life, along with Christ only knew how many others Theodore Harnes had left locked up to rot.

I coasted past the stone lions, out from beneath Harnes' arcing name twisted in metal, and Nick Crummler disengaged from the convulsing shadows. He stepped out into the open and walked toward the van. I stopped and he got in.

Even seated he kept himself crimped, low and tensed. Streams of water slithered across his face and ran down his badly trimmed beard, pooling in the seams of his black overcoat. He was soaked, but somehow didn't appear to actually be wet, as if only a moment of blotting with a handkerchief would have dried him completely. Someone so used to being out in the elements had a thousand ways of countering cold and rain, most importantly by ignoring them.

"What are you doing here?" I asked.

The wary edge in his shrewd, discerning eyes lifted a little. "Rummaging through their garbage, of course, what else? Figured there might be lots of good food going to waste. I was right."

It was only partly a joke. The odor of fresh shellfish and dill sauce flowed off him, and I could tell that Harnes had served crab meat quiche for appetizers. Nick Crummler's gaping pockets were stuffed with crumbling bits of hors d'oeuvres. I would have offered to take him out to dinner if I wasn't so sure he'd turn me down.

"How do you know Harnes?" I asked.

"I don't," he said. "Let's go."

We got moving again. The van handled well in the mud; all the sports cars were going to have trouble making it back to the highway later tonight. Nick rolled the window down just enough to let a nasty wind whistle come tearing across

the front seat. It didn't bother him. Apparently nothing did. I
kept seeing Zebediah Crummler come bursting into the restaurant covered in ice, capable of walking miles with the burning wire inside keeping him heated. What made such men?
I'd stood in the rain for two minutes ringing the doorbell,
complaining the whole time.

"You were in Panecraft."

"Yes."

"Tell me about it."

"No."

"I saw your brother."

"I know, I was watching you."

"You got past the gate?"

He huffed, the whistle underscoring his words as we swung
up the looping back roads. "You forget that kids like to go
tearing up the fields and the thickets behind the hospital? A
lot of the fencing has been cut through or torn down, they go
there to rip up the grounds with their trucks and get drunk and
get laid. Bet you been back that way with a girlfriend or two
yourself in your day. I didn't get too close, they've got three-
man random patrols, but I saw you leaving. Is he making it?"

"So far."

"They won't bother him for a while, not until after they get
him off the murder charge by considering him incompetent.
A mental deficient. They won't touch him for a few months.
Maybe longer. Then it will get bad." Nothing changed in his
voice, but I heard his neck and shoulders crackle as he tightened. "Eventually Shanks will probably kill him. There's a
lot of empty acreage on that property. A lot of bodies buried
on it, too, I'd bet. Who the hell would ever care? Potter's Field
isn't the only resting place for the destitute and schizo-
phrenic."

"Has Harnes always paid off Shanks?"

"Sure, Shanks has been there at least twenty years." The
keening kept up with him, musical strains rising and falling,
cold rushing my face and the rain starting to seep and run
down the inside of the window. "Theodore Harnes has got a
lot of enemies, or thinks he does anyway. A lot of wives and
bitter girlfriends, right? I'd think there are accountants who

caused him some trouble along the way, too. A few pissed-
off bastard sons. Some business partners? It makes sense. It
isn't hard for lawyers to get a drinker committed for ten days.
Or get somebody hooked up with cocaine. Or oversex them
with prostitutes and paddles, living the good life for a while,
then pull the whole magic rug out from under them. How
about one of his wives or mistresses with post-partum depres-
sion. Once they go in for the ten days, they're in for good.''

''Jesus Christ.''

''A nice set-up if you want to vanish somebody.''

Lowell had said the same thing. ''Why were you in?''

He simply shrugged.

''Shut that damn window, Nick. How did you get out?''

''I wasn't crazy, just had a period when I drank too much
and didn't handle it well. Made me talk to myself. But I wasn't
on Harnes' shit list, or anybody else's for that matter. Not
really. So they couldn't keep me in for long.''

''But you dealt with Shanks.''

''Oh, yes,'' Nick Crummler said, and the honed blade of
indignation slid into his tone. ''I dealt with him.''

The foothills of High Ridge came into view, rising levels
falling back farther and higher into the mountainside. Only
when I passed the statue of the lonely revolutionary war hero
did I realize I'd been on auto-pilot and heading toward Alice
Conway's home the whole time.

Nick reached for the CD player, checked Pachelbel's
''Canon and Other Baroque Favorites,'' and gave a satisfied
grunt. ''Good taste in music. You really know how to use
those hand controls well.''

''It didn't take long.''

''Yeah,'' he said. ''You can get used to almost anything.''

Alice Conway's brooding house showed through behind the
thick line of oak and hickory, that same single foreboding
yellow light shining in the darkness. The chipped and rutted
driveway tossed gravel up against the grille. Caught in the
heaving wind, those rotting leaves spun wildly against the
porch. The rain gutters on the east side of the house had torn
loose completely and lay on the lawn along with piles of crum-
bled wooden shingles.

"Why are we here?" he asked.

"I think Teddy Harnes might still be alive and hiding inside."

"I never did buy that cutting the face off thing. There has to be a reason for it." He changed tracks on the CD until he came to Vivaldi's "Concerto in C major: Minuet." "Harnes is out of his mind, so it makes sense his kid might be, too. Okay, so you think the ME is in on it, too?"

"No, but he may have been duped, and the sheriff didn't ask many questions."

"No reason why he should, when you think about it. So who's the corpse then?"

"I have no idea. A friend he double-crossed. Somebody helping him out until things fell through."

"Doesn't sound like you really believe it."

"I don't."

"Well, you know how to play the string out anyway. Why here? This his girlfriend's house?"

"Yes."

We stepped up on the porch; the stairs creaked loudly beneath me but remained silent under Nick Crummler. I thought I saw a blur of activity in the living room, like someone dropping back out of sight. Nick kept so low beside me that when I turned it took me a moment to spot him, hunkered below my shoulder. His coat snapped in the wind and he seemed at complete ease, as if nothing ever fell outside the reach of his own experiences.

I put my hand out to knock on the door, and he grabbed my wrist and held me in a rigid, impressive grip. Everybody was doing that to me lately and everybody was a hell of a lot stronger than me, too.

I said, "What?"

"You didn't hear that?"

"No, I didn't hear—"

"Shhh."

"What?"

"*Shhhh.*"

It took a few seconds to focus past the rain pummeling the porch roof and the rustling of overgrown brush pressing hard against the railings. I stepped closer to the front door and heard a soft but anguished groaning. I thought of Alice Conway's look of desperation as she attempted to talk to Harnes tonight, and could clearly see her being forced to choose sides: Teddy hiding in the house, arguing with her, Frost fighting and beating him, and Alice going to Harnes to tell him that his son had escaped his influence and was still alive.

"I'll go around back," Nick said, reminding me how much like a cop he sometimes acted. I nodded at nothing—he'd already slipped away into the storm. I waited a minute but the groaning became louder, more intense, until I was sure Frost was killing Teddy this very moment. I tried the door and found it locked, but the wood of the jamb was so rotted that all I had to do was lean heavily on the knob and the door popped open. Splinters shot against my legs.

I stepped into the foyer and the harsh sharp stink of blood smacked me in the face like it had been hurled from a bucket. I moved toward the living room. Moonlight sporadically cut through the windows and sliced the house apart into the great black-and-white slats. Dark clouds frothed and the front rooms filled with silhouettes, curling black shapes, and gray murkiness.

Brian Frost lay in the center of the floor, tied to an overturned chair. Frost's face had been pulped, his teeth broken, and his nose so shattered that it leaned too far to the left and the right at the same time. Blood hung from his eyes and ears. He tried blinking at me but couldn't quite do it. It looked like I'd interrupted somebody from doing the same thing to Frost as had been done to the guy in the cemetery, except this time there'd been no shovel handy. I kneeled beside him and rested a hand on his chest as he gurgled his pain. Despite it all his breathing remained slow and regular.

I faded backward to the wall, listening for Nick and whoever had done this. A creak from a kitchen floorboard caused my ears to prick up. I sniffed, but didn't smell the hors d'ouevres. It wasn't Nick. I hadn't heard a door or window open, so he might still be outside.

Another footstep. The house was cold and damp and the rafters groaned and the house shifted mightily with parts of the roof tapping and ringing like a kettle drum. I didn't know what kind of play to make. Frost probably wasn't in any real danger from dying of his wounds, but I didn't want to leave the kid lying in a ring of his own drying blood like that.

I progressed through the living room. From what I remembered there was hardly any furniture to worry about tripping over. Moonlight kept throwing my vision off, one moment lighting the room and ruining my night-sight, the next casting the place back into total blackness. Another footstep, somewhere behind me. I thought I'd take a lesson from Nick and hunker down, holding my breath, hoping not to misstep on a bad spot on the floor and give away my position. It worried me that he didn't care about the creaking; it meant that *I* didn't worry him.

He was moving around from the kitchen to the dining room, maybe trying for the foyer or heading for the back door. Could he see Nick waiting for him back there? Would he circle right into me? Bottled, he'd have to either head upstairs or make a launch for the front door. Was it Teddy Harnes? Or somebody looking for Teddy? And might Teddy still be in the house?

My cell phone rang.

Behind me, Freddy Shanks, my old pal Sparky, said, "Now that was goddamn stupid."

I agreed with him as the phone tweeted again and I spun, and a blackjack with one edge of its leather covering showing glinting metal beneath from so much continuous wear struck me low on the back of the skull, his exposed tooth shining with that ragged lip raised in a blissful snarl, his laughter loud in my head stuffed alongside the sudden black agony and knowledge that I deserved this for being so goddamn stupid.

ELEVEN

I STAGGERED AND SCRAMBLED AND he hit me some more, moonlight flashing off his tooth and sick eyes, as he struck down with splitting, glancing blows again and again, on my crown and just over the top of my right ear. He liked to toy with his mark, taking his time to inflict the most damage. Shanks had mastered his technique in the rooms of Panecraft, using the sap for maximum pain but without allowing me to pass out. His shadow spun around me, the blackjack gliding in first from one side and then the other.

My head became an old dirty sponge jammed with gravel and broken glass. Shanks kept making sounds, little venomous squeaks in between the twittering of the cell phone, until his weird huffing squeals were louder than the tweets. Through the shroud of pain I realized he was laughing. We performed a brutal ballet across the living room and I felt the wet heat heavy in my nostrils, filling my ears and dripping down my neck.

The pain had almost lifted to a floating ache of dull purple and yellow streaks, and new star systems erupted with each strike, but still nothing that would put me all the way under. I couldn't get to the phone in my jacket pocket. I couldn't even find my hands. Frost gargled on the floor and I fell beside him, scrambling to my knees and collapsing again.

Shanks switched the sap to his left hand, hauled back and waited until I'd floundered into the correct position for him to bash me over the ear once more. I managed to wheel aside just enough so that he hit my shoulder instead, and my arm went completely numb. I dropped over backward and lay there breathing hard, unable to see him clearly enough through the glittering haze to protect myself in the slightest anymore.

He knew it, too. A lamp snapped on and a harsh circle of white lit the far corner, igniting among the rest of the swirling patterns of blunted colors vaulting before my eyes. Groaning, I wanted to roll aside but couldn't. My gaze had shifted back to see Brian Frost weakly struggling to get loose from the chair, groaning right back at me.

I expected a lot from Shanks but not this new silence. It went on and on. I had the bizarre sensation of standing outside myself and running through the house looking for Teddy, moving in behind Shanks and pummeling the crap out of him. Unfortunately, it was only a sensation. He stared at me with the clear and innocent eyes of a Secretary of Defense. He was in no rush to proceed.

He said, "You know what the beauty of this moment is?"

Neither Frost nor I had any answer and we both sort of rocked and continued to grunt.

Nick Crummler appeared in the foyer, hands in his pockets, his wet hair slung down across his eyes. Trails of rain poured down his face, and when he blinked water squirted out like tears.

"Oh," Shanks said, and stretched and rubbed his bad back. "It's you."

"Hello," Nick said.

They approached as if to shake hands, and my chest tightened until I thought it might crack, and I wondered about how it all fit, with the two of them working together. I struggled to think and make connections but the throbbing became a steel-toed boot kicking me in the head. I tried to talk but my bottom lip hung a half mile beneath the roof of my mouth. He hadn't hit me in the mouth, but I must've bitten my tongue because it felt swollen and bloody and too heavy for words.

Nick glanced down at me and shook his head. He looked up at Shanks as they moved closer toward each other, then back at me once more, still nodding. Sparky broke into a run and rushed Nick with the blackjack raised in his fist, and I felt a great sense of relief washing over me as I started to vomit.

The blackjack came up high and angled down at Nick, but when it descended it slipped through the air uninterrupted. Nick moved that fast. Overextending that way threw Shanks off and he nearly hit himself in the knee. I couldn't turn my head enough to watch the whole fight: they swerved in and out of my line of sight, Nick feinting, keeping tight, blocking blows and without any indication of what he was thinking. I craned my neck and my skull flooded with a vat of molten metal. I would've screamed if I could have found the rest of my mouth.

Rain hammered at the windows like the hands of children. The wind roared. They kept circling behind me, where I could hear wheezing and the slap of fists on flesh, Nick's coat still snapping as he wheeled to avoid the sap. They'd come around in a wide circuit over and again, and each time Shanks looked a little sweatier and a lot happier, thin ribbons of blood dangling from his chin, the ripped lip tearing his face up with a vicious smile.

"I should have killed you a long time ago," Shanks said.

"It might've saved your life tonight."

"First thing I do when I get back to the hospital is break your brother's legs."

"You're not going back."

They stepped on Brian Frost's hair as they went dancing by and Frost didn't have enough left in him to even cry out. The floorboard in front of my nose thunked heavily with the weight of the blackjack. The cell phone was ringing and I couldn't tell if it had been doing so the whole while or if it had just started again. The back of Sparky's shoe brushed my nose.

Nick Crummler scooped up the blackjack and said, "I remember this." He hauled back his arm and brought up the sap. I knew what was about to happen. Nick showed nothing in his face but somehow the seething, irrepressible hatred he felt came through.

I tried to shout "No," but all that came out was a garbled, "Uhmmm . . ." The blackjack kept rising. "Uhmmm."

Those hands, with the power in them, backed by his incredible fortitude, his rage, all the grudges in his life, especially those against a tormentor, and his need to protect his brother, coming in and down toward that smiling face. The blackjack wavered just a bit like it had hit an air pocket, then straightened and speeded up, gliding in the ultimate course of action, and smashing directly between Shanks' eyes.

Sparky stiffened as his frontal lobe caved in, and he went back onto the balls of his feet, wavered there for what felt like a few minutes, and slowly toppled to the floor, dead.

"Now that's the beauty of the moment," Nick Crummler said.

He answered my phone and told Lowell what had happened. He lifted and carried me over to a divan in the back room, untied Frost and sort of propped him up against my shoulder, staunched our bleeding heads and said, "You're going to be all right. Tell them the truth. I can't get involved with this and you know why." He put the phone on my lap and ate some of the crab meat quiche. "I'll be around."

I sat on the divan with a towel on the back of my neck and listened to Frost mumble in his semi-conscious state, slowly regaining some feeling in my extremities. By the time I heard the sirens and the room filled with whirling red-and-blue lights, and Lowell's face suddenly loomed in front of mine, I could almost stand.

Lowell put a palm to my chest and gently pushed me back down. "Careful, you might have a concussion."

"I'm okay," I told him, but it came out as though I was conjugating Latin verbs.

Lowell kept his hand on my chest. "Whatever the hell you just said proves my point, don't you think? Just lie there."

The ambulance and other deputies arrived a few minutes later, followed by Keaton Wallace who, for a Medical Examiner, always looked a little put out by blood. He stared at the floor where Frost and I had bled and screwed up his face. He didn't know whether to bag Frost's splintered teeth or let one of the cops do it. He fingered his dentures in sympathy.

Wallace glanced over at me and said, "Jesus God, Jonny Kendrick, what the hell are you into now?"

The EMTs loaded Frost onto a gurney and rushed him into the back of the ambulance, taking his blood pressure and shouting numbers at each other. A petite blond with rubber gloves on and the fingers of a masseuse checked my pupils and scalp. She felt my lumps and washed me with something that stung like hell but also brought me fully back to my senses. She gave me a sweet smile that made me hurt worse. "We're going to take you in for a CAT scan."

I was ready to consent until the front door opened and a portion of Harnes' party-goers poured in: Anna and Broghin and Oscar, followed by a weeping Alice Conway, who stared over at Frost on the gurney. She hugged her elbows, and her knees were about to give out. Oscar realized she'd fall over any second and fumbled around trying to grasp her in his arms. Broghin pushed my grandmother into the foyer; he'd had a lot more practice with the wheelchair and could've maneuvered it up the rotting steps where Oscar probably couldn't have.

Lowell said, "Oh, Christ."

Sheriff Broghin remained extremely drunk, and the other deputies looked at him with the quiet, unhappy resignation of sons watching their father making a damn fool of himself.

Lowell nodded his head at me and asked the pretty blond EMT, "You taking him in?"

"He could use a CAT scan, to be on the safe side. Most of the wounds are superficial, a couple of deeper lacerations on the back of his head and neck, but you can't mess with a concussion."

Lowell stared at me hard, considering factors, friendship, the weight of murder. "I want to ask him questions first."

"I'm fine," I said, pretty shaky and sick, but at least my voice sounded a lot steadier.

"We've got to get that other kid out of here," she said. "He's stabilized, but still in bad shape. If he'd earned his muscles the hard way and wasn't swallowing steroids like me going through coffee he'd be a lot better off. A beating like that is a hell of a lot of trauma.'' She cocked a thumb at me. ''Bring him by as soon as you can.''

''Will do,'' Lowell said.

''Will do,'' I said.

She packed up her medical kit and joined the others in the ambulance, slammed the back doors and drove off across the lawn past all the traffic that had piled into the driveway.

''No comment about my hard head?'' I asked.

''You're fortunate he liked to play games.''

''I am?''

''Sap feels light, closer to three ounces instead of the usual five. If he wasn't taking his time toying with you, you'd be dead.''

Lowell watched Broghin walking around doing his best not to stagger. He didn't comment on the fact that the sheriff had given an open invitation to a crime scene.

''You ready to take it from the top?''

''Yeah,'' I said, about to get into it, but couldn't shake my curiosity about something. ''In just a second. What were you calling me about?''

''I'll tell you later.''

''Come on, let's have it.''

His stern face didn't soften as he decided whether to tell me or not. I knew it had to be bad then. When he realized I'd picked up on that he had no choice. ''Somebody broke into Katie's flower shop. Roy was doing his rounds downtown, saw broken glass, and checked it out.''

''Devington,'' I said. ''Or his mother.''

''It's not too bad, not like you might think. Just a few tossed plants and some busted pottery. No real damage. Wasn't even the front window, one of the little side panes.''

''Couldn't have been his mother then, she'd never have gotten in.''

''Roy cleaned it up, got some boarding to cover the window.''

My head started to throb again, not where the sap had hit, but over on the other side where Devington's fist had caught me. I wondered how that might be possible, feeling the specific pain just by seeing his face again, the bile rising in my throat. "Some people have a hard time learning lessons."

He gave me a long humorless stare. "I've noticed that myself."

My cell phone rang and white-heat anger and agony came spearing down directly through the center of my brain and ignited Mrs. Devington's chunky putty face. Lowell came over and pressed a couple buttons on the phone and said, "You can adjust the volume."

"Jesus Christ, thanks."

I answered. Katie sounded sleepy and eager for company, and I didn't know what the hell to tell her about my hideous night and what had happened to the shop. I decided to wait and did my best to act unconcerned, praying she wouldn't worry. I flubbed it. I heard the rustling of her covers as she shot up in bed and said, "What's wrong?"

"It's okay. It's nothing."

"I hate when you say things like that. Now I'm really scared."

It took a couple of minutes to ease her mind enough to where she'd let me off with the promise of having breakfast with her.

Broghin pushed Anna toward us, and she had to reach down and grip the tires to brake herself or he would've shoved her right into the divan. My grandmother smiled sadly and took my face in her hands the way Katie sometimes did. I liked when they were willing to do that for me.

She looked at Lowell and said, "How is he, Deputy Tully?" She knew he was incapable of lying, even to soothe feelings.

"Lucky."

She shifted in the wheelchair and asked me, "How do you feel?"

"Lumpy."

"Yes dear, I'm afraid you're quite correct."

Her fingers worked softly through my hair, and Lowell let out a huff. He needed to get answers. Oscar Kinion stood behind the sheriff and leaned forward on him, and Broghin leaned forward onto the wheelchair. They both teetered a bit and stared at the rest of us as though we were speaking Mandarin Chinese. I got a pleasant thrill at imagining Broghin passing out and snoring loudly at the murder scene. Alice Conway continued to sob, standing alone and occasionally glancing over at Shanks' corpse, waiting for somebody to do or tell her something.

Anna kissed my cheek, waiting—like Lowell—for me to start telling it. She had more resolve than anyone I'd ever met, and I wondered what that, coupled to Harnes' calculating nature, could do in the world. She continued smoothing my hair as I told Lowell everything that had happened in the house. I kept out the fact that I'd picked up Nick Crummler outside of Harnes' estate and said I'd met him on the road much closer to town. I could feel the silky strands of secrecy wrapping around us, with my grandmother unwilling to let me in on whatever it might be she was keeping to herself.

When I brought the situation up to the moment Nick answered my phone, Anna stopped rubbing my head and sat staring at me. I stared back and we came to the silent understanding that when we got home the rest would have to be unraveled.

"Who the hell is Nick Crummler?" Lowell said.

In a faraway voice, as if he were trying to struggle back into himself and couldn't quite get there, Broghin said, "Zachariah Crummler's brother. Thought he'd be dead by now."

"Crummler has a brother, and everybody knows this except me?" Lowell called Roy over and passed on the information I'd given him.

"Haven't seen him in damn near fifteen years," the sheriff said sleepily. He was breathing only out of his mouth, taking large gulps of air like a hooked trout tossed up on the dirt. "He ought to be dead."

"I don't think you'll catch him," I said.

"Why?" Lowell asked.

"He reminds me too much of you."

"That's about as left-handed a compliment as I've ever been given."

His attention turned to Alice Conway and she drifted over like she'd been called to the head of the class. She worked her large, pouting lips, the deep brown circles under her eyes looking like they might eventually scrape bone. He said, "Do you know anything about what happened here tonight, Alice?'' He wasn't really asking. He wanted answers and knew she probably had at least a few of them. A man had died in her living room and a friend of hers had bled so much that the wood of the floor would be permanently stained.

Anna said, "Take your time, dear."

Without further prompting, the sentences rippled from between her sobs. "Mr. Harnes drove my father out of business. Daddy put up a hell of a struggle but it didn't come to much. We lost everything less than two years ago. When my parents died last year there wasn't even any insurance. My father had been driving drunk. He drank a lot at the end."

Anna drew a short, noisy breath, and perhaps I did, too. My parents had died in a car accident, initially blamed on my father's drinking before we discovered that his best friend and business partner, my Uncle Phil, had actually rigged the brakes and murdered them. Anna had been in the car and crippled in the crash that night.

Alice sat on the divan where Brian Frost had bled, and the camera flashes went off in the other room, capturing Sparky's corpse from every angle. "Mr. Harnes doesn't care about anyone or anything, but most of you know that already. Look at this place." She made a sweeping gesture to show the extent of the house's emptiness. "He took it all. I'm telling you, he killed my mother and father, really. Really, he did. You should have seen them, how happy they were. How they used to dance, they loved to waltz, right here in this room. He's evil."

Lowell opened his mouth to ask a question but Anna put an arm around the girl, cradling her gently. My grandmother said, "And you and Brian plotted against him?"

Lowell's gaze flitted from Anna to Broghin and back again, and he must've found it more troublesome than not to get all of us out of here at this point. His cheeks and forehead had the barest touch of red. Anna liked words like "plotted" but Lowell sure as hell didn't. Neither did I. It sounded as if she might be defending Harnes.

"Teddy loved his father," Alice said. "He tried talking to him, to stop him from driving my dad out of business, but it didn't do any good. Mr. Harnes didn't even care that Teddy and I wanted to get married. Teddy tried getting some capital for me so that I could keep the house up, but that wasn't any good, either. He never actually had any of his own money. It was all his father's. Teddy didn't understand, he could afford to play around with art and philosophy, he'd never had to pay a bill in his life. Brian started arguing with him constantly after my folks died. Brian was only trying to help me."

Broghin and Oscar both had their eyes closed and had pinioned themselves against each other, nearly asleep standing up.

"Help you in what way?" Lowell asked. He looked proud to have sneaked a question into his own investigation. His face grew even more crimson, and I could tell he felt the whole night slipping even further out of his massive hands. He needed to interview Alice, but his eyes flicked constantly to Wallace handling Shanks' body, the other deputies searching for physical evidence, taking samples and bagging. His fingers trembled slightly because he knew he'd have to catch the sheriff soon. "What was he going to do?"

Alice couldn't answer right away. Her weeping had gotten so out of control that she was on the verge of hyperventilating. Anna pressed the girl's face to her shoulder, making *shushing* sounds hoping to quiet her. It took a while. I sat there with the towel on my neck, and Lowell and I looked at each other, both of us feeling lost. A part of me remained suspicious enough to wonder if Alice was actually only biding her time in order to get her story straight, but her sobbing was as real now as it had been at Teddy's funeral.

Finally Alice could continue. Her voice took on a harder tone. "I was desperate," she said. "That bastard . . . that rotten bastard. Nobody would help. I was losing the house. Teddy turned out to be useless. We broke up, more or less, but I was pregnant by then. Brian stood by me through it all."

"You poor child," Anna said. "What you've been through, alone." Alice Conway looked nothing like Diane Cruthers, but my grandmother, patting Alice's back, peered at her as if seeing her long-lost bridesmaid.

"Brian thought if I had the baby then Teddy or his father would feel obligated to care for it. For me. Teddy would want to, I knew, but he didn't understand how things worked. He loved his father too much to see what kind of a man he really was. Mr. Harnes wouldn't feel any responsibility, but I tried talking to him anyway."

I picked up on how she kept calling Harnes "mister." Like Dr. Brennan Brent calling Sparky "Mister Shanks." Even angry, or scared, they showed proper deference.

"Brian wanted me to go to the papers and cause a stir. We knew Mr. Harnes had had lots of difficulties and bad publicity with women before, but never where Teddy was concerned. It was wrong. I know it now. I knew it then, but I didn't see any way out. Brian threatened to go to the papers and we said we'd cause trouble. Teddy was devastated." She frowned and shrugged off Anna, and an even sharper edge entered her voice. "He was so stupid, he just didn't get it. What it was like to have creditors calling all the time, county taxes, they were going to foreclose. Look at this place, just look at it. Falling apart. Even the man who'd cut my parents' tombstone threatened to repossess it, can you imagine? Taking back a gravestone? Can they do that? Why would anybody want to do such a thing?"

"What happened when you approached Theodore Harnes?" Anna asked.

"Nothing. Nothing at all. He didn't even get mad or anything. He's a man who enjoys a standoff. He said he liked me. That drove Brian crazy. Brian said we should go to the papers and say Mr. Harnes and I had an affair. Brian used to be Teddy's best friend, but he learned to hate him so much in almost no time."

"Why were you at the gathering tonight, Alice?"

"Mr. Harnes invited me," she said. "Maybe to scare me. I was already scared, way too frightened to say no. After Teddy died I wanted to tell him we wouldn't do anything. Brian and I wouldn't cause any waves, we'd let it all drop. I guess he didn't believe me. I lost the baby. I just wanted somebody to help me a little."

"Did Frost know Shanks?" Lowell asked.

"Is that the dead man? I don't know him. I don't think Brian does, either."

"Shanks never threatened you?"

"Nobody ever threatened us."

"Why don't you get along with Daphne Kupfer?" I asked.

"Oh, that. She liked Brian. She likes lots of young guys. She was always running after him."

Such a simple answer, so much more believable than when I'd let my imagination snag me into thinking that everybody I knew was Harnes' bastard kid.

Why would anyone cut off his face?

I didn't believe Teddy had faked his death anymore, but I needed to gauge her reaction anyway. "Was Teddy hiding here?" I asked.

"Teddy?" Alice's bloodshot eyes rolled and focused on me. "Hiding?" She looked at me as if I were insane. She wasn't alone. They all looked at me as if I were insane.

"Do you think Brian might have killed Teddy?" Lowell asked.

One on one, down at the police station in his office, the question would have had a greater impact, but the rest of us diffused the situation. He was hoping to pull her off-guard and see how real her tearful act actually might be. It failed miserably, with Anna's arm around Alice as the girl's shoulders shook. Lowell undermined himself as well, forced to suddenly reach out to grab Broghin and Oscar firmly by their elbows before both men went toppling over. Each of them snorted loudly and blinked at him.

Anna breathed softly, "Oh, my heavens."

"No, no, of course not," Alice Conway said, frowning. "Brian couldn't have. He wouldn't have."

"You said he learned to hate Teddy."

"He was angry about everything, but he never would have hurt anybody."

I thought about roid rage, how I could almost feel Brian Frost's venomous thoughts wishing me to die the day I'd visited. I thought he could have very easily murdered Teddy Harnes, and that Alice could have made him do it by simply asking. I looked into her eyes and thought I saw the fangs of the dragon there.

No wonder Nick Crummler had been afraid of Felicity Grove. All of us who lived here seemed to possess the beast, or to have been bitten by it.

TWELVE

I LAY ON ANNA'S COUCH with another ice pack on my head, Anubis sitting rigidly beside me as I stroked his back.

Bitter crimson early morning sunlight foisted through the one window with open curtains. More reporters would probably be around today after what had happened last night, but I thought they might be tired by now of getting nothing besides a close-up of Anubis' snout. I watched the dawn trickle through the thickets across the street, patchy frost on the panes slowly burning off.

Lowell had driven Broghin and Oscar home last night while Anna took me to get a CAT scan. After sitting around the nearly empty emergency room for over an hour, I'd decided that if I wasn't yet smelling odors any stranger than Oscar's aftershave or hallucinating that my eyebrows were threatening to eat Cleveland, I'd probably be okay. Anna, knowing how thick the head of a Kendrick could be, agreed.

As in times of past crises, for some reason I felt more comfortable sleeping on the couch. Maybe because it reminded me of my parents, or because I found a certain solace in the books and photo collages. Anna and I always slept only six hours, and virtually nothing could change our internal clocks. We both quietly got dressed as though afraid to alert the other to our presence.

The swelling had gone down a little, leaving only a few crusted abrasions and sore knots the size of peach pits. I emptied the lukewarm water from the ice pack and refilled it with ice. At his worst, loaded every night, my father used to hide gin in the rubber bladder, and despite the years it still smelled faintly of liquor. Anubis caught a whiff and snorted happily, tongue poking out an inch and his tail thumping loudly. I always suspected my father didn't like to drink alone.

I heard nothing more from my grandmother's bedroom, and sat wondering what kind of revelations might be heading my way and how bad they would be.

Before leaving the Conway house, I'd had a brief but compact discussion with Lowell on everything that had happened during the day. He stood with a completely stone countenance, the way Nick Crummler might have, and silently seethed as the bodies in the Grove piled up. Sheriff Broghin got sick all over the floor before they'd even finished bagging all the evidence. Keaton Wallace, another drinking partner of my father's back when they'd wandered home together, shirtless and singing "The Loveliest Night of the Year," looked pleased with himself; even at his most intoxicated Wallace had never fouled up a crime scene or vomited across a chalk line. Lowell listened to me, the muscles in his jaws looking hard enough to withstand a thrown brick, knowing he had to get Crummler out of Panecraft, but realizing they were both too mired in the system.

Thinking about some of that, still stroking Anubis, I fell asleep.

When I awoke the second time Anna sat reading Charles Williams' *Go Home, Stranger* in the living room. I checked my watch: 7:30. Over an hour had passed, but Anubis still sat at my side and my hand was still on his back. He turned and looked at me inspecting the damage, or wanting more gin. He didn't shove at me to take him for a walk the way he used to do. I had a feeling he'd never want to go for a walk again.

Anna said, "Good morning, Jonathan. How are you feeling?"

I sat up and my neck cracked so loudly that it echoed in the kitchen. "I don't think I can honestly answer that in mixed company."

"How is your vision? Blurred at all?"

"No."

"That's reassuring. Still, we should not have been so hasty to leave the hospital last night. Such a ridiculous place, to keep us waiting over an hour."

She took the ice pack into the kitchen and refilled it with even more cubes, returned and placed it on the top of my head. I felt significantly silly. Anubis wagged his tail some more, thinking there was another few shots in it for him. My grandmother took my face in her hands the way she had last night, and I got that same sense of my adulthood crumbling between her fingers until I was a little boy again. "Do you feel hungry? Would you like some breakfast? There is an egg-white omelet and French toast still heated on the oven."

"No, thank you, I'm going to have breakfast with Katie."

"Good, you haven't seen her much the past few days."

"I need to talk to her. I need to talk to you, too."

She dropped the open book in her lap, bending the spine in a fashion that made me cringe: the dry, dissolving fifty-year-old glue gave up the long battle of holding in yellowed pages. She loved to read but, like Teddy, didn't love books. "Have you decided on definitive plans for your future with her?"

"No," I told her, and felt foolish saying it, as if the woman I loved and our unborn child deserved only my fear and not enough of my time. "I need to tell her that someone broke into the shop last night."

"There is such a thing as a floral thief?"

"Vandals."

"Oh dear, was there much damage?"

"Lowell says no."

She didn't even have to consider it for long. Sunlight drifted over her legs and caught in the spokes where it danced, giving her a silver sheen. "And you believe it might be your former teammate?"

"Arnie Devington, yeah."

Anna sighed, something like a sound of defeat, but not

quite. It scared me a little anyway, and I perked up in my seat.
She must have also smelled the gin, and been thinking some
of the same thoughts as I was, the dead past always clutching
like inflexible fists. "Do you plan to wallop him further?"

"I think I've had enough of that lately."

"I agree. Despite his fixations he is someone more deserv-
ing of pity, from what you've told me."

"Maybe. It's a moot point, more or less. He's gotten a few
extra licks in, maybe he's flushed it out of his system."

"Perhaps you have as well, Jonathan. You don't appear
nearly as agitated as before."

"I said what I had to say, but instead of cooling him off I
may have just pushed all the wrong buttons. He hit the shop,
but not when Katie was there. I think he must've realized he
was breaking the rules. Same as when I made that crack about
his wife."

"And you feel, after all this time, rules must be applied."

I tried to find that rage I'd felt that day in their yard, but
all I could come up with was the sickness of seeing that family
so tied to their own losses, the busted glass in their overgrown
grass like the regrets and broken expectations of their lives.
"Yeah, I suppose I do, though I'm not sure why."

"Because you must follow an honorable course," my
grandmother said, "even if it brings you into contact with
miscreants."

My head began to throb worse, sending a surf of pain into
the back of my eyes. Everything we talked about seemed to
be merely preamble.

"Deputy Tully may be in a better position to cool him off,"
she said.

"That would involve walloping, I think."

"Maybe not."

I thought of calling Katie, but about now she'd be in the
throes of morning sickness and heading back to bed for another hour of sleep. Anna read the Williams novel, tugging
too hard on the frail pages so that every so often I heard the
soft snap of paper peeling free from the spine. My stomach
spun in time with the thrumming behind my eyes. I cared too
much about books. I should've been capable enough to stick

them on the shelves of the flower shop and watch over an infant crawling across the carpet. I should've been bold enough to go out to lunch at Pembleton's and eat purple stuff every day like the rest of them. So where did all the resistance come from? The kind I hadn't even felt last night while Shanks stood this close to beating me to death.

Anna said, "We must talk."

"Okay."

We kept silent for a few more minutes.

She shifted in her wheelchair and *Go Home, Stranger* fell from her lap and struck Anubis across his toenails. As if he was playing the shell game, he immediately moved his paw and covered the title.

"You apparently feel at odds with me. Or worse, you feel I am in conflict with you. That isn't the case, Jonathan, nor could it ever be. You're concerned that I am not being completely open with you about this investigation."

Like "plotted" and "case," my grandmother enjoyed the word "investigation," even though all I'd learned so far was how little I knew. I no longer accepted the possibility that Wallace had been bribed or duped by a fake passport—an idea that had drifted like smoke, like the life of Teddy himself. I still had no idea why Teddy had been murdered, or why Crummler had been set up, or what Harnes planned to do with him, especially now that Shanks had been killed as well. Above all that, more meaningful to me at this minute, remained the fact that I was extremely worried about all my grandmother *wasn't* telling me.

"Yes," I said. "I'm concerned."

Anna pinched her chin between thumb and forefinger and I realized we were going to skirt that issue entirely and get into the rest of it instead. Maybe she'd picked up enough from Harnes to make sense of the situation. I remained torn. I didn't want to get into all of this now. Brent would be scared as hell today. I looked at my watch again. I should get down to the shop and check out Roy's patch-up job before Katie saw the mess. Lowell would be learning everything he could about Shanks and Nick Crummler. I slid forward on the couch and the crick in my neck caused more crackling noises. Sharp pains skittered up and down my skull. I should have stayed for the CAT scan last night; my brain felt slung over to one side of my head. The ice pack dropped to the floor. Anubis saw the bladder and started wagging his tail and doing a fair imitation of the flamenco, kicking further hell out of the book.

"Brian Frost, perhaps in an effort to protect Alice Conway, may have murdered Teddy," Anna said.

"I thought of that myself."

"The possibility also exists that Alice is lying. She may have, in fact, orchestrated the entire blackmail scheme."

"Yes," I agreed. I believed Alice's sorrow, but that didn't mean she hadn't killed her own boyfriend.

"Or unbeknownst to her, Teddy may still be alive."

The face. Why had they. . . . ?

I'd gone to the house to hunt for Teddy or find proof of whoever might have taken his place, but I'd never even made it up the stairs. "I had a hunch, but after being in that house last night, I'm leaning against it. If Teddy had been there he would have either been working with them in blackmailing his own father, or Frost and Alice would've had to keep him under lock and key. If he was with them, he'd have helped Frost. If not, I'm assuming Shanks would have let him go."

"Did you search the house?"

"No."

"So Teddy, if he truly is the hand behind these ugly circumstances, might possibly still be there. Or there may be evidence of some other sort that Alice is concealing. I am not positive that she told us the complete truth about her relationship with Teddy."

"Neither am I. Lowell must've searched the place thoroughly, though. Since we don't know anything about Teddy, and there's been no real evidence that he's still alive, maybe we'd do better to concentrate on only one line of reasoning."

"I agree."

"He's dead."

"Why would they have mutilated his features?"

Once again I felt something from her life seeping from her. I wanted to find those invisible wounds and cover them with my hands, and keep her from dissipating into the air around me.

"Do you trust Nick Crummler?" she asked.

"He saved my life."

"By murdering Freddy Shanks. And why would Shanks involve himself directly in such a manner?"

"I don't know, it seems out of character."

"For such a brute."

"And for Harnes, as well. Harnes is way too smooth to let things get so messy. He could have simply given Alice a little money. Or more to the point, Harnes could have allowed Teddy to be with Alice and accept his responsibility where the child was concerned."

I had no doubt that Anna would be amused by my saying that, and wonder just how much of it was intended as a parallel to my own situation with Katie and our baby. The conversation could have easily shifted, but I knew she wouldn't harp on it.

"You fear I am in love with Theodore Harnes," she said.

"No," I answered honestly. "That's the only thing I'm sure about, that you're not in love with him. At least not anymore. But you're holding something back, and that chafes me, Anna."

"Not only held back from you, but perhaps from myself."

"Oh cripes, what does that mean?" She didn't seem to know. "What did you and he talk about?"

"Very little of consequence, actually."

"You were with him alone all night."

"In the library, yes. I was, foolish as it may sound ... studying him. I find it fascinating that he has no moral convictions whatsoever, and yet is capable of great feats of merit, at least where his accumulation of wealth and entrepreneurial deeds are concerned. He talked of his business ventures, his wives, and even his more notorious affairs. He is forthright about such matters. He spoke of his son at length, yet offered nothing that might shed a new perspective on Teddy's death and Crummler's implication in the crime. He sentimentalized without any real sentiment. He adored his son, but in a way that a man might prize a car. He offers up all the authenticity of a poor actor in a bad play, and yet he's honest in his lack of sincerity.''

"Could he have killed Teddy?"

"Certainly."

I'd asked her once before if she thought he'd murdered Diane Cruthers—I couldn't call her Diane Harnes, she remained too alive in the photos, outside his influence now—and she hadn't answered. I asked again.

Anna said, "I know he did. And I realize now how very close I came to having been her. It could easily have been me left behind dead."

Anubis, keyed to my grandmother's nuances after so many years, picked up on any subtle shifting in mood and tone. The air thickened with attitude and history. He stirred and began to whine.

I started to get up and said, "Oh no."

"You see," she said. "I once tried to kill Theodore Harnes."

I fell off the couch.

Coming up the Leones' walkway, I caught an odd, sharp perfume rising from around the trellis. Only tangled dead vines remained twisted between the slats, and I was convinced Katie would do the pruning this year. I saw no rose buds but maybe hidden in the gutters of the shrubs some wildflowers were already blossoming. I didn't want to think that a concussion might actually be filling my brain with phantom scents.

As I entered the boarding house, I could smell the heavier, savory, more substantial aromas from the Orchard Inn's kitchen. Mr. and Mrs. Leone banged pots and pans and sang alternating stanzas of "Funiculi, Funicula," sounding just slightly more in tune than my father and Keaton Wallace had when parading around town without their shirts. I turned and leaned in the doorway, watching leaves scuffle in the breeze. I looked out at the rest of the street.

The weather had taken a contradictory turn again, bypassing mild and heading straight into summer heat. People took advantage of the day. I heard lawnmowers and hedge clippers from down the block. A paperboy on a four-hundred-dollar bicycle with tires so thick they looked like they were belted flung copies of the *Gazette* onto the neighborhood lawns, the way I used to do. The house next door actually had a couple of whiffle balls and bats lying in the grass, and a plastic pitching machine grounded in the center of the yard. I wondered if I could ever get used to living in the Grove again.

I shut the door and a draft spun the floral chintz curtains. Mr. Leone, still singing, walked into the day room and turned on the television, where he grew entranced by one of the Italian soap operas: two men in the middle of a knife fight snorted at each other, while a woman wept and prayed and tried to keep them apart. The choreography had a true operatic quality, the guys tussling without really touching, staring wide-eyed with pursed lips. I figured she'd be accidentally stabbed by one of her lovers. Maybe they'd wring every bit of melodrama out of the scene like the American soaps and have her get it in the belly from both men.

Mr. Leone sat and scuttled forward to the edge of his seat. The woman threw her arms out and the camera came in for a close-up on her shocked face; the men shrieked and held her dying in their arms. They were all covered with a thick red liquid that looked more like tomato paste than blood. Mr. Leone let out a loud, "*Madonna*!" The dead girl tried hard not to blink. The two men started to cry, and Mr. Leone looked like he might do the same any second.

I took a step inside. He turned and said, "Uyh, Jonny, you don't look so good. You kids and all your stress, it'll kill you. Relax, drink some *vino*, it's good for your heart, you listen to me. You and Katie, why don't you go have fun, like go bowling? Or better, you stay in tonight and let me cook a good meal for you. I was right, wasn't I? That fish in that goddamn Frank's Bistro, it makes you sick. I'll get some breakfast, okay? And you make your girl eat."

"I'll do my best."

"We still got the *pasta fagioli*. It doesn't go bad, you listen to me. You want that?"

"Maybe something a little lighter," I said. "She hasn't been feeling well lately."

"Yeah, yeah, she looks pale to me all the time, I told you."

He nodded knowingly, and I caught him glancing at the crucifixes and statues of saints as if praying for my soul. "*Aspetta minuto*, I make some peppers and eggs. *Biscotti et caffe*, it sounds like a spicy meal, but it's not. It'll help. A little. I have three sons, I been through this before."

"Thank you."

"And it'll help you, too, you must have one big headache. I saw the news on the television early this morning. I'm not gonna ask about it, you tell me later when you want. All right?"

"All right."

"Well, okay then."

I watched some more of the Italian soap opera. Soon the dead woman roused and the men crossed themselves and thanked God and everybody appeared to be friends again. In ten minutes Mr. Leone brought out a tray of coffee and cookie-like biscuits, two plates of fluffy omelet with thinly sliced red and green bell peppers. "You can bowl a two-thirty easy when you eat this. Jonny, the back of your head looks like you got an eggplant growing out of it."

I took the tray upstairs trying not to think of that image, knocked lightly on Katie's door and opened it. She stood at the mirror doing her hair and let out a heavy sigh when she saw me, perhaps like an exasperated mother, perhaps as if she'd been holding her breath for the past two days. I noticed how all her muscles slacked at once. She dropped back on the bed, and I sat beside her and put the tray on my lap.

"Here, we're going to bowl at least a two-thirty now."

"Oh my, and just when I'd given up hope."

I brushed the hair from her face, and drew my thumbs across her dimples. The set of her lips remained the same, and then slowly the lines around her mouth deepened, the frown causing a trench between her eyes. She sounded trapped between annoyance and relief. "I've been worried as hell, you know."

"I know. Did you see the news earlier?"

She nodded, and the light in her eyes glowed and dimmed and glowed. "There's a lot of conjecture about you and why you're always getting into trouble."

"I'd like to know the answer to that myself," I said.

Only half-finished, her hair rolled out to one side and twisted down across her face into her mouth. She kept brushing it behind her ear. "Is Crummler out of danger with this sadist gone?"

"Maybe out of immediate physical danger, although his brother told me they wouldn't have touched him for a while anyway. Still, I don't trust the doctor in charge of Panecraft."

"Do you trust the brother?"

I gave the same answer as before. "He saved my life."

"God, you're lucky that maniac Shanks didn't fracture your skull. Let me see."

She touched the back of my head with talented, trained fingers. She could have been a doctor if only she'd loved the profession enough to continue with medical school; I thought about all the hospitalized men who would never get a cheap thrill out of her touch. I looked around her room. She'd chosen this—she'd preferred Felicity Grove over southern California, where most of us used to dream of moving to after high school.

"What is it?" she asked.

"Nothing."

"Come on, you seemed a little flustered. Is Jesus bothering you again?"

I took her in my arms. "Let's go back to bed for a while."

She grinned and the light in her jade eyes flashed more brightly. "Those Italian love songs always get you in the mood."

"If you're lucky I'll serenade you with my rendition of 'Summertime in Venice.' "

"You devil."

"Do you feel up to some breakfast?"

"Yes, I'm starved, actually," she said. "Are you going to tell me about it?"

"Uh . . . let's eat first, then."

I'd stopped at the flower shop earlier. Lowell had been right—not much damage had been done to the place, and Ray had done a solid job of patching up the small side window. I'd cleaned up a few broken pots and scattered bags of plant-growth. The cash register hadn't been worked on though it looked like a couple of flowers had been lifted from the refrigeration unit. Devington hadn't had much of a fight left in him. Maybe he stole a corsage for his new girlfriend. Maybe this would be the end of it, or at least the end for another ten years before his mid-life crisis or his bitch of a mother spurred him back after me.

It came as a surprise that Katie had an appetite, and that her face had a pleasant pink shade to it. Like most bachelors, and a vast percentage of married men, I was woefully ignorant about the arcane workings of female biology in general, and about pregnancy in particular. Though she'd stressed that morning sickness was common, it worried me to see her so ill so often. I'd batted around the idea of abortion for her health's sake, which made it even worse to think about.

She waved me on with her free hand while she scooped peppers into her mouth. I told her about the shop and she froze in mid-bite. "Tell me it's not bad."

"It's not bad."

"Tell me you're not just telling me that."

"I'm not just telling you that. Almost nothing was touched."

"Who did it?"

"Arnie Devington."

"That bastard, why'd he have to pick on me? Did they catch him?"

"No, there's no proof it was him. Lowell might go out there to roust him a little, or maybe he won't."

"Well, how nice for everybody." Her sarcasm didn't have much sharpness to it, maybe because she didn't want to look bad in front of Jesus. "I know this might seem a peculiar time to bring this up, seeing as how I've just been vandalized, but have you thought any more about moving the bookstore?"

"Yes," I said. "I have."

She scanned my face, trying to glimpse lies or terror or desperation. I didn't know myself what might be showing in there, but she grinned, apparently appeased, and nibbled on the *biscotta.* "Okay, so back to last night and you getting attacked by this psycho. You think Theodore Harnes sent him?''

"I'm not sure," I said. "Maybe Sparky thought he would get in better with the boss if he took some initiative.''

"That's generally not the way to get in better with the boss.''

"That's why it doesn't feel right to me.''

"So what did Anna have to say about all this?''

I told her what Anna had explained to me back at the house. I tried to keep my voice steady but wound up sounding like a crotchety old man who'd been having trouble with his regularity. Katie took it in stride, and continued eating until the plate was empty. Everyone had a much calmer demeanor than I did, and it was pissing me off.

"You look surprised," she said.

"Aren't you?''

"That she nearly ran him down? Hell no. Don't you know anything at all about your grandmother? It's not like it was a conspiracy to commit murder. Anna was only nineteen or twenty years old, her friend comes to her distraught, wanting to leave Harnes, who, as we've already established, has got some *serious* issues, and asks for help.''

"She might've killed him.''

"She was trying to help her friend get free from a bad situation, and the son of a bitch wouldn't get out of the way.''

Katie hadn't seen the expression on Anna's face: the self-righteous glint in her eye, but with some doubts surfacing even after all these years. "Still . . .''

"Still nothing. I think it was wonderfully brave of her, and you should be proud of what she did. You know what it was like back then, women terrified to leave their husbands, the stigma that went along with divorce.''

I could picture the scene clearly, each detail properly placed as my grandmother had told me.

Diane Cruthers seeking help from Anna, knocking frantically at an embarrassingly early hour when only a milkman like my grandfather wouldn't be in bed sleeping. Anna, a newlywed herself, unsure of almost everything at the sudden shift of her own life, in a new house not yet a home, married to a virtual stranger she'd known only a few months, startled before sunrise as she stood at the sink cleaning breakfast dishes. My grandfather always had five sausages but never ate the tips, leaving the ten crispy black ends lined in the center of his plate. Diane Cruthers, on the verge of enraged hysterics, had come for help . . . but what could Anna do? Only nineteen, Anna understood insecurity well enough.

Without knowing the reasons behind her friend's panic, she could only think of flight as her distraught friend badgered her for some kind of support, never explaining what had happened. Not a mark on her, and Diane Cruthers wasn't even crying. Perhaps Anna understood Harnes' capabilities already, or merely gave him the benefit of the doubt. Theodore Harnes, only a teenager himself, without much presence even then though not quite as *tranquil* as today, void of some necessary part of the human essence, but with a potential for reaping so much, was capable of real evil, and they knew it. They got into the car—a lumbering ten-year-old Airflow DeSoto haphazardly washed because my grandfather refused glasses and could never quite get the entire roof or hood done. Where were they going? She had no idea.

Was she only aiding Diane Cruthers, or had Anna decided her marriage had been a mistake? But they got in, my grandmother a poor driver at best back then, having just learned only a couple of weeks earlier, fumbling with the starter and crowding the clutch, stalling time and again while Diane let out raspy, bitter breaths beside her.

Harnes had found them, of course, and pulled up carefully to the curb, taking the time to lock his car door before moving up the walk to stand nonchalantly at the end of the driveway. He waited calmly without a word. Finally the DeSoto squealed to life, and Anna worked the clutch correctly to get into first, and they began to slowly roll forward. Harnes didn't move, and didn't seem to mind. Anna wouldn't stomp the gas but she also wouldn't stop. Not even after Diane gripped her by the arm and growled for Anna to step on the brake, she didn't stop.

So it had all come down to this: Diane caving in at the last moment while Anna, without understanding why, continued the struggle. Harnes smiled as the car barreled toward him.

No wonder they could talk like old friends. The mutual respect, regard, admiration, and *hate* they must've felt at that moment would have been memorable for a lifetime, neither altering their course, as the grille loomed closer to him and he stared contentedly ahead. The DeSoto hit him flush and Harnes piled over the hood, bouncing across the front yard as the engine sputtered and died. He hadn't even left a dent.

Diane Cruthers went to him then, and doomed herself.

Alice Conway had explained Theodore Harnes simply and efficiently: a man who enjoys a standoff.

"But after all that," I said, "she went back to him."

"He had the money and she had nothing. No job, maybe no family. She was pregnant, right?"

"I don't know about then. She was pregnant when she died." *What pregnant woman commits suicide?*

"And Anna thinks Harnes killed her friend?"

"She said she was certain."

The phone rang, and Katie answered and handed it to me. "It's Lowell. He sounds displeased."

"He usually does."

I took the phone and Lowell said, "Change your battery, that sucker's drained already."

I checked, and found there was only a static-filled buzz. "My walkie-talkies would have lasted longer."

"Frost died a couple hours ago," he said.

"Shit."

"You remember what the cute EMT mentioned about kids and steroids? Remember how they used to bleed on the field?"

"Yeah."

"Besides shriveling your nads and giving you hard-ons in math class that won't settle, there's a risk of heart attack, stroke, and liver disease, among other wonders. This guy was probably strong as a bull but a real mess on the inside."

"Shanks didn't exactly help him on the road to recovery."

"I put a little pressure on Dr. Brennan Brent today. He knows I have no legal right, but he's a nervous pissant. Shanks' death has him rattled."

"Maybe he thinks Harnes will send him into the fray next."

"Or knows the fray is coming after him."

The fray came after us all. "I wonder if we look hard enough in Panecraft . . . maybe we'll find out what really happened to Teddy."

"You leave that to me," Lowell said. "You keep looking into things on your own and you're going to wind up without a face too, Jonny Kendrick, and won't that be a damn shame?"

"I kinda think so."

He hung up and I racked the phone, knocking aside two books I'd given Katie last month that had been lying open on her nightstand with a paperweight slapped on top, the dust jackets already crumpled. Nobody seemed to care much about the condition of books. I thought again of Teddy having once been in my store, the way he'd worked on the books with his tiny print about paints and colors, and the folded pieces of artwork hidden behind the inner flaps. I tried recalling the young man I'd seen in the photo standing between Alice Conway and Brian Frost. Had he come down to the city just on a book-buying excursion or had he led another life that no one had known about, a kid far different from this phantom with no real persona? More likely he'd visited Fifth Avenue's Museum Mile, the Guggenheim, Museum of Natural History, and wandered downtown to the Village to peruse the shops and Soho galleries. Or maybe he was a pervert hooked on the peep shows who ran around with the prostitutes who had gone to the east side after Times Square was taken over by Disney.

"You don't have to keep going on with this," Katie said.

"Crummler might be safe from Harnes at the moment, but he's still in an asylum for something he didn't do."

"We hope. So what happens next?"

"I need to go back to the city."

"When? Today?"

"Yes."

"Why? What do you expect to find there?"

"I just had a thought."

"Oh." Her jade eyes filled with that irritated glow again, and I sucked in my breath. The pink in her cheeks faded and the thick drops of sweat formed on her upper lip. "Oh, you had one of those. And no doubt you intend to keep having more of them, too. Well, while you're having your thoughts, I have to go find out what your friend has been doing to my shop. You wouldn't happen to know the number of a good window repairman, would you?'' Her lips turned the color of ashes. ''Oh God, watch it . . . move, let me get to the bathroom.''

THIRTEEN

THE CAB RIDE FROM JFK to the midtown tunnel took nearly an hour due to a closed center lane, traffic bottlenecking for over a mile at the toll booths. A water main had burst at 33rd and Park Avenue, and the cops had closed both directions. The staccato of blaring horns did nothing to make anybody more pleasant or move any faster through the gridlock. The entire time I had to listen to the Russian immigrant driver badmouthing the Pakistanis for taking over the city, telling me in broken English how they all ought to go the hell back home. I hopped out and took the 6 downtown, and when I came up out of the heat I noticed that another Barnes & Noble had gone up seemingly overnight only four blocks from my place.

My store smelled of dust and acidifying paper, an oddly agreeable mixture reminiscent of potpourri and dry leaves. It was ten degrees cooler inside, and the sudden change made a chill ripple up my neck.

There was a nearly desolate sense of vacancy here, I thought, an emptiness in the despondent dark as I snapped on the lights. Again I realized just how much I'd taken my former assistant Debi Kiko Mashima for granted. She not only handled the nearly infinite number of small and irritating daily tasks about the store, but she added a genuine and often blithe liveliness to the place. I wondered if I gave her a twenty-buck raise she'd leave her new husband Bobby Li, the billionaire software writer.

I had less than five hours before the next flight upstate out of JFK. I checked my online orders and found a great deal more than I'd expected, enough to make up for whatever might have been lost by my closing down for the past few days. A part of me wanted to accept the idea that seventy-five percent of my business had nothing to do with face-to-face customer service, and another part of me didn't want to believe that so few people liked to peruse the stacks and smell the books anymore.

I thought about that photo of Teddy Harnes. Alice Conway could have lied. It might not have been him, but his amiable countenance, leaning into the camera, one arm around Alice and the other around Brian Frost's shoulders. Pulling his friends to him gave him a certain credence in my mind, as if he'd been born to make up for his father's lack of descriptive character. Alice had said, "He loved to read, and read everything he could get his hands on. He returned all the books for credit or gave them away."

I checked the art and philosophy shelves, spending a half hour glancing through books and finding nothing. Eventually I realized I had to tackle the storage room, and heartburn started edging through my chest. Dozens of sprawling stacks and a hundred boxes filled with thousands more books stood chest-high, all of it in disarray. My inventory constantly shifted and fluxed, moving in and out of storage with all the order of a lingerie fire sale. Just because some novel sat three feet at the bottom of a box didn't mean it hadn't been brought in only a week ago. Debi had kept on top of changing shelf life, but I'd let it slip into a hopeless snarl of tilting heaps.

I left the door open in case Nick Crummler had returned to the city after killing Freddy Shanks. He wouldn't abandon his brother, but he might've come back to Manhattan to regroup and figure his next step. I tried to beat him to it, but just kept seeing the vacant look on his face that somehow showed the irrepressible contempt he felt when he brought the blackjack down onto Sparky's forehead.

If he knew anything about the Grove at all, he'd know that Lowell would never stop searching for him.

I went to work.

Two and a half hours later I picked up a copy of E. A. Strehlneek's *Chinese Pictorial Art,* Commercial Press: Shanghai, 1914—a cloth copy I'd originally purchased at a bargain price from an auctioned lot the family of a bibliophile had let go too cheaply—light-blue silk binding over boards with gilt decoration with its original dust jacket and a seventy-three page supplement. In the same box was Raphael Petrucci's *Chinese Painters: A Critical Study,* 1920 cloth and boards with twenty-five illustrations in duotone. I'd priced each of the books at $200, and must've been dumbfounded to have discovered them returned for credit. It was something I shouldn't have forgotten, but I had.

Teddy had made further extensive handwritten notes in that tiny, clear print, and also drawn on the inside back covers. It amazed me he would write so much about painting and not keep the book to reread later. In the center of the Strehlneek book were several more ink drawings Teddy had done of the same woman.

I looked out at the city I'd tried to make my home despite the jealous and perpetual draw of Felicity Grove. Greenwich Village always had a vigorous disposition, the downtown culture and club kids, students, poets, insane crackheads and homeless crammed to within a few feet of each other. The museum owners, sculptors, and painters keep art in front of your face like soldiers performing a necessary but dangerous duty. Music shops kicked it out into the streets with band names I couldn't even pronounce, and the dogwalkers, Rollerbladers, and professional dominatrixes shopping at the Pink Pussycat kept you busy just making it down the sidewalks.

I sat at my desk inside a room empty except for ten billion words, and put my head back against the window and listened to the street humming as though everyone were reading aloud. Two kids in NYU sweatshirts walked in and hunted around the back stacks. I watched them grab and scarf comparative theology texts and science fiction, skimming and discussing content the way I usually did myself when I found somebody who cared. They spoke resolutely but with the absorbed manner of people in love. Enamored with each other, and with thought, and perhaps art. I could have spoken at length about C. S. Lewis and Henri Daniel-Rops, Spider Robinson, Alfred Bester, and Roger Zelazny. When they left I locked up and hailed a cab for the airport, carrying Teddy's books under my arm. I thought of the woman he kept sketching.

Who was she?

The hot breeze blowing across Lake Ontario felt like Santa Ana winds coming off a desert. In winter, the Lake Effect chill added a dozen feet of snow to the area, but in spring there were odd thermal drafts that swooped over the country and brought on stifling heat. I got off the plane already sweating, my mouth dry and thoughts full of Teddy's artwork, knowing I had to return to Panecraft.

Crummler had been trying to warn me and give up answers, and some of the slippery pieces seemed to be sliding together, if only I could hold on to them long enough.

I walked into the airport lobby to get a cab and spotted Theodore Harnes' white Mercedes limousine waiting at the curb.

Jocelyn stood on the sidewalk, facing me resolutely, holding the car door open. Sunlight caught her at just the right angle to make the slant of her hair, cheeks, and chin shimmer. She wore a silver top and black skirt slit up the side, and a businessman spun and marched into a SkyCap. Every guy within eyeshot was walking with a staggered step and looking back over his shoulder at her. She motioned for me to get into the car.

"Not even a please this time?" I asked.

The dead gaze didn't waver. "Please allow us to drive you home."

"No," I said. "I don't think so."

She simply continued staring, those lips flattened with just the right sheen laid on by her tongue, glowing and faultless as though they'd never been kissed or chewed or touched with makeup, not even once turned into a pout. That face like nothing so much as cloth or canvas, smooth and maddeningly beautiful. Her flesh so perfect. I kept searching for a solitary crease in her skin, a mark of violence or lust over the years. Had she fled Hong Kong and been a virgin on the streets of Bangkok or Rangoon or Hanoi, sold into prostitution to the highest bidder? Those hands had never been used to sew or stamp in any of Harnes' factories. Did he plan for her to be the mother of more of his children? Had she been mistress of the erotic arts, used to teach Teddy the finest points of pleasure?

"Please," she repeated without inflection. "Allow us."

"No. Thanks, anyway." I got a step closer, and another, and one more until we were nearly nose-to-nose. Even her nostrils were alluring. She scratched her thigh lightly along the slit of her skirt, but didn't even leave one of those fine, chalky lines on her skin. The draft from the limo's air conditioning blasted against my legs. I could make out the silhouette of Theodore Harnes in the far corner of the back seat, sitting rigidly with his hands laid across his knees.

"Get into the limousine you annoying pissant fool," she told me.

"Well," I said. "Since you asked nicely."·

I got in and she slipped in beside me. I held tightly to Teddy's art books but nobody noticed. Sparky's seat seemed entirely too empty, and I wondered if Harnes would find another malicious guard in Panecraft to act as a replacement in this entourage. The driver appeared even more spectral than before—starved perhaps, the poorly fitting black suit draping off his scrawny frame. He smelled worse, too, and there were scabs on his throat like he'd gone for exploratory surgery. I realized he must have cancer, and the chemo and radiation weren't delaying the inevitable.

Harnes continued to stare straight ahead as we pulled out, his hands still hanging open. Jocelyn smoldered beside me, or at least I hoped she did, though her voice hadn't changed at all, even when insulting me. The two of them looked as inorganic as the portraits at the top of Harnes' grand stairway, like all the dead women from his past.

The living pressure known as Theodore Harnes kept exerting itself upon me as we drove toward Felicity Grove. I thought about how he'd allowed Anna to run him over, as if he couldn't quite comprehend that the physical laws of the world should ever be impressed upon him.

Jocelyn glanced over at me, and the dying driver glared into the rearview mirror, but no one said anything. This might have made a good Sergio Leone spaghetti western, lots of close-ups on our squints, each noise magnified on the soundtrack. The chauffeur drove effortlessly, even when abruptly caught up in a coughing fit. I slowly became aware of Harnes' breathing, as though it was only within the last few minutes that he'd learned how to do it, or even needed to do it. I knew we didn't quite share the same reality.

"I did not appreciate your attendance at my home," he said.

"No," I said. "I imagined you wouldn't."

"You sought only to provoke and irritate me."

"That sounds about right."

"Why do you pursue in this aggravating manner?"

A man who enjoys a standoff.

"Whatever I've been doing it's been getting me a lot of nice rides in this limo."

The sound of breathing became displaced for a moment, and suddenly I became aware of Jocelyn's chest rising and falling, as though they shared one pair of lungs and couldn't use them at the same time. An undercurrent of tranquillity and calamity ran through the car, each of them feeling different things at different times, in perfect counterpoint to one another. She seemed to be getting angry now even while he calmed. In a way I was reminded of how things worked between me and Anna.

Harnes flexed his fingers, once. "Let us talk of the untimely death of Freddy Shanks."

"I thought it was pretty timely myself. Any later and the bastard would have killed me."

"I do not believe you," he said.

"I've still got the lumps to prove it."

He had no people skills. "Tell me what occurred that night."

"If you already don't believe me then what's the point?" I asked.

"Be that as it may, I require you answer my questions."

"You didn't ask any."

That tickled him, almost. Something crawled around in his eyes, and his fists opened once more and then shut. "Tell me all that happened."

I told him.

"I do not believe you," Harnes said.

"I sorta figured you'd say that."

My attention snapped to Jocelyn as though caught on barbs. I watched her frozen visage for a moment, wondering how much hate or love might be hidden there, if any, and if so, for whom. The charge flowed and returned to Harnes.

He said, "My son is dead and the man who murdered him has been put away. Why do you persist in involving yourself in my affairs?"

His calm demeanor rattled me. The car seemed to roll and crest with sodium pentathol, all of us unable to lie about anything. The stink of death rising from the driver perhaps lulled us toward our own ends. My heartbeat tripped along. Theodore Harnes had enough wealth and influence to build, buy, or steal whatever he might want, but chose to converse pleasantly about a boy who'd had his face cut off, an innocent man locked in an asylum, and a sadist dead on the floor with his brains spilled. I started to sweat. I imagined how many of his enemies might be cowering in restricted areas D and E of Sector Eight in Panecraft, gazing down at me as I stood looking up.

And Crummler, locked away, still waiting for my help, too terrified to think of happier things because it was so much easier to survive that kind of sorrow if you accepted hell as your fate.

"Why did you send Shanks to kill Brian Frost?" I asked.

"I did no such thing."

"I don't believe you."

Only the barest movement from those hands, as they closed slightly to cup his knees. "That does not concern me."

"Does anything?"

"Nothing you could know."

"You're probably right." It was my turn to breathe as we

hit the outskirts of town. "Alice Conway was blackmailing you."

"Indeed not," he said, so sedate that I looked at his eyes to see if the pupils were dilated. "She performed a poor masque meant to threaten me. It did not. Hence, by definition, there could be no blackmail."

"Still, she was making the attempt."

"I found her company pleasant, for a time. As did my son. There is nothing more to say on the matter."

"She was going to have Teddy's kid. Didn't that matter to you?"

"No," he said.

I took a breath. The air had come back around to me. "You're a real piece of shit."

A brutal growl ripped up the back of Jocelyn's throat and she stirred in her seat and slapped me. The heel of her hand drove into my jaw and my skull flared with that now familiar spatter of color and pain. Even while my mouth filled with blood I felt a genuine sense of hope, and even grinned as I turned with the expectation of seeing a frown or sneer, her lips marred and curled by unsheathed anger. Even just a single misplaced strand of hair, anything, a casual crease around her eyes, or dimples in the chin. I smiled and blood flooded against my teeth.

Absolutely nothing had changed in her face.

The driver stopped at a red light on Fairlawn, four blocks from the flower shop. I said, "Let me off here."

"Enjoy your day, Mr. Kendrick," Harnes said.

I wiped the corner of my mouth with the back of my hand. "You, too," I said. "Thanks for the ride."

"You are most welcome."

"One more thing," I told him. "Stay away from my grandmother."

"No."

My face tightened as I grew flush, and my fingers flexed, once, the same moment his did. Jocelyn got out and I followed. I stood on the corner as the stink of the dying driver wafted out on the air conditioning. Jocelyn got back into the Mercedes and I held the door open before she could shut it.

If Harnes didn't believe that the physical laws of the world were meant for him, then what could he possibly think of moral precepts? We waited like that for a while.

Finally, at long last, he looked at me.

"Did you murder your first wife and unborn child?" I asked.

"Yes," he said.

Jocelyn slammed the door, and the limo pulled off.

FOURTEEN

I WALKED INTO THE SHOP and immediately noticed that the window had been repaired. They'd done a fairly sloppy job with the frame, and I'd have to repaint. Dust motes spun in the shafts of sunlight that layered against the unused room. If my desk was in there I'd have to pull the curtains every day at four o'clock to avoid a face-full of glare. I scratched the top of my head thinking that if I needed ten thousand more excuses for not moving the bookstore here, I could no doubt find them. I could probably even hold my breath until I turned blue and wail and pound my fists against the floor while I thrashed all over the place.

Katie stood in the back shoving various bins of flora aside in the humming refrigerator. She'd had no trouble cleaning up the few strewn flowers, torn plant-growth bags, the broken pottery and glass. Her frozen breath clouded around her throat. She'd been too preoccupied to notice the tinkling bell. I moved to her as she closed the refrigerator door. At the sound of my footsteps she wheeled and flung herself sideways with a startled gasp, barely stepping over the spider plant Anubis had been gnawing on. She grinned and let out an uncomfortable giggle. That usual sense of amazement I got from seeing the

imples flaring at the edges of her lips took such hold that I
almost didn't spot her real fear.

"Oh, you're back already," she said.

"What's wrong?" I asked.

"I didn't hear anybody come in."

"You're trembling."

"I was just working in the fridge."

My grandmother might be highly accomplished at control-
ing her demonstrative side, but Katie didn't quite have the
nack. I thought I might be able to let the things slide for
maybe five minutes, and decided to give it a shot. I rested my
elbows on the counter and she leaned over from the other edge
facing me, and we kissed for a moment as I touched the nearly
invisible blond down under her ears, brushing its softness back
across her cheek.

"Sorry about the mess this morning," I said.

"It could have been a lot worse. Thanks for cleaning up
before I got here."

"Anything missing?"

"Just a couple of orchids. They were crushed in the street,
where he'd stepped on them." I could see Devington doing
something spiteful like that, useless and without meaning. The
least he could have done was bring the flowers to his mother
and sister instead of dumping them in the gutter. Katie
shrugged, still holding back. "Did you find out anything that
might help Crummler?"

"I don't know yet. I need to talk to him."

"Will they let you in again?"

"I think so. Lowell probably rattled Dr. Brennan Brent's
cage a little more by now. After Freddy Shanks' death, Brent
knows there's some focus on the hospital. He'll probably be
more careful and want to appear completely candid about his
patients."

"The murder, you mean," she said.

"What?"

"You said 'Freddy Shanks' death' as if it occurred naturally, like he died in his sleep. He was killed by Crummler's
brother, who promptly ran off and is still hiding in town someplace."

"I thought maybe he'd gone back to Manhattan."

"That doesn't jibe with what you told me about him want
ing to help Crummler. Why would he leave?"

"I don't know."

"You wanted to see him in the city?"

"I was hoping he'd stop in again."

Her lips looked too wet, the crimp between her eyes deepe
than it should be. "It was murder, wasn't it? He did kill th
man."

"And saved my life," I said. I'd been able to curb m
concern for all of three minutes, which I thought was sti
pretty damn good considering the kind of day I'd had. I feare
for the baby, and wondered if she'd miscarried.

"Tell me what's wrong, Katie."

"My tires were slashed this morning."

I exhaled deeply and it felt like the last stored breath share
by Jocelyn, Harnes, and me had been squeezed out of m
chest. "What?"

"Three of them anyway, and busted a headlight. Wasn't i
nice that the son of a bitch didn't go for all four tires, so h
could save me a few dollars? It didn't matter, though, what'
the point of buying only three new ones? The car's got fifty
two thousand miles on it, so I had to go for a full set anyway
Same with the headlight, I had a new pair put in. I don't thin
Duke weighted the tires properly though, the right side seem
off. I'm going back to have him do it again."

"I'll get them done right now," I whispered. I sounded ver
far away from myself.

"I know how you are when you talk like that." She cam
into my arms and kissed me hard, and kissed me again, mor
gently as the icy sweat slid down my back. "Don't do any
thing crazy."

"Me?" I said.

It took Duke a half hour to correctly weight the four new tires
and he muttered and grimaced because I stood there watchin
him work the entire time.

"You don't have nowhere else better to be?" he asked.

"Believe it or not," I said. "I do."

He finished and wanted to charge me extra and instantly saw I wasn't having any. He tried to get me to thank him for putting in so much extra time and effort, instead of owning up to the fact that he'd fouled the job the first time.

I drove out without another word and pulled up outside McGreary's discount store at about four-thirty, where I waited almost forty-five minutes before seeing Kristin Devington leave for the day. I hoped to seem careless in my approach, but the gravel crunched loudly underfoot and I sounded like a lost water buffalo moving through the parking lot. She heard me coming and wheeled and waited for me to step up.

"Hi, Jonny."

"Hi, Kristin."

"You don't plan on causing any more trouble for Arnie, do you?" she asked. "Not just for his sake, because it took my mother two days to calm down. She's got high blood pressure and diabetes. She's supposed to take a couple of different medications and watch her diet, but she only swallows some of the pills and she eats a half pound of peanut brittle almost every night."

"No," I said. "I don't want to fight with your brother anymore."

"That's good to know. What brings you here then?"

"I thought we might talk for a few minutes."

"Okay."

Neither one of us had grown so much as an inch since we were seventeen, and she reached exactly the same place on me as back then, just about my shoulders. I put my hand on her arm, thinking about the night I'd taken her to her junior prom. I remembered how lovely Kristin had looked that evening when I'd pinned the corsage on her, both of us lit by the bug light on her front porch, back when Arnie and I and the rest of the team used to wrestle in the mud of the high school fields and go drink beer in the moonlight behind the gymnasium or the bleachers.

"What's been happening at your house?" I asked.

"He's been fighting with my mother something awful the last few months. She'll put her teeth in somebody's throat to defend him most of the time, but when she's alone in the house

with him it's a different story, all right. It gets ugly a couple
of times a year, and Sheriff Broghin had to put handcuffs on
her once just so she'd settle down in her recliner long enough
to keep from killing Arnie's dog with the meat cleaver.'' She
tipped her chin aside and I saw her mother there in her face,
lurking below. ''Stupid dog died anyway a couple of weeks
later from eating rat poison over in the tool shed. Arnie got
out his shotgun and blew up the roof a little, aiming for the
weathervane.''

''Did he ever hit it?''

''No, but some of the shot nailed a passing crow and
brought it down into the blueberry patch. He was pretty happy
with himself over that.''

''I'll bet.'' I could see him plugging at nothing and laughing
morosely, creeping around that quarter-acre of crabgrass covered with trash and shards. The mold and ivy was so thick
and heavy on the gingerbread trim that he must've felt as if it
covered him as well. He'd be wishing his wife was still with
him, his father back from the grave. Christ, we weren't so
different after all. None of us.

''Why don't you leave?'' I asked.

She shrugged with the same despondency I'd seen in most
of my high school crowd after they found themselves still
living with their parents ten years after graduation. ''Where
am I going to go?''

I watched the pedestrian traffic go by, thinking that Katie
might be right, the bookstore could have a fair flow of business
between ten and six. The Barbara Cartland and Danielle Steele
shelves would turn over quickly because of sorrowful women
who had nothing better to do than scarf down peanut brittle
the *Mission M.I.A.* and *The Executioner* series would be selling well due to the NRA enthusiasts flocking over from Oscar's hunting goods store.

Kristin didn't seem to mind just standing here at the back
of the parking lot with me. Her mother's features rose for a
moment like a drowned woman's face bobbing to the surface.
Maybe Mrs. Devington had been going for a wrench the other
day, or maybe Kristin had just wanted to brain me with that
broom handle.

Abruptly she said, almost too softly to be heard, "I'm
orry."

Arnie Devington wouldn't have slashed tires. That showed
plenty of rage, all right, but directed toward Katie. Arnie
hadn't broken into Katie's shop or mashed the orchids in the
street. "Why'd you do it?"

"I don't know exactly," Kristin said. "I guess . . . I guess,
maybe, because when you showed up at the house the other
day, it reminded me of the prom, how handsome you looked,
and the way I thought it was going to be, you know, one day.
With you, or maybe with just anyone, but it never was. I
ironed the corsage between two pieces of wax paper, still have
it saved in the bible on my nightstand. You never asked me
out again."

She was wrong, we'd had a couple more dates afterwards.
Then she'd joined her family in badmouthing me in order to
keep what little self-respect they had in the wake of their life-
long failures. I thought she might cry, but she didn't appear
to be particularly abashed.

"Sometimes," she told me. "I wish it hadn't been that stupid dog that ate the rat poison. I should've done it myself.
You ever feel like that, Jonny?"

Nothing I could do would change anything. There was nothing left to be said except what I came here to say. "Please,
Kristin. Don't go near her again."

The gentleness in her eyes as she'd watched her brother and
I tearing it up on the lawn had fled; she had her own harbored
resentments to deal with. Or those she'd failed to deal with.
The orchids stepped on in the street, like a flattened corsage
kept between pages in a book, might still haunt her years from
now.

Kristin looked at me the same way she had the other day;
as if she knew this wasn't over, and might never be.

The spacecraft continued to rise into the reddening sky, silhouetted
in the rotund face of the full moon breaching the sunset. Rest-
less clouds curled, parted and twisted in argument, then
thinned and drifted away. The air grew heavy and began to

still, and the temperature dropped significantly in only a few minutes.

I drove up to the black-and-white striped semaphore arm at the front gate checkpoint, and the same guard performed another extravaganza of looking for my name on the pages of his clipboard.

I said, "Just call ahead to Dr. Brent."

He didn't pick up the red phone in his little booth, and wouldn't do so until he'd gone through the rest of his paperwork. I leaned out of the car window and scanned the tiny cubicle again. He actually had a bookmark placed in the men's magazine so he wouldn't lose his place. If he was really reading the articles in a magazine called *Gozangas* then no wonder he had to entertain himself with his clipboard. He must've desperately wanted to pull his firearm just to fend off the tedium.

I didn't think Brent would let me inside without a growing series of threats that might culminate with my reaching for the red phone myself and finally giving the bored guard a chance to wave his gun around. I waited while the guy ran his finger down another sheet. He said, "Yes sir, Mr. Kendrick. Enjoy your visit." I shot up in my seat as he palmed the button that opened the gate, and waved me on.

So, Brent wanted to see me.

Or perhaps Harnes wanted Brent to see me.

I found the parking lot and left Teddy's books in the back seat, but took his folded sketches and put them in my back pocket. I got out and scanned the thickets in the distance where Nick Crummler had told me he'd been watching from when I'd first visited the hospital. I didn't see him anywhere but that didn't mean he wasn't out beyond the fields and back fence, where Michelle and I had made love years ago. At the main doors two guards gave my identification a cursory viewing. I was frisked much more poorly this time and wasn't even told to turn out my pockets. They let me keep my cell phone.

The same guard, Philip, escorted me up to the sixth floor again, and back to Brent's disinfected white office. I got used to the fluorescent brightness quickly this time. We were all getting used to one another. The decontaminated white walls, chairs, and floor appeared to be even cleaner, if possible.

Dr. Brennan Brent sat at his desk sucking his pipe loudly. For a man who should be on edge he looked annoyingly serene and self-possessed. The murder of his right-hand employee raised his confidence level, now that he wouldn't have to call a subordinate "mister" anymore. His mustache continued to skitter on its own, but like a friendly cat it perked up some when he spotted me. He smiled pleasantly. I thought perhaps my plan had already been foiled.

He nodded to the guard and said, "Thank you, Philip. Proceed with your rounds." Philip spun on his heel and slid down the hall, and I felt my chest hitch with an overwhelming sense of *déjà vu,* as if the hospital had a piece of me now that would forever play out these exact same scenes.

His smile widened, and he showed the stubby brown teeth on one side of his mouth where he'd been gnawing the pipe half his life. "And what can I do for you today, Mr. Kendrick?" He said it like a clerk behind a counter.

"I'd like to see Zebediah Crummler, please."

"Yes, certainly."

The good doctor made no move though, resting in his chair peacefully, as though he'd just been walked on by a Geisha girl with sandalwood slippers. I shifted and tried to appear indignant. His eyelids lowered to half-mast and he let out a sigh. I was not exactly impressing him with my self-righteous contempt. If he'd had a desk piled high with files, books, and personal momentos I might've reached over and swept them onto the floor in a gesture of scorn. I didn't think I'd get the same effect by knocking over his No Smoking paperweights.

"It's all falling apart, Brent," I said. "How many new cases came in this week?"

"Twelve."

"I'll guarantee that one of them is undercover, a cop or a reporter who'll be keeping carefully detailed notes about this facility."

At least his eyes opened wide again, though he didn't appear to be concerned. "This is one of the leading rehabilitation clinics in the state. Who do you think you are threatening in such an insolent manner?"

"Better I should threaten you in a respectful manner?"

His mustache appeared to want to leave his face, sidle up to me, and make friends by rubbing itself against my ankle. "You are not an officer of the law."

I figured I'd push the bluff. "Are you sure?"

"Yes."

So much for bluffing. "I'd like to see Crummler now."

"Certainly."

"You already said that. Let's go."

He almost pouted, and the milieu between us shifted as if he considered himself some exasperated but beloved uncle of mine. "I must say," he whined. "Your grandmother didn't behave in such an impolite manner."

"What?"

"She is a woman of refinement, manners and *gentility*."

"My grandmother? My grandmother was here today?"

"Certainly. With Mr. Harnes."

For a moment I thought he might be lying, but recalled the signs posted around the hospital showing it to be fully accessible to the physically handicapped. While I'd been at Duke's garage and sitting out front of McGreary's store waiting for Kristin, Anna had been here, with *him*—the emperor of the asylum.

Brent and I walked down the corridor and passed that same room with the murals of cliffs and cloudscapes, the kids already battling drugs and liquor seated in a semi-circle among the older faces that regretted too much of their own lives. A few were crying, most of them looked annoyed and angry that their parents, wives, and husbands had forced them into rehab. Maybe some of them, like my father, would get the help they needed to stop robbing their families and taking off their clothes and singing "Green Dolphin Street" at five AM and finally manage to straighten out.

Brent nodded to the counselor pontificating in front of the two fuming teenagers. We went up to the twelfth floor, down the winding maze of hallways to Crummler's cell. I noticed the small plastic window had a smear of dried blood on it.

The migraine burst full-blown into my head so suddenly that I nearly pitched forward. My heart began a slow crawl up my throat. Cold sweat exploded across my face and I wondered if I really should get a therapist to help me control my temper. The tapered lighting seemed to draw the world back into one corner, and again Crummler lay in the darkness where I couldn't see him.

"We've had some troubles recently. Zebediah has grown torpid to the point of becoming cataleptic. He refuses to shower or even use the toilet."

"How does a catatonic wind up bleeding on the door?" I whispered.

"He had a psychotic outburst two days ago, hammering himself, wailing to be set free. He forced us to use restraints so he wouldn't bring further harm to himself."

The sound of the door unlocking drove a spike into my headache, and it took me a moment to realize that my palms weren't wet simply from sweat, but also because I was squeezing my fists so tightly that my fingernails had cut them open.

Brent didn't bother with a cheerful greeting, but his voice sounded inordinately loud anyway. "Hello, Zebediah, your friend Mr. Kendrick has returned to see you."

The brown blanket lay draped on the bed but couldn't quite hide the arm, leg, and chest restraints. Crummler stared straight up at the ceiling, eyes full of bewilderment and despair, his upper lip occasionally quivering. His baby's face had a shadow of his former beard across it; his shaved head showed specks of hair. There were dried salt tracks down his cherubic cheeks and in the corners of his eyes. I sat beside him. Not only had his manic happiness and the ecstatic fire and passion gone out of him, but so had the terror and horror and his imprisonment.

Brent had let me see Crummler because he knew I wouldn't be able to do any good for my friend. His nostrils and lips had crusts of dried blood on them. I didn't doubt that he'd rammed his face against the little plastic window. I would have done the same. I spoke to his inert form for about fifteen minutes while Brent gazed on complacently, but Crummler didn't stir in the slightest. I wanted to show him the sketches but he wouldn't even see them. Anna probably sat beside him and put her hand on his head and kept it there for a moment,

knowing better than to waste her time trying to talk to him. I
tried to coax and placate his steaming mind, but nothing got
through. He would know when I possessed the power to free
him, and he understood—even from his black slumber—that
I couldn't help him at the moment. Without his duty of bur-
ying the dead, he had no life himself.

Harnes didn't need Freddy Shanks to torture or kill Crummler.

He'd be dead in a couple of days if I didn't get him out of
here.

We left the cell and Brent escorted me to the elevators. I
thought about my friend Lisa Hobbes again, locked here for
a time before being sent to jail for murder, and what it must
be like to so easily lose yourself into these walls, into the
clouds and cliffs painted there.

The migraine dissolved in an instant, and I was slowly able
to open my fists again. "Teddy met somebody here, didn't
he?"

Brent said, "What do you mean?"

I stared at him and grinned, and wondered if I was half as
repugnant to him as he was to me. "Who was it, Doctor? Who
did he recognize?"

"I have no idea what you're talking about."

"Teddy volunteered at the hospital, didn't he?"

"What makes you think that?"

Teddy wasn't very good with painting murals: the size and
texture of the wall apparently threw him, but he'd made a
decent enough attempt to fill his work with the qualities of
Chinese art he admired so much. The way the clouds and
whitecaps curled, that sharpness of each angle of rock and
wave. "Who did he see in here while he worked in that group
counseling room? Was it his mother?" I unfolded the sketches
and swept them under his face. "Is Marie Harnes still alive
and rotting under your supervision?"

The mustache looked like it was having an epileptic fit,
scampering all around his face so badly that he had to snort
to clear his nostrils. "I believe she's been dead for over twenty
years, Mr. Kendrick." He motioned for one of the guards, who

quickly came to attend him. "And it's you who should be seeking psychiatric help."

"I know what kind of care you dole out, Brent, I think I'll take a pass."

I wondered, was it possible?

Marie Harnes trapped here for over twenty years?

"If you continue to harass and threaten me, Mr. Kendrick," Brent told me. "I promise you our next meeting will be a most unpleasant experience."

"Certainly," I said.

I sat in the parking lot of the hospital, looking at the visitors, nurses, and patients wandering the grounds despite the oncoming chill. Several people were underdressed, but they so valued their time outdoors they didn't mind the cold. I gazed up at the rows of cube windows and settled on the highest one in the farthest corner of the building. No matter how stable Marie Harnes might have been going into Panecraft, she'd be totally insane now.

I pulled out the cell phone and saw it was blinking angrily at me. The LOW BATTERY flashed. I searched my jacket pockets but realized I'd left the second battery recharging in Anna's van. I still got a dial tone, though, and called my grandmother.

"Hello," she answered with a faint barb that nobody would have noticed but me. From just that single word I could hear that her voice was thick and weighty with frustration.

"What the hell is going on, Anna?"

"What is the matter, Johnathan?"

"You tell me. You're with him?"

"If by 'him' you mean Theodore Harnes, then yes, in a matter of speaking I am. Actually, at the moment I'm putting on a sweater, it is getting quite brisk out again. Did you dress warmly, dear?"

I repressed a sigh of irritation. "I'm not in my Mukluks but I'll get by. Why are you spending the day with him? Why did you go see Crummler with him? And for heaven's sake, what happened when you did?"

The barb hooked a little deeper. I got the feeling she was doing her best to control a great and painful passion within her. It had been brought out in both of us. "I wanted to see Theodore Harnes in his natural habitat, as it were, acting his most characteristic," she said. "I was hoping to humanize Crummler in his eyes, but I fear that none of us has ever been quite human in his regard, not even his son."

"I know why you went, Anna, but why did he go?"

"Perhaps because he feels most at home in his burrow."

"That's not why he did it." I thought about it for a minute, the way he followed me and Anna, skulking about the streets of the town in his limo, slowly circling Panecraft. "He's fascinated with you, and has been since you nearly ran him over fifty years ago. I also think he's trying to lure Nick Crummler out into the open."

"Why?" she asked.

"Nick knew Shanks from his time in Panecraft. Maybe he knows something about Harnes, too. Harnes has lost his right-hand psycho. Who knows?" I asked. "Maybe he wants Nick to replace Sparky."

"Yes. Perhaps Theodore Harnes believes Nick helped his brother murder Teddy."

"There's still more going on here than we know about."

"Or less. I fear we haven't handled this situation very effectively."

"That's an understatement."

I heard a few snaps, a tinny voice, something being clicked. "Is that my micro-tape-recorder?" I asked. "What are you doing?"

"Testing it. I failed horribly today in not bringing it with me earlier."

"Why? Is he opening up at all?"

She did something then I had never heard her do, not even in the hospital the day my parents died, when she'd had tubes and needles plunged into her thin arms pumping painkillers throughout her system while the massive casts held her shattered legs and spine immobile.

My grandmother *cackled*; a high, painful, and somehow loathsome noise that drove an icicle against my spine. I shivered so hard I nearly dropped the phone.

"There is nothing in him left to open," she said. "He is

completely guileless in a most heinous and unsettling manner. 'm thoroughly convinced he genuinely did not have anything o do with Teddy's murder, or, if Teddy is still alive, with his on's disappearance. He is not honest due to any conscience or moral fiber on his part. He admits to the truth because he s the incarnation of baseness, so utterly at ease with his own vices.'' Her breath caught in her throat, and my hand shook worse. "He and I have spent the day in his limousine discussing how he murdered my friend Diane—''

"Oh, good Christ.''

"—and speaking at length on any number of his other crimes, including the poisoning of Teddy's mother. Apparently he had no need to find exotic toxins. Simple household cleaning products mixed into wine can often prove untraceable. He is quite knowledgeable about a whole host of such lethal misdeeds, and prefers to handle them himself rather than entrust minions to accomplish such tasks.''

"He admitted her murder to me as well. Why didn't you call me, Anna? Did you call Lowell?''

"What, dear?''

"Why didn't you call me?'' I shouted.

"I had a chance to finish it fifty years ago before any of he real horror began. And I did *nothing*.''

I could feel her getting further away from me. "Anna, listen, I'll be home in twenty minutes . . .''

"I won't be here by then. Jocelyn is mounting the front steps even as I speak, Jonathan. They have been idling outside while I changed into heavier clothing. My day with them hasn't ended yet. Don't worry, dear, I pose no threat to him.''

"Yes, you do, we both do.''

"His ego needs an audience, you see. And now, as when I first met him, I'm a spectator to his dementia. I'd like to catch some of what he relates on tape, though ultimately I fear it will be useless in a court of law. I shall be home early, dear. 've left some roast beef in the refrigerator, help yourself.''

"Anna, do *not* go with him!'' I started the car and jammed he accelerator and spun in a tight circle heading for the gate.

"You see, Jonathan—'' A sob nearly broke within her, but he caught it on the cusp and quickly reined herself. "You see, dear, he enjoys talking of murder. We needed only to *ask*."

She hung up and I gunned it, trying to dial Lowell's number and stay on the road, watching the patients wandering the grounds staring mournfully at me as if begging to take them home.

A woman, staring emptily at me.

I gasped when I spotted her, and the world grew insanely white and too wide. A male nurse frowned and his patient blinked as the new tires on Katie's car squealed. I suddenly spun the wheel tightly and roared off toward a pine tree over-hanging a splintering wooden bench. One of the guards stood his ground and put his hand on his firearm. I jammed the brake, jumped out, and started yelling, "Help! He's in my back seat trying to escape! Somebody stop him!" I waved my hands about my face because they did it in the movies.

The guard drew his weapon and came over while I hopped around some more. The nurse and the patient he'd been stand-ing with both stirred; the woman appeared to be self-assured, giddy, and frightened at the same time.

The guard said, "Who's in there? What happened?"

I stopped hopping, turned, and swung at him as hard as I could, connecting with his chin in such a beautiful display of action and reaction that I gave a grunt of pleasure, watching him fly over the hood of the car the way Harnes had done five decades ago when my grandmother had nearly run him over. His gun went off and the woman almost smiled.

I grabbed her hand and pushed her into the passenger seat while several nurses came running after us. I slammed my foot down and drove through the semaphore arm while the guard at the gate popped his head out of the little cubicle. I'd been wrong. He didn't want to pull his gun, he just wanted to be left alone to finish reading the socially and politically absorb-ing articles in *Gozangas*. The woman stared at me and sud-denly giggled.

She was the lady Teddy had sketched—and because of her, for some reason, I knew, he'd been murdered.

FIFTEEN

LIPPING OVER A CLAWING TREE line, the bloated moon wobbled through the clouds, looking ready to keel over backward and roll out of sight. The woman smiled as we drove along the empty back roads toward Harnes' estate. She took my hand briefly, let it go, and then grasped hold again. Her teeth glowed in the flow of moonlight. Shadows twisted and filled her face. I spoke to her, trying to explain the situation, but she clearly didn't understand a word I said. Her small, strange smile remained firmly affixed.

Teddy was at once a better and worse artist than I would've believed; he managed to capture so much of her likeness, but not quite enough so that I could've pieced it all together days ago in his own bedroom, when I'd searched through the books he'd bought from me. Irony settled heavily on my shoulders. If only he'd been a slightly better artist.

I called Lowell and listened to phantom echoes of his voice, the phone battery so low and the static so awful that we had to scream at each other to be heard. He yelled, "You know what you've done? That's kidnapping. The feds will be involved now. What the hell are you doing? You finally lost your bird?"

I shouted, but in a few seconds the green power light

dimmed and the phone went dead in my hand. I tossed it in
the back seat and jammed the accelerator, pressing seventy
along the snaking road and waiting for FBI helicopters to start
swooping in low. The woman clapped and giggled some more.

When we passed the two rearing stone lions at the entrance
to Harnes' private road, she nearly jumped out of her seat and
started wailing and slapping me in the arm. I pulled over,
unsure of what to do. If I let her out and anybody else found
her in the state she was in, dressed like a hospital patient, I
suspected they'd only toss her back in. Besides, showing up
with her might be the trick I needed to pull. She scrabbled at
the door like a dog scratching to be let out. I spoke plainly
and calmly, and though my words meant nothing to her, I
hoped my tone would get through.

She kept hitting me in the arm and keening loudly.

I took firm hold of her shoulders and said, "You have to
trust me. I need your help. I don't work for Harnes the way
those doctors do. I'm your friend, and we're going to get away
from him." I took my hands away, hoping she wouldn't leap
for the woods. "But he has my grandmother, and only you
can help me get her away from him. From him and Jocelyn."

She quieted and looked straight ahead. I waited. Her face
drew in on itself and became composed, revealing almost
nothing. The corners of her eyes were filled with cracks from
years of squinting in fury. She gestured for me to proceed,
and despite the skittering shadows, she now appeared almost
anxious to see him. She let loose with a string of sounds and
folded her hands in her lap. I drove on.

The stately electric gate stood shut, and that arcing iron
name HARNES above seemed an extension of the man, loom-
ing over me. The stone wall surrounding the mansion was too
high to climb, even if I managed to belly the car through the
dense trees and climb onto the roof. I got out and could hear
the buzzing of the amperage in the intricate ironwork. The
metal wasn't that thick, more stylish than practical. I hoped. I
gazed at the computerized connecting lock and the stone post
in which it had been set.

He had my grandmother.

I got in the car and backed it up to the mouth of the private

road. I'd heard you couldn't get electrocuted in your car because the tires would ground you. It was the kind of Ameri-
cana I didn't trust, but it would have to do in a clinch. I
continued in reverse down the road for a couple hundred yards
more. I revved the engine and enjoyed the brusque howl and
shriek coming from it.

"Can you say 'fuck it'?" I asked.

She continued to simply stare ahead. Sweat trickled down
my neck and my bruises and lumps burned. I reached over
and put her seat belt on her.

Finally she got hold of my meaning and said, with a ten-
tative but laughing lilt, *"Fuckit."*

"I'm glad you agree."

I floored the gas.

Trees streamed by in a rushing black wash as we hurtled
forward. I threw on the high beams and they punctured the
night like twin glittering blades. After crashing through the
lightweight semaphore arm I felt used to smashing things.
Even at this speed the car glided. Duke had done a good job
the second time around. The gate loomed and we accelerated
straight for it. Katie wasn't going to be thrilled with me. I
gripped the steering wheel hard, and then the woman covered
her face and let out a tiny but fierce scream. Or maybe it was
me.

When we hit, the headlights exploded, the grille wrenched
wildly, and steam burst from the engine, but despite the gate's
screeching lightning hum and burst of red sparks, we didn't
fry. The gate tipped on top of us and crumpled part of the
roof. She screamed but began clapping again, that giggle such
a peculiar underscoring to the sound of tearing metal. The
safety-glass windshield cracked and crimped inwards at the
driver's corner but didn't shatter.

The car sputtered feebly as the mansion emerged in the
moist moonlight. Hundreds of panes of glass like menacing
eyes marked my—our—return. The woman said something in
a hushed mixture of awe, fear, and anger. I looked at her and
she repeated it, and again and once more. I nodded. Whatever
she was saying, I felt exactly the same way. We pulled up to
the house behind the limousine, and I motioned for her to stay

in the car. She tucked her chin to her chest and gazed at the front door. I hoped to Christ that Lowell had understood me through the static. I took off my watch and noted the second hand, and showed her that I wanted her to come inside in ten minutes. She looked at me as if I were insane.

The dying chauffeur sat in the limo, slumped back in his seat, coughing into a bloody, phlegm-flecked handkerchief. He didn't even have the strength to go to his room. His heavy, wet wheeze made it sound like he was slowly being crushed under a board with rocks on top of it, and he only followed me with his eyes because he couldn't turn his head anymore. I wondered if Harnes had actually been poisoning him with a mixture of household products, too.

The chauffeur said, "What the hell was that noise?"

"Me," I told him. "Come knocking. Cops will be here soon. Hold on."

"What are they headed here for? Nothing they can do. He won't hurt your grandma. He hates her, but he won't hurt her. That's what he likes."

"Why aren't you in a hospital?"

He went into a coughing fit and spasms coiled him in his seat. I heard something break away deep inside his chest. "No medical."

In the hard-boiled novels Anna read, the protagonist would have a host of choices to make: he might throw himself through the front window; roll on the floor in perfect tune with the room, some psychic sense aiming his gun for him; or he might climb and enter through a skylight left carelessly open, and then swing down into a plush room where a blond had moments earlier finished showering and stood naked with a thin smile at his entrance; or he might just grab the dying chauffeur and hurl him through the window and follow with a roar in the acrid air.

I tried the door, opened it, and walked inside.

In the library, my tape recorder lay on the table, turned off, the cassette beside it.

Anna sat with Theodore Harnes by the window where they'd spent the night talking during the party. Jocelyn stood beside them, looking at me, waiting expectantly. I couldn't tell what kind of charge was already in the room, but we all knew a conclusion of some sort was at hand.

My grandmother appeared extremely tired and weak. Her cheeks were ashen and she rubbed her wrists together to heat her hands. A full glass of wine rested beside the tape recorder, and I realized she'd never be able to look at that chateau the same way again, much less drink it after hearing of Harnes' exploits in poisoning women.

I would have to lead the dragon from its lair.

There wasn't much light in the library, and gloom en-wrapped us all. Jocelyn's incredibly long, intensely black hair seemed to draw her further into darkness, like a suitor wanting to dance. A phone rang distantly, and I realized it had been ringing for some time. That would be Brent calling to report the escape from Panecraft. It was a nearly plaintive sound in the dim recesses of the house, the night soaking inside.

Jocelyn said, "Leave."

"Boy, you have got to be kidding."

I walked past her and moved to Anna, who reached for my hand. Jesus, her fingers were freezing. Had she sipped any of the wine? A nervous gurgle boiled in my throat, but she grinned and softly said, "My, I hadn't realized how the time had galloped away, dear." She glanced at Harnes and tipped her head as if to thank him for such a lovely day. "Well, Theodore, we really must be going now. I have so much to do at home. The place is an absolute *shambles*."

"What with all the dusting," I said. "And cleaning out the rain gutters."

The nondescript persona of Theodore Harnes slid against me once more, a pressure without a living force wallowing within his body's residence. I thought if I looked closely enough I could spot the seams where they'd stuffed him full of sawdust and cotton.

He said, "I'm afraid I cannot allow that just yet."

Anna's hand didn't warm quickly enough in mine. We both released long sighs. I tried to get into Harnes' thoughts for a minute but still nothing clarified. He was a man who enjoyed a standoff and needed an audience. He used people at his whim, and when finished he either murdered or imprisoned them. His methods took months or years to play out. He delighted in watching the plight of his prey.

Anna said, "Theodore, you are a stately sophisticate, a brilliant industrialist, and a terrifyingly refined psychopath."

"Yes," he responded.

Jocelyn inched forward and so did I. Although she stood completely stationary, her lithe form still seemed to be floating around me, on the air and threading through my hands. In another minute we were going to be into it and somehow, without her ever having done anything remotely threatening, she had become one of the very few people I'd met who actually frightened me.

My grandmother, smiling now, allowed the beginning of that cackle to escape her once more. She let out fifty years of anger, scorn, contempt, and heartache for her lost bridesmaid and also herself, and she never raised her voice. Her chilled hand slid on top of his, and the iciness startled him. She patted him with a disdain that actually brushed Harnes back in his chair.

She said, "For Diane, and Crummler, and all your other victims, but more so for myself, I will do everything in my power to see that you not only pay for your heinous crimes, but that you suffer for them, and suffer dreadfully."

I sighed even louder. Anna shouldn't be threatening a wealthy, psychotic killer during our attempted getaway.

Jocelyn glided forward and I moved to meet her.

Nick Crummler stepped into the room.

I whispered, "Oh shit."

He appeared to have spent the last several days in the woods, perhaps around the Harnes estate, or hiding in the back fields of the hospital, or somewhere in the cemetery where he could seek occasional shelter inside his brother's shack.

"Hello," he said.

Harnes stood and approached him. "Hello, Nicodemus."

"No need to get up on my account."

"You shouldn't have returned."

"You shouldn't have gone after my brother."

"He murdered my son."

"No, he didn't."

Nick had proven to be the wild card, somehow a part of all that had transpired, and yet not really of it. He remained too far outside the rest of us. He'd saved my life but I didn't know what that might mean anymore. Jocelyn drifted back into a darkened corner of the room. I quickly checked around. There wasn't much to grab, not even a bottle of wine, a letter opener, nothing.

"What are you doing here, Nick?" Anna asked.

My grandmother had been right: sometimes all you had to do was ask. I suddenly realized with an awful clarity that no one, so far, whom I'd spoken with since Teddy's murder, had actually lied to me.

"I had an affair with his wife, Marie, a long time ago," Nick said, reaching into his pocket and retrieving a hardened piece of cheese. He swallowed it in one bite and proceeded to look so relaxed and untroubled in Harnes' home that I was beginning to feel extremely uneasy.

"And you, I presume," Anna said. "Are Teddy's biological father?"

He grimaced and shook his head. "Hell, no. Vasectomy when I was twelve. There are places that still do that to orphans." He went through his pockets, found the stub of a cigarette, and stuck it in his mouth. "I used to work for him. I was his chauffeur once upon a time, back when I wasn't much more than a kid." When he couldn't find any matches he dropped the butt back in his coat. "By the way, you need a new driver. The one outside is dead."

Jocelyn descended through the ink trails of the room and reappeared like a dark angel landing. I spun toward her and we met face-to-face, as if about to kiss. She pressed a silver .32 she'd probably bought from Oscar Kinion hard above my heart as I looked deeply at the dragon that Crummler had seen murdering a boy in his cemetery.

"You'd do anything to protect him, wouldn't you?" I asked. "But you don't have his light touch or his patience. He enjoys the slow drag and you like the quick finish. That's why you had Shanks kill Brian Frost. What are you after?"

"You ordered Freddy to do such a thing?" Harnes asked.

"Yes," she answered.

Nobody seemed too concerned about the gun jammed into my chest except me.

Harnes' brows drew together in a scowl of disappointment. "That is not my way."

No, he had his own methods. Theodore Harnes enjoyed a standoff, the panic and passion and dismay of others he could leech to fill his own vacant shell, but she clearly hated all of us; everybody.

"Have we not dealt with these pretentious American fools long enough?" Jocelyn asked. Something displaced beneath her face, like the slow but irrevocable movement of a leviathan thrashing from the depths toward the surface. "A moronic, arrogant brute daring to *demand* money for a weak, simple-minded girl? Attempting to disrupt our lives with lawyers and reporters? And you abide their impudent threats instead of putting a stop to such insolence?"

"Empty threats mean nothing."

"They are an affront to honor. America is unbearable. A wasteland of privilege without principal."

"It is that, and more. My son wanted to come home, and so did I."

"It is not my home."

The timing had to be right. Ten minutes had gone by, but Nick hadn't made any mention of the woman. Had she run off? Jocelyn dug the barrel of the .38 along the groove of my ribs. It hurt like hell, but I did my best to keep my face as straight as hers. I didn't do so well. Anna wheeled forward and my heart sank even lower. If she could have seen what I'd seen in the wake of the dragon—the elimination of a boy's face in the name of hate—she would have stayed back. Or perhaps not.

Anna said, "There is no need for this."

"Quiet, you foolish, nosy old woman."

From the doorway came, *"Fuckit."*

Jocelyn drew back out of my range before she would even turn her head. Then she glared at the woman. Neither she nor Harnes showed any change of composure. Harnes said, "Li Tai." I finally knew what to call the woman. Her mouth fell open for a second and then she closed it. Jocelyn said something to her in Chinese. They began a slow chattering that rapidly built to a singsong quarrel. Harnes put in a few words himself, and they all fell silent.

"Jocelyn is your daughter," Anna said.

"Yes," Harnes admitted.

"And you had her mother confined to a mental institution? Why?"

"I did not want her in my life any longer and she threatened to cause a stir with Chinese officials. She managed several of my factories overseas, and had a great many political affiliations in Hong Kong. This course proved to be most beneficial for me."

"So long as you had her you could control these politicians."

"No, money did that, until Hong Kong reverted back to mainland China's rule. Then it became more advantageous to simply leave."

Anna's lips flattened and went white until she found the air to say, "That was nearly two years ago. Why not release her?"

He looked mildly amused. "And why should I?"

I made eye contact with Nick Crummler but couldn't read anything. Jocelyn hadn't pointed the gun at him at all, I'd noticed. Harnes sat, crossed his legs, and straightened the seam of his pants leg.

I said, "You returned from Asia two years ago and left her imprisoned that long for no reason?"

"No, it has been over twelve years," he confessed with the cool alacrity I wanted to set fire to. "I brought her from Hong Kong under the auspices of visiting Disneyland long before my son and I stopped traveling the world and settled back in America."

At the word *Disneyland* Li Tai squeezed her eyes shut and one massive shiver ran through her body.

"And Teddy didn't know."

"He believed her to be dead. My son was . . . a benevolent soul. He would not have understood."

"It was stupid of you to bring her here," Jocelyn hissed at

me. "What could you possibly have hoped to accomplish?"

"This." I unfolded Teddy's sketches and showed them to Harnes. "You didn't know that Teddy volunteered at the hospital, did you? He drew murals in the group therapy rooms. He must've spotted Li Tai there several weeks ago. She was your wife in China, wasn't she? He'd been raised by her."

"For some years, yes."

I turned to Jocelyn, watching all that had laid coiled and under control for so long rising and struggling to get free. I shoved my chest against the gun, hoping it would make her feel empowered enough not to pull the trigger.

"A woman he hardly remembered, and believed to be dead. He came to you, didn't he? He finally realized the kind of man his father was, and he came to you, hoping you'd side with him. How he must have loved you to have trusted you. His sister. He thought you hadn't known your own mother was still alive. But you did know. And you didn't care. That's what Crummler saw that day he came out into the hailstorm. He saw you two arguing. He knew what you were capable of. You terrified him."

"Shut up about that brain-damaged caretaker. He means nothing," she said. "Teddy never understood the man our father was. If he had, he would not have acted so intolerably."

"What did he want to do? Go to the police? Try to get your mother out on his own? He chose to talk with you alone while he visited his own mother. He must've gone to the cemetery every day for a while. He respected the dead."

"He did not respect father."

"And you'd do anything to protect your father," I said. "So you murdered Teddy."

Harnes cocked his head and said, "What?"

"Father . . ."

"What?"

"Farther, it had to be done."

"You? You . . . killed my son?" Harnes said. His voice seemed to come from someplace other than his throat—perhaps Jocelyn still had his breath, or maybe I did—so that he was only a man mouthing silently in a vacuum. He still showed no emotion, other than the slight hint of confusion. "You did this?"

I saw the dragon emerging in Jocelyn's eyes, and stared in lost captivation as it began to overcome her—the lizard beneath the beauty, cold and primordial, jealous and savage.

"Once Teddy was dead you became even more brazen," I said. "You approached Shanks to handle Frost. Your rage was showing." In fact, it started to show again in her loveliness, the shadows moving in her features, and I had trouble speaking and watching at the same time. "Why his face? Why did you cut off his face with Crummler's shovel? Because you saw too much of yourself in it?" *Yes, yes, look at her.* "Teddy didn't turn against his father. You did."

"Father," she said. The word held such extreme importance for her that she seemed to be saying prayers and making sacrifices upon an altar. "He'd betrayed you. It could not be permitted."

"You did this?"

Jocelyn flicked her wrist casually toward me and I knew the black night she had wrapped inside of would all come rushing out in this moment. I dodged toward Harnes hoping she wouldn't fire if I was too close to him. The shot sounded impossibly loud and Anna lurched sideways, rising slightly—it seemed as if she might actually be standing, about to take a step toward me. I reached and she flopped into my arms, and said, "Oh, dear."

I found my grandmother's blood on my hands and the world grew tight and too painfully well lit. I closed my eyes and opened them again.

Jocelyn twisted and pointed the gun at me. I wheeled blindly and flung myself aside as she fired. Nick Crummler backpedaled and hurled himself at Li Tai as Jocelyn straightened her arm and aimed at her mother. She fired twice more before I dove onto her. We dropped to the floor heavily and rolled into the darkest corner, where we belonged now. Shadows tore at us. Her façade fell in on itself and her nostrils flared, and I saw all the welts of her strange soul rise to the flesh. I watched her became a hideous caricature of beauty, her face haggard and deeply fissured, nose drawn into a snarl and lips skinned back in a sneer. She tumbled against me, desiccated, more terminal than the dead chauffeur.

Everything stilled. I knew my face looked the same as hers. She fired again. I felt warmth slithering out of me. I reached down and grabbed Jocelyn's wrist and brutally pulled it backward, wanting and needing to hear the bone snap. She easily squirmed from my grip and brought the heel of her palm up viciously into my jaw. More blood spurted, but I didn't mind the dragon's bite now. It felt too good letting loose my own beast.

Nick Crummler rose and punched Harnes once in the mouth, and the madman who had poisoned his wives and imprisoned the mother of his own insane child slid to the floor where he stared at me. I pulled my fist back and drove it forward into Jocelyn's stomach, and still she sneered at me. She smashed me in the mouth once more and I slugged her on the chin as hard as I could.

A soft sound faded in.

A second later I heard it again, and once more, much sharper, and knew it as my name.

"Jonathan. I'm all right. I'm all right, deer. Stop it, you'll kill her!"

I got my hand around Jocelyn's neck and squeezed as tightly as I could, not caring where the next minute took me so long as it took me away from here, but before I got there she was suddenly gone, yanked backward by her long hair into Harnes' lap. He reached for the wine glass, broke it against the edge of the table, and tried to slice her throat open with the shard of the shattered stem. He wasn't angry, not even while he calmly tried to hook her jugular. "You killed my son. My son."

Nick punched him in the mouth again, took the broken glass out of his hand, and looked around the room.

For a man who had been a denizen of Panecraft and lived inside a cardboard box, eating garbage in the street, he sounded damn sure of himself.

He said, "All of you are crazy."

SIXTEEN

I KNELT BESIDE MY GRANDMOTHER. The bullet had passed through the thick folds and layers of clothing near her neck. The heavy sweater had scorch marks on it, and her hair had been slightly singed. I tore the tiny rip open wider to get a better look, and vaguely wondered why I was using my left hand instead of my right. The ridge of her shoulder had an inch-long crease that had mostly crusted, yet still dribbled a little blood.

"I'm fine, dear, I'm fine."

"You're bleeding."

"No, look," she said. "It has already stopped. Let me attend to you."

"Me?"

I stared down at myself and saw my right hand still opened into a claw as though waiting for Jocelyn to press her throat back into it. My arm dangled oddly and was entirely drenched with blood.

"Jesus," I said. "I don't feel it."

"Jonathan, you're in shock."

"That's pretty helpful."

"We've got to staunch the wound." She stretched like she would hug me or pull me down onto her lap. Instead, she lifted my jacket and un-tucked my shirt. "You're not wearing a belt."

"So I put on a little weight. I think you're supposed to tear the hem of your skirt at a time like this."

"Perhaps if I was your love interest and we were fleeing *mafiosi*."

My arm kept leaking. I shook free of my jacket and Anna yanked out the lining, making a tourniquet. It wasn't until she said, "There," that I started feeling woozy.

Lowell hadn't used his siren. Like Nick Crummler, he simply appeared in the room, his gun drawn but pressed down tightly to the side of his leg.

I hadn't realized Nick was even still in the house. He looked over his shoulder at Lowell and muttered, "Oh hell."

Lowell took it all in, stood beside me, and said, "Your phone ain't worth shit."

"I've begun to realize that."

"Ambulance is on its way."

Harnes and Jocelyn lay unconscious on the floor, tangled in the dark corner that reminded me of the tapered lighting effect of Crummler's cell. Li Tai sat in the center of the room, her hands folded in her lap, showing no emotion besides a ruddy glow of vindication lighting her visage. Nick and Lowell eyed each other very carefully.

"This is Nick, huh?" Lowell asked without really asking. I nodded. "Think you can explain this all to me in less than an hour, Jonny?"

I thought it would take a month to clear it up, but the short form only took ten minutes.

"Who killed the guy out in the limo?"

"Maybe cancer, or maybe Harnes poisoned him."

"Why?"

"He's a psychopath."

"Christ, we're going to have Wallace exhuming bodies for weeks."

Nick Crummler scratched at his beard and said, "Well, now that we all know my brother is innocent, I guess I'll be going."

"You killed a man," Lowell said.

"Whatever he was, he was less than a man. If you'd seen him in action you'd understand that and would've done it yourself. I saved the kid's life."

Lowell was actually three months younger than me. He nodded and said, "I know, but you realize I can't just let you leave."

"I have to admit I was hoping."

"I'd appreciate it if you didn't give me a bothersome time here."

Nick cocked his head, considering it. "I understand your situation, Deputy Tully. But if I get taken in there're a lot of reasons a man like me can get put away for good that have nothing to do with what I'm arrested for." He pointed at Harnes, but Lowell didn't turn his head. "It's happened before, and I wound up in that asylum under the care of a bastard who liked to wear steel-toed boots to crack ribs and sap somebody three times a day for the fun of it." He smoothed his beard again. "I'm sorry, I can't go with you."

"I wasn't actually asking," Lowell said.

"No, I figured you weren't."

I'd helped to put an innocent man inside the perverted corridors of Panecraft, and had been forced to watch him slowly dying in sorrow because I hadn't had enough faith in him to help out when I should have.

Shit.

Anna knew what was coming and said, "Oh, Lord."

I spun and caught Lowell in the stomach with my left. It was like smashing my knuckles into a marble statue. He looked more startled than hurt, but dropped back a few steps with his mouth open and raising the gun. Nick had already vanished. Lowell let out a short bark of disgust, his bunched muscles shifted beneath his uniform, and I wondered if I should shut my eyes or take it like a man. I shut my eyes. He hit me only twice, but it hurt worse than when Sparky had licked the crap out of me all over the place. I went to my knees trying to suck wind and retch at the same time. It was like that for a minute, and then my mind whirled pleasantly for a moment and I felt warm and comfortable. I screamed from the bottom of my nuts when he jerked my wounded right arm, snapped the cuffs on me and dragged me across the yard and threw me into the back of his parked police car without a word. I sat staring over at the dead chauffeur's head lolling against his steering wheel until the ambulance and other police arrived. Lowell took me to jail without a word.

Five days later I sat in a hospital bed with my good arm cuffed to the railing, trying to think of something to do besides play with the tiny cups of mashed potatoes and gelatin. Sheriff Broghin came in and took a slow gander at me. He seemed highly pleased with himself that the wheel of our situations had turned again. The last time I'd seen him he'd been vomiting on Alice Conway's floor. Now I was under arrest for obstruction of justice.

He said, "Lowell had a reason to put you in here, but he wouldn't give me all the details, and now he's changed his story some."

"When did he do that?" I asked.

Broghin smiled and his enormous gut shook with the force of the laughter he continued to swallow. He took deep breaths and let out little sniffles of giggles. "Two days ago. So I'm forced to let you go, you pain in the ass." He grinned as he uncuffed me, and leaned so far over the bed I had to pull back or be smothered. "I'll tell you this though, Jonny Kendrick. You pissed off about the only good friend you had, and he's truly a man to be reckoned with. I've got the feeling that the next time you tangle with him he's really going to put the serious hurt on you." He picked up the little cups and headed for the door. "Now you just lie there and reflect on that some."

I did.

The cops finally got the full story and released Li Tai late the following afternoon after an interpreter flew up from Manhattan and translated the woman's entire twelve-year-long imprisonment, as well as her preceding years as Theodore Harnes' mistress. Since she didn't understand English, and never spoke, Dr. Brennan Brent had allowed her to participate in all activities, despite her constant attempts at escape. The

uards called her Rapunzel because of her long hair and flair
or pleating together ropes in the recreation room which she
ad at various times used to attempt climbing from her win-
ow, strangling Brent, and hanging herself.

Anna, Oscar Kinion, and I sat at her kitchen table eating
reakfast. Even before Broghin stole my hospital food I'd been
tarving. Oscar had his arm around me and occasionally
ugged me to him during his sporadic but generous fits of
motion.

"She's got a case that will net her millions," Oscar said.
The way these reporters are trolling around the Grove, we're
oing to be seeing her on talk shows for a long time to come.
he'll be the queen of Hong Kong when she get's back!"

"If she does indeed return," Anna said. I noticed the stiff-
ess in her shoulder was nearly gone already as she speared
ore sausages and placed them on Oscar's plate. "Apparently
i Tai has always wanted to see America, and despite her
wful travails she has never let Theodore Harnes steal that
assion from her. Her first stop will be Disneyland."

"I've never been there, either," I said. "What's going to
appen to Harnes?"

Oscar jabbed loudly at his food, and Anna's lips drew into
pale line. "He's gone, of course. Fled the country during
he night. His lawyers were extremely effective, and there truly
n't much concrete evidence against him. Not until the bodies
f his victims are exhumed."

"I was hoping he'd wind up in Panecraft."

She smiled. "Yes, poetic justice would be *so* fulfilling."

"And Jocelyn?" I asked. I knew the answer but didn't want
 know it.

"He took her with him."

"Damn it."

My grandmother put her arm around me even as Oscar did
e same, and years spun from the three of us. I thought they
ight elope one day soon, on a gorgeous morning like this
e.

SEVENTEEN

KATIE AND I WATCHED CRUMMLER dance with Anubis among the headstones.

They were both wild and happy and clung to each other like long-lost friends. Every so often one of them would race past us or flail over an exposed root and take a head dive, and the other would pounce. "I am Crummler!" Crummler would announce giddily. "I am here!" His beard and wiry hair would be back in no time, the stubble already thickening. He snapped his fingers rapidly and jitterbugged along, trembling with his nerve endings burning again. "I have fought brave battles! I am home!"

"Yes, you are."

Anubis led him away in a game of tag and Katie asked, "They let him out like that, even in the condition he was in?"

"The administration isn't going to cause any fuss, not with all the troubles they're in for now."

"Did his brother say goodbye to him?"

"I'm not certain, but I tend to think so."

Not far away Keaton Wallace stood by the grave of Mari Harnes, overseeing the exhumation. He already appeared tire after finishing up the autopsy on the poisoned chauffeur.

The wind brushed Katie's hair against her jade eyes and

stroked it back into place. "Lowell will forgive you."

"No, he won't."

"In time."

I shook my head. "Not until he captures Nick Crummler."

"In time he will."

"Will you marry me?" I asked. She stared at me and slowly blinked. "Sorry, I didn't mean for that to sound so non sequitur."

She smiled, but I could see a faint cast of bitterness edging her lips. She could read my heart, my love, and my fear. "We've got time for that, Jon. We can wait another few months, or longer, maybe even until after the baby is born. If we still want to go through with it."

"Or we can get married now," I said.

She pressed her chest to mine and said, "So you actually want to move back to Felicity Grove?"

"Yes."

"And buy a house? Take care of a yard with a gigantic, gnarled ancient tree and an old tire swing?"

"Yes."

"Did I ever tell you about Ronnie Helmstead, my first boyfriend?"

"Talk about non sequitur," I said. "Yeah, the guy with acne."

"Not acne, he broke out in nervous rashes. He liked this cheerleader, used to date her behind my back and tell me that he was working late at his father's VCR repair shop. He'd get hives, turn crimson, and start pouring sweat and scratching himself everywhere." I just looked at her. "Let me tell you, you're a worse liar than him, Jon."

I'd have to practice my poker face a little more. "You're what's most important to me."

"And you are to me," she said. "I know you feel pressured."

"It's not that . . ."

"I know you do. I love you, but I still think we need some more time to get used to how things are going along."

I'd first met her when we were seven or eight, and she came out from San Diego to visit with her aunt, Margaret Gallagher, and she'd forced me to eat one of those Easy Bake Oven kiddy cakes. Despite only knowing her a couple of months in our adult lives, I understood I'd love her like this for the rest of our lives. I needed something, but it wasn't time. She needed that.

I pulled her to me and cradled her, wondering if she'd start crying soon. No matter what the situation, my ex-wife used to whine dreadfully whenever I hugged or held her, which should have clued me in on how things would work out. I waited and watched Katie's shoulders quivering, and I touched her chin and turned her face to me to see her laughing.

Our lives had become as entwined as anyone and everything in the Grove.

"Have I mentioned that twins run in my family?" she said.

"Oh boy."

Anubis flung himself against my knees. Katie fell back and giggled harder. Crummler danced as if he could see our children dancing with him, and I took my love in my arms and we waltzed along with them.

A JACK FLIPPO MYSTERY

DOUG SWANSON

UMBRELLA MAN

PUTNAM

< A FELICITY GROVE MYSTERY > # THE
DEAD PAST

Tom Piccirilli

Welcome to Felicity Grove...

This upstate New York village is as small as it is peaceful. But somehow Jonathan Kendrick's eccentric grandma, Anna, always manages
to find trouble. Crime, scandal, you name it...this wheelchair-bound
senior citizen is involved. So when the phone rings at 4 A.M. in
Jonathan's New York City apartment, he knows to expect some kind
of dilemma. But Anna's outdone herself this time. She's stumbled
across a dead body...in her trash can.

BERKLEY
PRIME
CRIME

☐ **0-425-16696-1/$5.99**

Prices slightly higher in Canada